MAGO HALMI
MOTHER OF ALL

PATRON GODDESSES

| MOON RABBIT GODDESS | NINE-TAILED FOX GODDESS | MOUNTAIN TIGER GODDESS |

THE GIFTED CLANS

TOKKI
INFUSERS

"Kindness and heart"

CLAN COLOR:
GREEN

GUMIHO
ILLUSIONISTS

"Beauty and influence"

CLAN COLOR:
SILVER

HORANGI
SCHOLARS

"Knowledge and truth"

CLAN COLOR:
RED

THE
LAST
FALLEN
STAR

A GIFTED CLANS NOVEL

BOOK ONE

BY GRACI KIM

RICK RIORDAN PRESENTS

DISNEY • HYPERION   LOS ANGELES   NEW YORK

Copyright © 2021 by Graci Kim
Introduction copyright © 2021 by Rick Riordan

First Edition, May 2021
1 3 5 7 9 10 8 6 4 2
FAC-020093-21078
Printed in the United States of America

This book is set in Corton, Goudy Trajan Pro Medium,
Goudy Old Style/Fontspring
Stock images: watercolor 61613686, sun 89398255,
moon 1471622636/Shutterstock
Designed by Joann Hill

Library of Congress Cataloging-in-Publication Data
Names: Kim, Graci, author.
Title: The last fallen star : a Gifted clans novel / by Graci Kim.
Description: First edition. • Los Angeles ; New York : Disney-Hyperion, 2021.
• "Rick Riordan presents." • Audience: Ages 8–12. • Audience: Grades
4–6. • Summary: After thirteen-year-old Hattie Oh casts a dangerous spell
so her adopted sister, Riley, will get a share of her inherited magic, Riley
must undertake a near-impossible quest to save Hattie from death.
Identifiers: LCCN 2020027526 (print) • LCCN 2020027527 (ebook) •
ISBN 9781368059633 (hardcover) • ISBN 9781368061285 (ebook)
Subjects: CYAC: Witchcraft—Fiction. • Sisters—Fiction. •
Quests (Expeditions)—Fiction. • Goddesses, Korean—Fiction.
• Korean Americans—Fiction. • Adoption—Fiction.
Classification: LCC PZ7.1.K556 Las 2021 (print) • LCC
PZ7.1.K556 (ebook) • DDC [Fic]—dc23
LC record available at https://lccn.loc.gov/2020027526
LC ebook record available at https://lccn.loc.gov/2020027527
Reinforced binding

Follow @ReadRiordan

Visit www.DisneyBooks.com

To my eomma and appa, whose love is the reason I exist.
To my sisters, Ally and Joya, whose love
is the reason this story exists.
And most of all, to my Spudman, whose love
(and patience) is the reason this book exists.

Contents

Why didn't somebody tell me about this stuff sooner?

THAT WAS MY FIRST THOUGHT WHEN reading *The Last Fallen Star*. Graci Kim does such an amazing job of blending Korean mythology into the modern world, I am now wondering how I ever lived without knowing all this cool information. Turns out, right under our noses in Los Angeles, there is an entire society of Korean witches with deep connections to the Godrealm. I am *so* glad LA finally has something to brag about besides being the entrance to Hades's Underworld.

Which of the six gifted witch clans would you choose to be in? Each one is amazing, with its own patron god and special powers. I'd love to be Miru—the protectors—because their patron is the Water Dragon Goddess, but there's no way I could be that fast and strong. I'm big into reading and history, so the Horangi clan is appealing, but as you'll soon see, this clan of scholars doesn't have the best reputation right now. In fact, they've been exiled from the other five clans. Bummer.

I guess my next choice would be the Gumiho. I've always liked the Nine-Tailed Fox Goddess. Being able to cast illusions could be really helpful. On those mornings when you're in a rush and don't have time to get dressed, just cast an illusion on yourself and look however you want! Their motto is

Beauty and Influence. I think they'd get along really well with Aphrodite's kids!

The hero of our story, Riley Oh, isn't sure where she belongs. Her family is in the Gom clan—the great magical healers—and Riley would love to get confirmed as a healing witch when she turns thirteen, like her sister, Hattie, is about to do. Unfortunately, Riley is a saram—a person born with no magic at all. She was adopted, and her biological parents weren't witches. Riley's adopted parents are awesome, however, and she gets along great with her sister. Still, it's super hard being the only one in the family without magic.

Then Hattie has a brilliant idea. They will cast a spell during Hattie's initiation that will let Riley share half of Hattie's power! Sure, the spell is forbidden. They'll have to steal it from their parents' safe. They'll also have to perform the spell in front of the Council of Elders and the entire congregation of the five clans on temple day, but what could possibly go wrong?

Um . . . you can probably guess how that turns out.

Riley discovers that her past is a whole lot more complicated than she realized. By trying to share Hattie's power, she unleashes an avalanche of unintended consequences, and brings secrets to light that were meant to stay buried forever. If she is going to save her family, the witch community, and the entire mortal realm, she had better discover her true powers quickly, and figure out who she can trust among the mortals, witches, and gods.

I have to admit, I fell down on the job while I was reviewing Graci's manuscript. I started reading and immediately got hooked. I was halfway through the book before I remembered,

"Oh, right, I'm supposed to be editing this." Then I went back and looked for stuff to edit, and I just got hooked into the story again. That's how good it is.

You're going to fall in love with this world right away. Riley's best friend, Emmett, is the kind of guy you want on your team. He loves baking and bringing you treats. He likes to dress up pets in strange costumes. He claims he is allergic to emotions, which just made me want to give him a big hug! He totally needs to meet Nico di Angelo and share a batch of cookies. Hattie is the best big sister, and she and Riley have the sweetest sibling relationship even though they're so different. The families in the witch clans are all so messy and loving and complicated—just like real families! And did I mention the food? Oh. My. Gods. Tornado fries. Bulgogi tacos. Gimchi salsa. Miniature donuts. Sign me up.

Speaking of eating, I ate this book way too fast. That's one of the bad things about getting an early look, because I devour the book and am ready for a sequel before the first volume is even published. *Burp!*

Well, at least I get to share *The Last Fallen Star* with you! I know you'll love it. When you're finished, let's get together and compare notes on which clans we like best and where we're going to eat a magical lunch next time we're in LA!

Rick Riordan

1.
My Family of Healing Witches

So here's the thing.

There are only two days left until my sister's initiation ceremony. In two sleeps, Hattie will turn thirteen, and she will have to prove to the entire congregation of gifted clans in Los Angeles that she has what it takes to become a witch. A healing witch. A *real* Gom.

And she's gonna be amazeballs, of course. I mean, it's her birthright. Healing magic flows in her blood, as it flows through our parents' blood, because we, the Gom clan, are descendants of the Cave Bear Goddess—the patron goddess of service and sacrifice.

Well, except me.

Sigh. Yep. My own thirteenth birthday is only a month away, but unlike my eomma (that's my mom) or my appa (that's my dad) or my sister, I'm a normal, non-gifted person without a lick of magic. I'm a saram.

I was adopted. And don't get me wrong. My parents try super hard to make me feel part of the gifted community, and

I love them so much for it. But the truth is, the harder they try, the more I realize how much of an outsider I really am. I'm *different*.

Hence why I'm here, sitting behind the reception desk of the Traditional Korean Medicine Clinic that my parents run, doing mind-numbing data entry instead of practicing healing spells like my sister.

The bells chime on the clinic's door, and I jolt up in my chair as an old, dark-haired man limps in. He looks like he could be Korean, but I don't think I've ever seen him at temple.

"Welcome to the clinic!" I say. "How can I help you?"

"Good morning," he says, wincing as he wobbles up to the desk. "My name is Robert Choi. I've just moved here from New York, and I was told to ask for a James or Eunha Oh. I think I've sprained my ankle."

He slides his wrists together, and the water in his Gi—the cylindrical glass charm on his bracelet—sloshes a little as it rubs against his skin. An image of two suns and two moons appears on his right wrist with the motion, and the symbol glows green.

Ah, he's a Tokki—an infusing witch. All witches get the same gifted mark on their wrists when they do magic, but it reveals itself in different colors depending on which clan they belong to. The mark is also how we can tell which patients are gifted and which are saram. If they're saram, we have to make sure they don't know we heal with magic. The infusers make special memory-erasing potions for that.

I know what you're thinking: Why would you keep such an awesome skill secret from the world? Well, Appa says if the saram found out about the gifted clans, that would bring grave danger to our community. People don't like what they can't understand. It scares them, and scared people do foolish things. I guess that makes sense.

"You've come to the right place," I say, smiling brightly. "James and Eunha are my parents. And sorry to hear about your ankle, Mr. Choi. Appa has just finished up with a patient, and there's a free slot for you now if you'd like it."

"Ah, you must be Hattie." He nods knowingly at me. "I hear you have an initiation ceremony coming up. I hope you are well prepared."

I shake my head. "Hattie's actually my sister. I'm not... Well, I can't..." I trail off, and Mr. Choi frowns.

"That's odd. They said the Ohs only had one daughter."

Oof. The comment spears right through my chest, but I stay silent and put on a well-rehearsed fake smile. What I'd really like to do right now is take out my Gi bracelet (if I had one) and heal his ankle right here and now, to prove how much of an Oh I really am. Or at least stand up for myself and tell him I'm part of this family, too. That's what Hattie would do if she were in my place.

But I'm not my sister. I'm not brave like she is. I prefer to keep my head down and stay out of trouble. Trust me, it's easier this way.

A warm hand squeezes my shoulder, and I look back to see Appa standing behind me. I didn't hear him come to reception. "This is Riley, most *definitely* our daughter, and the most dedicated Gom I know." Appa beams at me, and then extends his hand to Mr. Choi. "Welcome to our humble clinic, Robert.

And welcome to LA. Come with me, and let's get that ankle looked at."

Appa leads the hobbling Mr. Choi down the hallway, and a stinging heat builds behind my eyes. *Sigh.* Yet another day in the life of Riley Oh—the wannabe witch living in an exclusive gifted world.

"Riley!" Hattie runs up to the reception desk, puts her elbows on it, and rests her chin on her palms. Her rounded cheeks are pink, and her hair is damp with sweat. "Please come save me. Eomma is driving me up the wall. She's making me repeat the incantations a billion times, and I don't know what they mean anymore. I mean, honestly, what are words, even?"

"She just wants you to do well at the initiation."

Hattie rolls her eyes, but she knows I'm right.

A successful initiation ceremony is the most important rite of passage in a witch's life. She's got to perform three spells that satisfy the elders in the gifted clans council, and then say her vows in front of the whole congregation at temple. That's hundreds of people from five different clans, not to mention our patron goddess, who will be watching from the Godrealm.

Then, and only then, will Hattie get to wear her Gi around her wrist without adult supervision. Without it, she can't do any magic. So yeah, basically, it's a *big* deal. I mean, no pressure or anything.

Hattie fiddles with the earth-filled charm that's attached to a gold chain around her wrist. Eomma usually keeps my sister's Gi in her enchanted safe, and Hattie only gets to wear it when she's practicing spells with our parents. "Okay, but can you come with me anyway? Eomma's all cranky and flustered, and I need moral support. Please?"

I make a serious face and pretend to be preoccupied with the patient database. "I'm kinda busy."

"Pretty pleeease?" She gets all up in my face and makes big puppy-dog eyes at me. "You can have my favorite sweater. And I'll do all your chores for a week. Come on, Rye, have a heart!"

I hold off as long as I can before laughing. "Okay, okay, you twisted my arm." I push her sweaty mug away. "Just wanted to see you beg. Looks good on you."

"You'll pay for that!" She slaps me on my shoulder but grins, and then drags me out of my chair and down the hallway to Eomma's consultation room.

Eomma is inside, pacing back and forth while holding the family spellbook up to her nose. Her glasses are foggy, and her black perm is bouncing like a halo around her head. "Hattie, there you are! Now come back and practice the wound-closing incantation again." She points her finger at a Korean word in her spellbook. "And remember this time that the *p* is aspirated, so don't be shy—put your whole diaphragm into it. *Puh! Puh!* See? Like this—*puh!*"

Hattie drags her palms down her cheeks and gives me an exasperated look. I stifle a laugh. Eomma is in fine form today. She pulls off the *plugged-into-a-power-socket* and *rest-is-for-the-weak!* looks better than anyone I know.

As Hattie reluctantly follows Eomma's lead to aspirate her *puh*s, I study their two faces. And, for the billionth time, I wish I looked more like them.

I'm told my biological parents were of Korean ethnicity, too. But that's about where the similarities end. Where my Gom family are round, petite, and unblemished, I'm tall and freckled. I'm all pointy chin and high cheekbones, with more angles than curves. I'm the one people raise their eyebrows at when they look at our family photos.

Before I know it, my eyes are burning and I quickly wipe them, embarrassed. Ugh. Classic me. This is what my best friend, Emmett, calls my "leaky-bladder eyeball problem." You see, I have a slight issue controlling my tears. When I'm sad, I cry. When I'm angry, I cry. When I'm frustrated, I cry. I'm basically *really* talented at crying.

Hattie says it's a good thing—that I'm "in touch with my feelings" (more like drowning in them...). And Eomma and Appa say I'll grow out of it. But let's face it—compared to my confident-and-composed family, I'm flawed. It's yet another piece of evidence that I'm not a true Oh. That I'm weak and don't belong.

Eomma has now prompted Hattie to practice her vows, and my sister reluctantly obeys. "I vow on the name of Mago Halmi, mother of the three realms, mother of the six goddesses, mother of mortalkind and all creation"—Hattie's lisp is making an appearance, which only happens when she's tired or stressed—"to carry out my sacred duty to heal those in need. To uphold the Gom clan motto of Service and Sacrifice... and... and..."

She trails off, forgetting the words, and I finish the sentence for her. "And I understand that with my gift comes great responsibility—to my clan, to the gifted community, and to our ancestor, the Cave Bear Goddess, who blesses us with her divine power." I might not have a Gi or magic running through my veins, but I know my stuff.

Hattie gives me a grateful look. *Thanks,* she mouths. She puts her hands on her hips. "See, Eomma? Riley is *so* much more ready for an initiation than I'll ever be. Have you spoken to Auntie Okja about Rye being allowed to do one, too?"

I stick my hand in my pocket and squeeze my onyx stone to calm my nerves. It's shaped like a curved teardrop, and it's the only thing my biological parents left me. Hattie thinks it might be a family heirloom or something, but I just like how hard and real it feels in my hand. It's only a stone (and not nearly as cool as a Gi), but sometimes I carry it with me, because touching it reminds me that I came from somewhere, too.

"Sorry, girls. Your appa and I have been trying to find a good time to tell you...." Eomma sighs. "Auntie Okja tried really hard, but the other elders just won't budge."

I lower my eyes, mostly to hide the new trickle of disappointment forming on my eye line. My stupid leaky-bladder eyeballs fail me again. "Oh . . . that's okay," I say, even though that's far from the truth. "Thank you for trying."

Hattie raises her eyebrows at me. "No, it's *not* okay." She turns to Eomma. "You and Appa are always pushing for more inclusivity in the gifted community. This is the perfect opportunity to make a statement, isn't it?"

Eomma looks sheepish. "You're absolutely right. But change takes time. Some of the clans aren't as progressive as we are. They're arguing that, without a Gi, Riley wouldn't be able to cast the spells anyway. And if the council can't witness the spells during the initiation, they can't make a fair assessment."

I shrink, but Hattie pushes back. "But that's the whole point. Rye knows the words to all the healing spells, back to front. If the council just gave her a chance to prove herself, maybe the goddess would be convinced and grant Rye a Gi, too." She rolls her eyes. "They've got it all backward."

"I understand, sweetheart. You know I do. But the other elders think it's asking too much of the Godrealm to bless a saram with magic. That it would be impertinent of us. Disrespectful, even. Your auntie is only one voice among five."

Hattie raises her hands in exasperation, and I want to melt into the floor and disappear. I hate being the reason they argue. "Seriously, it's okay, Hat—" I start, trying to calm my sister.

"What's disrespectful is not even giving Riley a chance," Hattie continues. "If she tanks the initiation and the Cave Bear Goddess doesn't give her a Gi, then fine. Or if Riley doesn't want to do it, then that's also fine. But not giving her the freedom to choose? That's wrong on so many levels."

When Eomma doesn't respond, Hattie squeezes my hand, and a determined look appears on her face. I call it her "boss face," because no one in their right mind would mess with Hattie while she's wearing that expression. "As soon as I'm old enough," she says, "I'm gonna run for Gom elder. And when I do, mark my words, I'm going to shake up that place. The whole secret-society thing is *so* outdated."

"I have no doubt you will achieve that, and so much more," Eomma says, and I totally agree. I mean, why stop at council elder? Hattie for president! I can see the enamel pins already.

I squeeze Hattie's hand back and feel a warmth spread through my chest. For everything I don't have, I definitely won the jackpot as far as my sister goes. She is literally the Best. Sister. Ever.

"It's a shame you can't just do a spell to share your magic," I joke, trying to lighten the mood. "One where the recipient doesn't need a Gi. That would solve all our problems."

A grin spreads over Hattie's face. "Crowdsourced magic. Now *that* would jolt the clans into the twenty-first century, right, Eomma?"

We both look to Eomma, and she laughs nervously.

Hattie and I share a glance. Eomma only laughs like that when she's hiding something.

"*No. Way,*" Hattie says. "There actually *is* a spell for sharing magic with a saram, isn't there?"

My jaw falls to the ground. Impossible!

Eomma mumbles something under her breath but still avoids our eyes, and *that* is a dead giveaway. "It's not that simple, girls," she finally admits. "It's dangerous, and even if it worked, it wouldn't be permanent. The spell would have to be redone again and again—"

"What's the name of the spell?" Hattie interrupts. "And where can we find it?"

And were you ever going to tell me about it? I silently ask, my gut rolling into a tight knot.

Eomma closes the spellbook in her hands with a decisive *thud.* "This conversation has gone on long enough." She looks at the clock on the wall and gasps. "And we're going to be late for temple! Quick, go get your appa. We're leaving in two."

She hurries us out of her consultation room, and I get my butt moving. I wouldn't miss temple for anything.

"Rye!" Hattie stops me in my tracks and grabs my arm. "Did you see Eomma glance at the book when I asked where we could find the spell?"

I shake my head. I hadn't noticed. I was too busy wondering why my parents had kept this from me when they knew how badly I wanted to become a witch.

"I know that book's only supposed to have healing spells in it," Hattie continues, "but maybe Eomma just told us that so we wouldn't snoop. Maybe the magic-sharing spell is in there, too. In fact, I'm *sure* it is. Where else could it be?"

I frown. We're not allowed to touch the family spellbook—not until Eomma and Appa deem us ready. And besides, breaking rules makes me erupt in hives.

"But, Hat," I start, "you know I was joking before, right? Even if the spell is in there, I could never ask you to share your magic. Besides, Eomma said it was dangerous. She wouldn't lie about something like that."

She snorts. "Who said I wanted your permission? Didn't you hear me drone on about choice before? If I want to share my magic with you, who are you to stop me?"

I stare at her, wondering what I ever did to deserve such a fearless sister.

Hattie lowers her voice, and there's an excited twinkle in her eye. "Looks like we need to get our sticky hands on a certain spellbook, wouldn't you say?"

As she drags me to Appa's consultation room to fetch him, I hear a small voice in my head.

Could I actually *become a healing witch—a real Gom? Could this be my chance to do my parents proud and prove to the gifted community that I belong?*

I know I shouldn't get my hopes up. It'd just be a recipe for disappointment.

But here's the *real* crux of the problem, folks: I, Riley Oh, have a sweet tooth.

And hope? Well, hope tastes sweeter than candy.

2.
Saturday Is Temple Day

H·MART IS ONE OF MY FAVORITE places in the world. I mean, it's hard not to love it. It's a grocery store full of the most delicious things: every variety of gimchi you could ever dream of, ice cream in the shapes of watermelon wedges and corncobs, and don't forget the little counter that sells tornado fries (basically an entire potato spiraled out and fried on a stick—*drool*).

But those aren't the only reasons I love this particular H·Mart. It's also one of the secret entrances to the temple. The gifted community is really paranoid about their secret getting out into the saram population, so the Gumiho clan (they're the illusionists) use their glamour magic to hide us in plain sight. Genius, really.

For example, right now, my family and I are walking through the refrigerated aisle of brightly colored milk drinks, past the sweet-potato-cake stand, and toward the counter that sells Korean fried chicken. To the saram eye, the cherubic-faced man at the counter might look like an ordinary chicken vendor. But those of us from the gifted clans know he's actually a Miru guard. The Miru clan are protectors descended from the Water Dragon Goddess. They have either superhuman strength or speed, which make them ideal for protecting our secret portals and entrances.

"Hi there. Could I interest you in some K-fry today?" he says brightly.

In response, Eomma and Appa each rub their wrists together, and their Gi bracelets reveal their gifted marks.

"These two are with us," Appa adds, nodding at Hattie and me.

The Miru protector checks out the gold symbols on my parents' wrists, and then he nods toward the swinging door to his left, which leads to the kitchen. "You may pass."

We push through the door into the bustling kitchen and immediately smell the delicious waft of sweet-and-spicy fried chicken. But it doesn't last long. As we continue over to the walk-in fridge and step into its chilly belly, we are transported to the lobby of a grand building with high ceilings and marble floors.

I come here every week, but the temple never ceases to take my breath away. At first glance, it looks like a super-fancy hotel. The Miru guards protecting the lobby could pass as doormen, and there's always soothing music playing in the background. A sandalwood fragrance lingers in the air, like those signature perfumes some hotels have.

But it's so much more than that. Once you jump into the elevators, you get a sense of the temple's true scale. There are eighty-eight levels, and so many rooms on each floor that no one can keep track of what's behind each door. Most of the rooms aren't accessible without the right keys, but Auntie Okja says some doors are portals to the various gifted temples around the world, while others house mythical creatures visiting from the Godrealm. They say there's even a door that takes you to the Spiritrealm (the place we go when we die), which, frankly, blows my mind.

"Hurry, girls," Eomma urges, pushing us out of the elevator at level 88 and toward the big bronze doors. "Mr. Pyo is going to make us pay for being late."

And she's right. As soon as we enter the sanctuary through the heavy wooden doors carved with animal heads, Mr. Pyo's booming voice calls out.

"Well, well, well. Good of you to join us, Oh family of the Gom clan. You've interrupted the service, but I'm sure you have a very important reason for being tardy. Please, why don't you find a seat while the punctual members of the congregation sit and wait."

We lower our heads and quickly sit in the Gom pews while hundreds of eyes follow our every move.

"Absolutely mortifying," Eomma mumbles under her breath.

"Ugh, he's the worst," I whisper.

"Agreed," Hattie and Appa echo.

Mr. Pyo turns his attention back to the service, and I eventually get the nerve to raise my eyes from my lap and look around.

The large hexagonal chamber is full to the brim today, with witches from the Gom clan, the Samjogo clan, the Miru clan, the Gumiho clan, and the Tokki clan all sitting in their respective pews, which fan out from the center. Each block of pews ends with a polished bronze plaque brandishing the clan's motto, beneath a tall statue of their patron goddess. The icons are made out of materials that match their clan's colors—jade for the Tokki, blue lapis for the Miru, gold for the Gom—that kind of thing. Of course, the Horangi clan's pews are empty. The sixth clan hasn't been allowed at temple for years.

As per custom, the five elders are standing in the raised center of the sanctuary next to the Gi cauldron, which is basically a large black urn with clawed feet. It has the symbol of the two suns and two moons branded on its side and is filled with sand from the beginning of time. Sticks of incense poke out from its top, reminding me of candles on a birthday cake.

The elders are all wearing hanboks in their respective clan colors, including Auntie Okja, who's in gold. She's my mom's older sister, and the Gom elder on the LA council. I give her a small wave when her eyes meet mine. She winks back in response.

"Now, as I was saying," Mr. Pyo continues, "today is not a normal Saturday service. It is a momentous day for my family and the entire Samjogo clan, as my granddaughter Mira turns one hundred days old today!"

The congregation claps enthusiastically, but my family all glance nervously at me.

Let's be clear—I love going to temple, I really do. But the one thing I hate about attending each week is the number of Gi ceremonies I have to endure.

When a gifted child turns one hundred days old, the Gi

cauldron assesses the witch's elemental balance and forges her Gi. Parents then keep the Gi safe until the child is old enough to start training for her initiation ceremony on her thirteenth birthday.

Auntie Okja once explained it to me like this: The world has five sacred elements—wood, earth, water, fire, and metal. If a witch can harness the perfect balance of all five, he or she can channel the power of the goddesses and wield the specific magic of their clan.

The catch is that witches are born with only four internal elements. Which is why they must wear the fifth element—the one they lack—around their wrist. A Gi is kind of like a car key. Each witch needs their fifth element to start their car, but the particular car each clan drives (i.e., the type of magic each clan can do) is different. It's in their blood. For us, the Gom, it's healing.

Mr. Pyo takes baby Mira from her mom's arms and carries her toward the cauldron. I instinctively shrink into my velveteen pew cushion, wishing I could melt into its softness and disappear.

"Mago Halmi, mother of the three realms, mother of the six goddesses, mother of mortalkind and all creation," Mr. Pyo starts, holding Mira up into the air with both arms outstretched. "Today I humbly present to you this child of the Samjogo clan, descendant of the Three-Legged Crow Goddess, for your divine blessing."

The Samjogo clan chants their motto, Leadership and Wisdom, while the four other elders take turns touching Mira's forehead with their activated gifted marks. Then Mr. Pyo steps toward the Gi cauldron and declares, "Mago Halmi, let your will be known!"

The congregation goes silent, and for a moment, nothing happens. Immediately, my heart starts to race and my palms get sweaty. A deep rumble emanates from the cauldron, and I count to ten under my breath as Mina's first element is revealed.

"Her dominant element is water!" Mr. Pyo announces first, as a swirling tornado of liquid materializes above the cauldron. "The symbol of abundance and grace. How fitting for a seer." Everyone cheers in approval.

The water tornado disappears, giving way to a glowing seed that grows into a tree in front of our eyes. "Her subdominant is wood," Mr. Pyo calls out. "The symbol of compassion and growth."

The cheering continues as the third element reveals itself—a pyramid of solid bronze, shimmering as if it had been dipped in glitter. "Followed by metal. The symbol of strength and power." Mr. Pyo beams almost as bright as the pyramid.

Finally, a blazing bonfire appears in the pyramid's place, levitating above the cauldron with its hungry flames. "And finally, fire. The symbol of transformation and will. Mago Halmi has spoken!"

My eyes lock on to the fire. I want to look away, but I can't.

"And so, Mira's Gi will be forged with earth—the element she does not possess," Mr. Pyo concludes. "The symbol of fertility and life, and the key to unlocking her perfect elemental balance. May Mago Halmi bless her future as a seeing witch."

As the fire dissipates, a small glass charm of soft earth

appears above the cauldron's mouth. It looks just like Hattie's Gi. The cylinder hovers expectantly in the air until Mr. Pyo carefully takes it in both hands and passes it to Mira's parents.

I clutch my chest, and Hattie takes my hand and squeezes it hard. She knows exactly what I'm thinking about right now.

My parents, being the progressive people they are, persuaded the elders to give me a Gi ceremony when I turned one hundred days old. And I'm sure they meant well. It must have been a landmark occasion for the LA-based clans to see a saram get blessed. Too bad it didn't go according to plan. . . .

The story goes that when the Gi cauldron was asked for my elemental balance, it sat silent and idle for an impossibly long time. Eventually, it spluttered and wheezed as if it had swallowed a fireball. Then it delivered its final answer.

First element: fire.

Second element: fire.

Third element: *still* fire.

Fourth element: Yup, you guessed it. Fire.

Then, instead of forging my Gi, the cauldron caught on fire. *Literally*. The entire thing lit up like the Christmas tree at the Grove.

The thing is, no one ever gets two of the same elements, let alone four. That's just not how it works. So the council considered the mishap proof that the saram shouldn't be part of the community, and I was deemed a fiery freak of nature. *Sigh*. As you can imagine, that was the beginning of the end for me.

"Who cares about Gi ceremonies when we have a magic-sharing spell to cast?" Hattie whispers in my ear. "Forget about back then. We have the future to look forward to."

I bite my lip. "But what if sharing means you'll lose your power? And remember, Eomma said it was dangerous."

"Sometimes you gotta burn your fingers to enjoy the s'more."

But it's different for me, I think. I love Hattie with all my heart, but she doesn't understand that things aren't as simple for me as they are for her. One false step and the council could ban me from temple altogether. Or, Mago forbid, what if they decided to wipe my memory with a strong dose of Memoryhaze potion? There's a reason I keep my head down and my mouth shut. It's safer this way.

Then again, seeing Mira get her Gi, and knowing Hattie's going to be initiated soon, it makes me wonder. . . . If I don't take this chance now, will another ever come again? Will I live the rest of my life regretting the one opportunity I had to fulfill my potential?

It's probably a result of my burnt nerves, but after a moment, I give in to Hattie's enthusiasm. As the sweet taste of hope returns to my mouth, I whisper back, "Guess we have to figure out how to open Eomma's safe, then."

Hattie's eyes light up so bright, I can see my reflection in them. "That's the smartest thing you've said in *years.*"

We both sit there pondering the mechanics of enchanted safes, when Mr. Hong, the Miru elder, begins making the community announcements. The first piece of news is that the date for the gifted library's grand reopening will be announced soon. The library has been closed for over ten years, so it will be a massive celebration for all clans around the world.

The second announcement is about an upcoming Saturday School trip to the traveling carnival. Saturday School is where kids go after temple service to learn more about the gifted clans and the Godrealm and stuff. Kind of like school for witches, but only once a week. As for the carnival, it's one of the highlights in the annual gifted calendar.

Suddenly I have an idea. "Isn't Professor Ryu teaching Saturday School today?" I whisper to Hattie.

She ponders for a second and then slaps me on the arm. "I like how you think!"

Professor Ryu is one of those super-liberal, ditch-the-lesson-plans-and-let-the-students-direct-the-learning type of teachers, and she claims there is no such thing as a bad question. She's also from the Tokki clan, and Kindness and Heart isn't their motto for nothing. She's one of the nicest people we know and probably our best way of finding out how to break the safe's enchantment.

"And for the final piece of community news," Mr. Hong continues, "a cautious word of warning for our loyal congregation."

The other elders visibly tense, including Auntie Okja.

Mr. Hong clears his throat a few times before speaking again. "It has come to our attention that the Horangi clan has attempted to make contact with some members of the council."

The temperature drops in the sanctuary and the hairs on my arm rise to attention. *No way.*

"The council has convened on the issue, and we suspect the excommunicated clan may be planning another attack on the community. We ask that everyone remain vigilant and take necessary precautions. If you see any of the scholars loitering around gifted property, report them to us immediately.

And if any try to make contact, it is imperative that you *do not* engage. They are dangerous and should not be approached."

Nervous murmurs ripple down the pews, spreading out from the center of the room like lava from a volcano. Eomma and Appa share a look of concern, and my eyes are immediately drawn to the empty benches in front of the red-jasper statue of the Mountain Tiger Goddess—the ex-patron of the Horangi clan.

The scholars weren't always cursed. In fact, they used to be the upholders of knowledge and truth in the gifted community. They were the keepers of the sacred texts at the gifted library, and they were well respected. Revered, even.

But then, almost thirteen years ago, everything changed. Auntie Okja said that under the leadership of their new elder, Ms. Kwon, the clan became obsessed with power. Ms. Kwon claimed she'd figured out a way for witches to become as powerful as the goddesses and that she would pursue it until the scholars became divine themselves. When the other five clans accused them of heresy, Ms. Kwon led a Horangi attack against the gifted community. You were either with them or against them.

Luckily, the scholars were stopped before a full war broke out. But not before a bunch of innocent witches were killed, including the Gom elder at the time, who happened to be my best friend Emmett's mom.

Anyway, as punishment for their actions, the Mountain Tiger Goddess disowned the Horangi clan and cursed them never to be able to wield her divine power again. And anyone seen colluding with the clan would be stripped of their own gift, too. As you can imagine, the council had no choice but to banish them from the community. The scholars' lust for power had made them dangerous, and it ultimately led to their demise. Sad story, really.

"And on that rather somber note, I conclude today's service," Mr. Hong finishes. "May Mago be with you this coming week."

"May Mago be with you," the congregation echoes in prayer.

Soon the kids start to gather near the elevator to go to Saturday School, which is held in the building next door. Hattie runs to use the restroom, and I see Professor Ryu's digital perm bobbing above the crowd of kids. My heart races. Our plan had better work.

"Riley, do you have a moment?"

I turn around to see Auntie Okja standing there in her beautiful golden hanbok. She looks as graceful and poised as ever.

"Of course, Auntie O." I smile at her warmly. "What's up?"

"I'm so sorry about your ceremony. I tried my best, but the council overruled me." She tucks a loose strand of my hair behind my ear, and I melt at the tender gesture. "You know I'm always looking out for you, right? That even if it might not always seem like it, I only want the best for you?"

I nod and look at my feet. "I know, Auntie O."

For a second, I want to spill the beans. I want to tell her our plans to steal Eomma's spellbook and to cast the magic-sharing spell. Maybe she'd talk some sense into me. Or perhaps she'd offer to help us. Like she said, she only wants the best for me. . . .

But the moment is broken when Mrs. Lee, the Tokki elder, comes and ushers Auntie Okja away for some urgent council business.

"By the way, I have some new plans for a diversity-and-inclusion campaign," she says to me before leaving. "Can I run them past you later?"

"Of course," I say. "Will look forward to it."

"The only thing you're gonna look forward to is getting half of my magic," Hattie whispers, pulling me away to join the other students. "And yes, I know what you're thinking. And no, we are *not* asking Auntie O for help."

I look away, hoping I can hide the guilt written in Mago-size letters on my face. You'd think I was a book the way Hattie reads me.

"But maybe she would?" I try.

Hattie snorts. "Oh, you have so much to learn, young grasshopper. She's a council elder. There's no way she would help us if Eomma won't. If we want to do this, we're on our own."

I frown so hard my eye twitches.

"If the tables were turned, would you do the same for me?" she asks.

"Without a doubt," I respond immediately. "You know I would."

"Then it's settled," she says, grinning. "We have ourselves an enchanted safe to crack."

3.
Even Witches Go to School

THE BUILDING NEXT DOOR TO THE H-Mart is a noraebang. *Norae* is Korean for *song,* and *bang* means *room.* So a noraebang is a song room—aka a private karaoke room. It's where teenagers go to hang out with their friends and sing their favorite pop hits at the top of their lungs. It also happens to be another secret entrance, this time to Saturday School.

"OMG, can you believe the news about the Horangi?" Jennie Byun, with her manicured nails and Ralph Lauren Polo dress, says in her annoyingly loud voice as we walk up to the doors of Gangnam Style Karaoke. Everything from her invisible braces to her perfect designer handbag irks me. "My mom told me our Samjogo elder received a vision this morning when he touched the fried chicken counter. And get this: The excommunicated Horangi elder—Ms. Kwon—was trying to break into the temple. Freaky, right?"

There are about twenty of us walking to class, and a good

three quarters of them hang on to Jennie's every word as if their lives depend on it.

"No wayyy," a few of them exclaim.

"You have *all* the good goss," someone else says.

Jennie smirks. "*Yes way.* You guys know our clan is basically the most powerful one, right? I mean, there's a reason the chairperson of the council is always a seer."

Hattie and I groan in unison. Jennie Byun—the most obnoxious human in the three realms—is a seeing witch. The Samjogo clan can get visions of truth simply by touching an item. They also have premonitions in their dreams, and the most powerful Samjogo can even see across space and time, which I'll admit is pretty cool. But the inside joke is that their clan motto should be Power and Ego, not Leadership and Wisdom. Appa says they're so full of hot air, it's a wonder they still have their feet on the ground.

"And you know what else I heard?" Jennie continues. "All those plans to reopen the gifted library are a lie. The council has never figured out how to reactivate the library since the scholars got banished. And now, with the potential threat of the Horangi coming back, the elders have all the strongest protectors guarding the entrance. Right, Noah?"

Noah Noh, a Miru protector, looks back over his shoulder as we walk up the stairs of the noraebang. "It's true they've got protectors working on a hush-hush project there. Don't know any of the deets, though."

I shudder thinking about the havoc the Horangi clan has caused. If it weren't for them, Emmett would still be part of the community. His mom married a saram (which makes Emmett half saram, half gifted), and she was one of the first champions for more inclusive policies in the clans. Eomma says Mrs. Harrison and my auntie Okja used to be best friends. Then, when Mrs. Harrison died, Auntie O took over as Gom elder.

"Anyway, my mom is never wrong, so you heard it here first," Jennie says. "You can thank me later." She tosses her hair back so forcefully, it whips me in the face. Which hurts more than you'd expect.

"Oh, *come on!*" I moan. "Haven't you ever heard of personal space, Jennie?"

She puffs out her chest and stares me down. "Don't you dare tell me what to do, you fake witch."

I shrink at the insult, which only fires up Hattie. "Watch your words, Jennie! Only cowards are bullies."

"I'm not a coward!"

"Then don't be a bully!"

Jennie harrumphs and storms off ahead of us.

Like I said, the most obnoxious person in the three realms.

When we get to reception, two people are waiting for us. They look like they could be college students. The girl is fixing her makeup (which is already flawless), and the pink streaks in her hair turn silver as she murmurs an incantation under her breath. Definitely a Gumiho illusionist.

Unlike the Gom, who, despite being healers, can't heal their own bodies, the Gumiho can glamour themselves. It has to do with their beautiful patron, the Nine-Tailed Fox Goddess. That's why they're so good-looking and why so many of them become K-pop and K-drama stars. In fact, all but one of the BTS members are Gumiho. Yup. True story.

The guy at reception is wearing a sleeveless blue T-shirt with an image of a dragon swimming in a river. The message P&P 4EVA is etched onto the dragon's chest, and I have to admire the dude's dedication. Their saram clientele would be none the wiser, but his top is a dead giveaway that he's a Miru protector. Provide and Protect is their clan motto, and blue's their color.

Professor Ryu rubs her wrists together and shows her green gifted mark to the witches. The Gumiho nods and signals to the Miru, who promptly disappears in a gust of wind. I have no idea where he goes, but in the blink of an eye, he's back—this time holding up an envelope. Superhuman speed must be so useful in LA's traffic.

He passes the envelope to Professor Ryu. "Room eighteen today, Professor." And to us, he says with a nostalgic look in his eyes, "Have fun, guys. I remember the good old days of Saturday School."

Professor Ryu leads us to room 18, and it's dim and windowless inside. It's about the size of my bedroom, and the air smells a little like Cheetos, root beer, and something sour I don't really want to identify. The large TV on the wall is flashing scenes from music videos and various song titles you can choose from. A large couch shaped like the letter C faces the TV, and between them is a low table with a few songbooks, a remote, some mics, and a feather boa. Cosette Chung, a super-pretty Gumiho witch (but unfortunately, Jennie's number one

27

henchwoman), immediately puts on the boa, and it's not fair how good she looks in a tacky piece of pink fluff.

Professor Ryu finally opens the envelope, revealing this week's glamour-reveal song. "'Fake Love' by BTS," she announces, to which everyone fist-pumps and grins. It's an oldie but a goodie.

"Now, when we get to Jimin and Jin's hook," she explains, "we just need to replace the words *fake love* with *secret life*. Everyone ready?"

She uses the remote to select the song. Music fills the room, and as the class stands in front of the huge TV with the scrolling lyrics, we sing our hearts out.

I'm so sick of this ~~fake love~~ secret life, ~~fake love~~ secret life, ~~fake love~~ secret life

I'm so sorry but it's ~~fake love~~ secret life, ~~fake love~~ secret life, ~~fake love~~ secret life

As soon as we say the last words, the Gumiho's glamour on the room starts to dissolve. The dingy walls shimmer as if they're made of silvery water, and slowly they melt like hot candles.

Before we know it, the noraebang has disappeared, and we are standing in a spacious, brightly lit classroom with large beanbags instead of desks and chairs. Three of the walls are painted with meticulous landscapes that look so realistic they could be photos.

One is of the sandy beach under Santa Monica Pier. (I recognize the Ferris wheel. They also have the best teeny-weeny donuts there—*drool*.) The second must be New York, because I see the Empire State Building, and I think the last mural is Lotte World—one of the world's largest indoor theme parks, which happens to be in Seoul. Gumiho witches change the murals from time to time, because, in addition to looking awesome, the images also double as portals. They're so well guarded by the Miru, though, you'd never risk sneaking through one—not unless you want to know what superhuman strength feels like when it's directed at you.

Professor Ryu encourages everyone to grab a beanbag and get comfortable, and Hattie and I camp out in the back, as usual.

"All right, class, I know you're all on summer break from saram school, but how lucky that you still get to come to Saturday School. A whole summer of learning! Oh, how *fun*. Would anyone like to start us off by suggesting a topic? Remember, there's no such thing as a bad idea. We're all here to feed our brains and, as I always say, everyone all together now—"

"There's no food like knowledge," the class chants back.

I glance over at Hattie and she nods. This is it. This is our chance.

"I have one." In my excitement, my hand shoots up before I have the chance to fully form the question in my mind. "So, um . . . how exactly would you go about opening a lock enchantment? Like on a safe or something?"

As soon as the words are out, I realize I should have been 1000 percent more subtle. "That is, *hypothetically*," I hasten to add. "Not for, like, really opening the safe—because there *is* no safe—but I mean, if I wanted to open a purely theoretical safe, one that doesn't actually exist. Like, academically speaking . . ." Ugh. Total facepalm.

My cheeks go hot, and I mouth a quick *Sorry* to Hattie. Why didn't I just let her do the talking? She's the smooth operator, not me.

Hattie smiles back, though. *Don't worry, you've got this,* her eyes say.

Professor Ryu taps her chin. "Well, that's a very specific question, Riley, but as I've said before, curiosity is the fore-mother to knowledge, and knowledge is the most powerful gift of all. So thank you for your contribution." She scans the room. "Before I provide my thoughts, does anyone else want to volunteer an answer? Remember, this is a *safe* space"—we all groan at her pun—"where everyone's opinion counts. Within these four walls, we *all* have a voice."

"Except for the wannabe witch." Jennie sneers over her shoulder at me.

"Just ignore her," Hattie whispers. "We have more impor-tant things to worry about."

I nod, but my eyes sting. Jennie is officially the worst.

David Kim, a rosy-faced infuser from the Tokki clan, pipes up first. "My mom has one of those safes. She keeps it at the restaurant for her really potent potions and tonics. Once, one of the waitstaff came into the kitchen and accidentally drank a triple dose of confidence potion, thinking it was juice. He then robbed a bank, because he was convinced he wouldn't get caught. Mom keeps all her stuff locked up now."

I think of David's family restaurant, Seoulful Tacos, and immediately feel saliva pool in my mouth. They have the best bulgogi tacos in the city. Which makes sense. Tokki witches have the ability to infuse food with magic.

"My older brother has an enchanted safe in his room, too," Noah Noh says, pushing his on-trend round glasses up the bridge of his nose. The Miru normally have a certain athletic look about them, but Noah's style is more hipster than jock. "I'm pretty sure he cuts off a lock of his hair, burns it outside the safe door, and then chants his password three times. Not that I spy on him or anything." He quickly glances at Hattie and his face goes a little pink. "I'm just observant."

Cosette giggles and flicks her hair at Noah even though nothing he said was remotely funny. Hattie goes unusually still, and I'm momentarily confused why there's a weird vibe between the three of them.

I would normally pester Hattie for details, but right now I'm too distracted by other matters. As I wait to see Professor Ryu's reaction, I pinch Hattie's thigh in excitement.

"You're absolutely right, Noah," Professor Ryu confirms, clapping. "A two-step enchanted safe lock involves the burning of hair and a password repeated three times." She leans forward and motions for us to come closer.

She lowers her voice as if she's about to tell us a juicy secret. "But if you want to be *extra* safety-conscious, some witches go one step further. They have a two-step lock and also require that a few gifted tears be dropped on the hair before it's burned. Then, voilà, they have themselves a three-step lock. Isn't that *fascinating?*"

I throw Hattie a nervous look. *Gifted tears?*

Our eomma is so meticulous, she would definitely use a three-step lock. That means we need to take a chunk of Eomma's hair, which I guess is doable. And considering I know all her laptop passwords, it shouldn't be too hard to figure out the one for her safe. But we're never going to get our hands on Eomma's tears. *No way.*

My heart drops, and I shove my hand into my pocket to fiddle with my teardrop stone. I *knew* this was a bad idea. I *knew* getting my hopes up was a sure way to get hurt. I shake my head in disappointment. I can't believe I let Hattie talk me into this.

"Don't worry," Hattie whispers, as if reading my mind. "We just need to brainstorm a little. We've got this." She sounds so certain, and I desperately want to believe her.

"Fine," I whisper back, getting out my phone. "I'll invite Emmett over."

"Good idea." She nods in approval. "We could use his smarts."

By the time we get home from class, Emmett is already waiting on the front porch. He's perched on the railing, and he's so short, his feet dangle freely. As usual, he's dressed from head to toe in black, and he's sporting his signature scowling resting face, which is basically the only accessory he ever wears aside from his silver ring and black cord necklace. There is a Tupperware container of donuts in his lap, and I fist-pump the air. Twice. Baking is Emmett's number one love in life, and his donuts are so good I once bedazzled a T-shirt to say DONUT TOUCH MY DONUTS! Uh-huh, I'm totes obsessed.

Emmett passes me the Tupperware. "Thought we might need some brain food."

I throw him a grateful smile and hug the donuts to my chest as we walk to the front door.

"Thank you for keeping the leaves out, door-sin," Hattie says to the door.

"You're so good at keeping the rain out, door-sin," I coo.

The door groans happily in response and unlocks itself for us.

Emmett, on the other hand, forgets to address the door-sin correctly. "You look so shiny and mahogany today," he says.

Sure enough, the door hits him in the butt as he walks over its threshold. Rookie mistake.

"Ow! I mean, you look so shiny and mahogany today, *door-sin*," he corrects himself.

Gifted homes are pretty special. Eomma says it's because they witness so much magic they become a little magical themselves. The walls breathe and the floors listen, and sometimes they whisper into our ears while we're asleep. Certain parts of the house—usually the ones we use the most—absorb so much enchantment that they come alive as spirits, or *sin*. The door-sin, the kitchen-sin, and the toilet-sin are the main ones, but sometimes you get others, too.

The house-sins protect our homes, but you have to make sure you say something nice every time you use them or they can make your life pretty miserable. One time Hattie forgot to give the toilet-sin a compliment, and for the next two weeks the lights kept turning off while she was doing her business. It was particularly scary at night, and I had to stand outside the door each time she peed so she wouldn't freak out.

We get to our bedroom, and Emmett starfishes out on my bed. "So what's this super-important thing we need to brainstorm?"

Mong, our fluffy white Samoyed, jumps on top of him to lick his face, and Emmett's black T-shirt is immediately covered in snowy fur. He could probably make a sweater out of all the Mong hair he picks up at our place.

Hattie and I update him on our plans, and he stares at us in disbelief.

"Wait, so you're gonna break into an enchanted safe, steal the spellbook, then cast a dangerous spell that your mom has forbidden you to learn?"

Hattie nods enthusiastically, but I frown. When he puts it like that . . .

He sits up on the bed. "And tell me, what *exactly* are you gonna tell your parents when they find out? Because, you do realize, they're gonna find out. Especially when Riley miraculously has healing magic one morning, just like that." He snaps his fingers in the air.

"Don't be such a party pooper," Hattie says. "You know how much Riley wants to be a witch. They'll come around— eventually."

He scowls at me and fiddles with his ring. It doesn't look like anything special, but the inner band has a secret compartment containing some of his mom's ashes. His dad had it made for him, and Emmett never takes it off. "Do you really need magic that badly? If your mom doesn't want you to cast the spell, there must be a good reason. Why put yourself in that situation when you don't need to? You're fine the way you are."

His compliment surprises me. *Fine* is not the most emotive word in the dictionary, but considering Emmett is allergic to emotions in general, it feels like a big deal. He's obviously worried about me.

I take a donut from his Tupperware and bite into it before answering. It's Nutella cream cheese, and it's so good it makes me want to drop a truth bomb. "Because," I confess, "I *do* need it. Having magic will make me fit in. Jennie Byun won't be able to bully me anymore, I'll finally be accepted as a Gom, and I'll be more confident and brave and strong, like Hattie. It's my answer to everything."

When he stays silent, I feel a spark of irritation. "Come on, Em. You of all people should understand. Don't you wish you could have stayed in the gifted community? Plus, your mom was the OG in the clan to preach about inclusivity after she married your dad and had you. We're doing her teachings justice."

"And look what happened to her," he snaps, crossing his arms over his chest. "Oh, that's right—she *died.*"

I immediately feel like the worst human being ever to have walked this realm. "Shoot, I'm sorry, Em. That was insensitive of me."

After Mrs. Harrison was killed by the Horangi, Mr. Harrison forbade Emmett from having anything to do with the clans again. He said he'd already lost the love of his life and he couldn't lose his son, too. As a result, he's *super* protective of Emmett and basically treats him like a baby. I forgot that, from where Emmett stands, magic could be blamed for stealing his mom away.

"But you're not gonna tell on us, are you...?" I mumble.

"Look, I know my dad treats me like I'm thirteen going on five." He talks through the muffle of Mong's thick white fur. "But he's right about one thing—magic is bad news. And I don't see why you think you need it. Look at me—*I* don't need it."

I frown and bite into another donut so I don't have to respond. Emmett must have inherited at least a pinch of magic from his mom. I'm convinced that's why his baked goods always make me feel better—because they have some Gom healing power. I know he's just got my back, but TBH, it's a bit rich of him to say I shouldn't need magic when he low-key uses it all the time.

Besides, now that I'm on board with Hattie's plan, I refuse to be talked out of it. This is my one chance to live the life I want to lead. Can't he see that?

He sighs and picks up donut crumbs I've dropped on the bed. "But I can see you've both made up your minds. And arguing gives me gas. So whatever. Do what you gotta do. Just know I'm coming with. Someone's gotta keep an eye on you two."

Feeling relieved, I jump on the bed to hug him, while still holding a donut in one hand. More crumbs fall onto the sheets. "I knew you'd come around. Love you, boo!"

He makes a face and pushes me away. "Ew, stop it. I've told you a million times, emotions are bad for your health. They give you wrinkles. Also, I'm getting you a bib for your birthday. No joke."

"Speaking of emotions," Hattie says, "we need to get our hands on Eomma's tears to open the lock. That's what we need to brainstorm."

We describe the three-step enchanted lock to Emmett and he immediately rolls his eyes. "Oh, come on, it's so obvious."

"It is?" I say. You can't force someone to cry and collect their tears. It can't be *that* obvious.

"What do we do every second Saturday night?" he asks, raising his eyebrows.

"Watch K-dramas and eat tteokbokki," Hattie answers.

"And why did we have to create a rule that your mom can't join us anymore?"

I groan. "Ugh. Because she's got horrible taste in Korean TV shows."

"Exactly." Emmett looks very pleased with himself.

Hattie scrunches up her forehead, trying to follow. But it suddenly clicks for me. "I knew there's a reason I keep you around!" I say to Emmett, grinning from ear to ear. "This way, she'll be pleased we invited her, *and* we'll get what we need. Win-win!"

Hattie's still looking confused, so I give her a hint.

"Let's just say there's a reason they call K-dramas tearjerkers."

4.
How to Open an Enchanted Safe

THE NEXT MORNING WE GET UP so early, it's still dark out. To be honest, I've hardly slept, because I've been so nervous. When I did sleep, I dreamed Hattie and I had opened our own healing practice complete with yoga lessons, barley-grass shots, and poolside meditation. The whole shebang. It was actually the perfect dream until the clinic got attacked by evil dokkaebi goblins who killed everyone in their sleep. So uh, yeah—not the best night.

Eomma and Appa are still asleep, and we pop our heads in their door.

"We're just taking Mong for a walk," I call out, my voice all shaky.

"We're gonna go the long route, so we may be a while," Hattie adds.

They mumble something sleepy and indecipherable from their bed and we quickly close the door before they can ask any questions.

We give the door-sin some nice compliments as we leave the house with Mong (who is looking rather surprised by this early morning walk), and we pause on the porch to make sure we've got everything we need.

"Lock of Eomma's hair?" Hattie asks, looking down at the checklist on her phone.

"Check." I tap the wadded tissue in my pocket. It was easier than I thought to cut off a bit while Eomma was sleeping. She won't even notice it's gone.

"Keys to the clinic?"

"Check." They were on the kitchen bench, where they're usually kept.

"Box of matches?"

"Check. And do you have the list of possible passwords?"

Hattie nods. "Check. They're on my Notes app."

"What about the tears?"

She holds up a small glass vial with the precious drops inside. "Yep, thanks to Emmett."

Last night we'd invited Eomma to our K-drama binge, which she'd happily accepted. Then we'd suggested we rewatch the final episode of her favorite series, *Stairway to Heaven*. It's super old and cheesy, about a woman who gets amnesia and forgets her first love and then goes blind. She gets new eyes donated by this other dude who falls in love with her. Super OTT and total eye roll, but Eomma *loves* it. And Emmett knew that it would make her cry, because it always does. That's when Hattie and I had kindly offered her a handkerchief, like the good daughters we are. After that, all we'd had to do was wring the moisture into a vial. Easy as that.

"He's kind of a genius, isn't he?" Hattie says.

I grin. "And he knows it."

When we get to the clinic, the sun is just starting to rise above the horizon, and Emmett is nowhere to be found.

"Where is he?" Hattie asks, checking the time on her phone. "He's late."

"He's always late." For all his great qualities, punctuality is not one of them.

"*Pssst!*"

We turn to see a figure in black stealthily crossing the street. His large sunglasses and wide-brimmed hat obscure most of his face.

"I can't believe you guys are making me do this," Emmett hisses as he approaches, pulling his hat down farther. "My dad is going to kill me if he finds out I'm helping you guys break in. You know it's a crime."

"You volunteered, remember? Also, we brought Mong to sweeten the deal," I say, passing the leash to Emmett. Baking and cute animals—that's basically my BFF in a nutshell. Oh, and *Battle Galactic*, an online game he's obsessed with.

He pretends to sulk but breaks into a full-watt smile as soon as Mong jumps up to lick his face. "Nice play."

Hattie checks her list for the billionth time. "All right, team, ready to do this?"

We nod and put our hands together for a huddle.

"For service and sacrifice," I say.

"For freedom of choice," Hattie says.

"For making sure you don't do anything stupid," Emmett says with a snort.

Hattie unlocks the door, and we're lucky there's no door-sin at the clinic. It would totally rat us out to our parents. With a final nervous glance at one another, we step inside.

The scent of a tonic is thick in the air—something warm and sweet and cinnamon-y that reminds me of the hotteok rice pancakes Appa makes on Saturday mornings (hands down my favorite meal). I take a good sniff, and I'm pretty sure it's the nectar Eomma gets from her Tokki supplier in New York. The infuser supposedly sources it from some old Greek dudes who work out of the Empire State Building, and the stuff really works. Took a sip once after I fell off my bike, and my cuts and bruises healed like they were never there.

"Mong and I will keep the coast clear," Emmett says, taking a seat at the reception desk in front of the shelves of dried herbs and roots in apothecary jars. Mong, thinking he's the size of a Chihuahua, promptly jumps up onto Emmett's lap, causing my friend to disappear behind an explosion of white fur. "But keep your phones on. I'll text you if I see anything suspicious out here."

Hattie and I enter Eomma's consultation room. A sigh of relief escapes my lips when we crouch down and pull back the black drapery to reveal a discreet wooden box in the corner.

The ancient wood is covered with a tawny lacquer that makes it almost look wet, and shiny brass cutouts of suns and moons decorate its front. The box gives off a slightly mildewed, nutty smell, and as I run my hand along it, coldness seeps into the pads of my fingers.

"Wow," Hattie breathes. "It's beautiful up close, isn't it?"

"*You*, old wooden box, might just change our lives today,"
I say to the safe, and I feel something flutter inside my belly.

I take the tissue out of my pocket and unwrap Eomma's
lock of hair. The clipping is dark and curly and thick. Hattie
gingerly passes the vial of tears to me.

"You ready?" I whisper, even though no one can hear us.

Hattie nods. "It's now or never."

I dip one end of the hair into the tears and use a matchstick
to light the other end on fire. It catches easily, and I drop it
into the vial. The flame goes out, but not before my nostrils
are filled with a terrible stench.

"Ugh, that's gross." Hattie cringes.

I carefully spread the smoke from the vial over the full
face of the safe, making sure to get all the edges and corners.
Hattie passes me her phone and, looking down at the various passwords we've brainstormed, I start chanting them out
loud, one by one.

"Gom, Gom, Gom." (Way too obvious, but worth a try.)

"Gimchi jjigae. Gimchi jjigae. Gimchi jjigae." (Eomma's
favorite food.)

"Mong. Mong. Mong." (Eomma's third child.)

"Jeju Island. Jeju Island. Jeju Island." (Where Eomma was
born.)

"*Stairway to Heaven. Stairway to Heaven. Stairway to
Heaven.*" (Eomma's favorite K-drama.)

I continue to chant the possible passwords—we even try
our names—but my shoulders get tenser and my voice gets
shakier with each unsuccessful attempt. Eventually, we run
out of words and the safe remains closed.

"The smoke's almost gone." Hattie frowns. "What else could it be?"

"Hmm..." I feel frustration bubbling up my throat, but before I give in to it, I close my eyes and put myself in Eomma's shoes. What would she consider strong and important enough to protect her safe? "What if it isn't a word or name?" I think out loud. "What if it's a saying? Like one of those motivational quotes people post on Insta?" It suddenly comes to me. "Wait, that's it! The clan motto. It has to be." It's the phrase she lives by. "Okay, here goes nothing. Service and Sacrifice. Service and Sacrifice. Service and Sacrifice."

There's a wooden *pop!* from the safe, and suddenly, the intricate brass cutouts start to move as if they are doing a choreographed dance. We both gasp as the suns and moons twist and turn and rearrange themselves on the wooden face until, finally, all but four of the cutouts remain. They lock into vertical formation—moon, sun, sun, moon—completing the symbol of the gifted. Then the whole front side of the safe swings open like a door.

"Rye, we did it!" Hattie hugs me tight and grins. Or at least I'm pretty sure she grins. I can't be certain, because tears have welled in my eyes, making everything blurry. And yes, happy tears *are* a thing.

Squatting on shaky knees, I peek inside. The interior is smaller than I expected—about the size of our microwave. But sure enough, next to Hattie's Gi is the spellbook containing all our family's healing spells, perfected and collected over generations.

My hand gravitates toward the precious volume like a moth

to light, and I pull it out. I stroke its soft brown leather cover as Eomma's words echo in my ears. *Our family spellbook isn't just a book, girls. It's a private conversation with the divine, connecting us right back to our ancestor, the Cave Bear Goddess. It is a privilege.*

I hesitate, my hand hovering over the book like an ominous storm cloud. What would Eomma say if she could see me right now...?

"Go on," Hattie whispers. "Open it."

That's all the encouragement I need. I eagerly turn the front cover, anticipation sparking in my fingers. If we're right, the magic-sharing spell is hiding somewhere within these pages.

My eyes gaze hungrily down at the first page.

Blank.

I turn another page.

Blank.

"What the...?" I flip more pages, only to find more emptiness. "I don't...I can't..." My throat starts to feel tight, and I pick up the spellbook with both hands, flipping the pages back and forth with greater urgency. But no matter what I do, they remain empty.

"Maybe we need to activate it somehow," Hattie says. "Here, let me have a look."

I place it in her hands, and immediately the spellbook starts making a soft murmuring sound. Slowly but surely, cursive Korean letters appear on the pages. First, they're just smudges, appearing in little smears like Nutella stains. But then they spread and grow, until each of the empty pages is filled to the brim with words and symbols.

Hattie looks apologetic. "Sorry, Rye," she mutters. "It must be spelled to activate when a blood Gom touches it."

I shrug and pretend I don't care. But of course I do. A lot. This is exactly why we need to do this spell—so I can stop being the odd one out.

Hattie skims through the book, and at first, all we see are healing spells. Spells for curing migraines to spells for clotting blood. They're all spells we're familiar with and, not to be a show-off or anything, I already know most of the incantations by heart.

But then we come across a chapter entitled "Miscellaneous."

"This must be where it is," Hattie breathes. We flip through the spell titles as my heart beats all the way up to my temples. And that's when we see it: the words *Temporary Gift-Sharing Spell* in big, scratchy handwritten letters.

"Oh my Mago, we did it!" I whisper-shout at Hattie. "I can't believe we found it!"

Eomma's door suddenly squeaks open and we almost jump out of our skins.

"Eomma?!" I squeal.

"Nope, just me." Emmett looks a little sheepish. "What's taking you guys so long? I've already eaten all the Choco Pies in the desk drawer. Can we go now?"

I wave him over to us. "Come look at this, Em!"

Even Mong comes to huddle over the spellbook with us, as Hattie, Emmett, and I silently read the preamble:

Casting this spell will allow a witch's gift to be shared temporarily with a saram subject for seven days. The witch's strength will be reduced by half for the duration of this period.

Two notes of warning:

(1) *This spell must not be cast between the gifted. Previous attempts have resulted in severe and unintended consequences, including death.*

(2) *Post-spell, all the saram subjects' memories must be wiped with a strong dose of Memoryhaze potion to preserve the privacy and sanctity of the clans.*

"*Pfft*, I am *not* having my memory wiped," I quip. "Not now, not ever."

"Defo not," Hattie answers. "That won't apply to you. You're a special case."

Emmett frowns and clutches Mong. "Guys, this sounds risky. I really don't think you should be messing with this stuff."

I ignore his warning and focus my attention back on the page. It's too late now to turn back—I'm too invested.

Instead, I follow my finger over the hand-drawn pictures of bellflower root, perilla leaf, and hongsam root, and read through the instructions. "So it looks like we make two potions with these ingredients—one for you and one for me. The clinic should have everything we need."

Hattie nods. "We drink half the potion before the incantations, in the presence of a council elder, then we do the

incantations and pour the other half into the Gi cauldron."
She pauses. "That's totally doable!"

I frown. "Uh, except we need to find a council elder who's
willing to be there. Not to mention we need to get inside the
temple to use the Gi cauldron. You know I can't get in unless
I'm with Eomma and Appa."

"Riley's right," Emmett says, pursing his lips. "Doesn't sound
that doable to me."

I exhale the disappointment from my system, now wishing
I'd listened to him. "I knew it couldn't be that easy. This is
never gonna work."

Hattie, with her eternal optimism, grins widely. "You guys
give up too easily. Don't you see this is perfect? In fact, we
couldn't make it more perfect if we tried."

Emmett and I cock our heads. Did she just read the same
words we did?

"My ceremony's tomorrow," Hattie reminds us. "I'll have
just gotten my Gi, we'll have easy access to the cauldron, *and*
all the elders will be there. That's when we'll do the spell."

I suddenly feel a little sick to my stomach. "Hat, we can't
do it at your initiation! It's your big day. What will people say?
You could get in *so* much trouble. You can't do that for me!"

Hattie shakes her head. "Don't you see? It is *the* ideal opportunity to make a statement in front of all the elders and the
congregation. Once we transfer half my magic to you, you can
prove you know the incantations to pretty much any healing
spell, which I know you do. And then the council will have no
choice but to let you do your own initiation ceremony when

you're ready." Her eyes light up. "It's going to go down in history as the day the gifted clans joined the twenty-first century."

The idea of being the center of attention as I recite the incantations makes me want to puke. But Hattie's right—I know the words to the spells as well as she does. I've just never had the Gi or divine support to power them. If this could help me gain the acceptance and recognition of the council, what else could I want?

That thought alone makes me feel warm and fuzzy, and I squeeze Hattie's arm. I can't find the words to express my emotions in this instant, but I know she knows. This means everything to me.

"I don't mean to be the resident party pooper, *again*..." Emmett starts. "But why do you think your parents kept this from you, Rye? Even I'll admit the spell doesn't seem impossible once you have the cauldron and the elder. So why hide it? It says it's only dangerous when cast between the gifted."

I swallow the lump in my throat. I've been wondering the same thing. "Do you think maybe...that perhaps...they don't *want* me to have magic? That they think I'm not good enough to be a healer and I don't deserve to be a Gom?" A lump forms in my throat, and suddenly tomorrow seems like a very, *very* bad idea once again.

"Don't be silly!" Hattie says, taking a photo of the spell and putting the book back in the safe. "You know Eomma and Appa are super supportive of you. They're just old school and never thought this was a valid option. We have to show them that some risks are worth taking. Easy as that."

I remain silent as she shuts the safe door and jumps to her

feet. "It's decided, then. We'll do the spell tomorrow, right after my initiation." She ushers us out the door and squeezes my shoulder reassuringly. "Trust me, sis, they'll come around. They all will. And we'll be opening up our own practice in no time."

As always, Hattie's words lift the weight from my shoulders. She's right. Eomma and Appa *have* always been supportive. And once I have my magic, they will be happy for me, too. I grab her and hug her tight, saying a thank-you prayer to Mago Halmi for my sister.

As we rush out of the clinic, excitement and nerves bubble up inside me like a shaken soda can.

One more day, and I will be a healer.

One more day, and I will be able to wield the power of the divine.

One more day, and my community will see me as an equal. They will accept me and embrace me as one of their own.

And then, perhaps, I'll finally belong.

5.
Time to Get Initiated, Witches

I WAKE TO THE FEELING OF something wet and sticky on my face. I jolt up in bed to find Mong sitting on my stomach, slobbering all over me.

"Ew, Mong, get off! Your breath stinks." I push him away and then do a double take. "Wait, are you wearing *clothes*?"

I hear Hattie chuckling from somewhere on the other side of the room. "It's an *outfit*, Emmett says. For the special occasion today."

I rub my eyes and follow Hattie's voice.

She's already up, sitting at her dressing table, brushing her long hair. The morning sun is shining through the gap in the curtains, pooling over her head and shoulders like a halo. "I don't know when he did it, but when I woke up this morning, I found Mong dressed like this with a little note on his collar."

She throws me the note. It reads:

For the special occasion today, I designed a celebratory outfit for Mong. *Guess who he is! Yeah, I know. I'm amazing. Also, for the love of all things baked, don't do anything stupid today. Well, not any more than what you've already got planned. . . I better see your faces after the ceremony. OR ELSE. —Em*

I study Mong's outfit. Black "scales" cover his body, making his big puppy-dog eyes stand out even more than usual. There is a single blunt horn on his forehead, framed by a great lion's mane, and around his neck is a small round bell. He looks part dog and part lion, with a tiny unicorn horn.

"Ha! He's the Haetae!" I squeal in delight.

Hattie giggles. "Pretty spot-on, right?"

The Haetae is a uni-horned lion beast, and one of the most-well-loved creatures in our culture. He's Mago Halmi's guardian pet, known for two things: his incredible loyalty, and his ability to manipulate time.

"Emmett really outdid himself," I say. "I wish he and Mong could come to the ceremony today."

"I know. Me too."

I roll out of bed and stumble over to Hattie, wrapping my arms around her shoulders. Our reflections smile back at us in the dresser mirror, and for a moment, there is no ceremony, no spell, no magic. Just me and my sister.

"Thank you for doing this for me," I say quietly. "And yes, yes, I know—you're doing it as a matter of principle as much as you're doing it for me. But still." I suddenly remember what else today is. "Oh, and by the way, happy thirteenth birthday!"

She smiles, and her cheeks glow warm with love. Then just as quickly, her smile turns into a grimace. "Ew, morning breath much? And to think you threw shade at our mini Haetae for *his* breath. A bit rich, Rye. A bit rich."

"Whatever do you mean, darling sister?" I say innocently as I exhale deeply into her face. "My breath smells like flowers. See?"

She shrieks and pushes me away. "OMG, you're the worst. Go brush your teeth!"

I chuckle and run out of the room before Hattie can retaliate.

Today is going to be the best day of my life, and it's already off to a roaring start.

Somehow, the morning passes in a flash, and before I know it, we're back in the sanctuary at the temple. Unlike in a normal Saturday service, the Gi cauldron is surrounded by a circular altar full of food offerings to our patron goddess. Among them are plump persimmons, savory gimbap, and sweet rice cakes drizzled in honey. Generous bowls of rice wine are dotted like milky exclamation points among them, and I gape at the size of the bae. The juicy Korean pears, each almost as big as a bowling ball, are stacked in a pyramid. Everything looks delicious, except for the plates of raw garlic and mugwort leaves. The Cave Bear Goddess apparently loves those, but I could definitely pass on them.

My parents and I sit in the front row of the Gom pews, eagerly awaiting Hattie's appearance. Hundreds of witches have gathered to watch her become a full-fledged healer, and looking around at all the expectant faces, I start to get cold feet about our plans to hijack the ceremony. I shove my right hand in my pocket and make sure the potion is still there and in one piece. I can't believe we're *actually* going to do this. . . .

Soon, a hush falls over the crowd. Hattie enters the sanctuary behind the five elders, and they walk in single file toward the Gi cauldron. My sister is wearing open-toed gold sandals, and her long golden hanbok ripples like gentle waves behind her. A fur headpiece sits grandly atop her head, sporting a row of sharp bear claws that make it look like she's wearing an ivory crown. Eomma and Appa let out quiet squeals of delight, and I beam proudly beside them. Hattie has worked so hard for this, and her initiation is going to be a breeze.

As she walks, her eyes search the crowd for me. And when they meet mine, she taps the side of her dress, reminding me that her potion is in the hidden pocket of her hanbok. I nod back, and she gives me a quick smile.

"Welcome, fellow witches, to a very special occasion," Auntie Okja says, starting the ceremony. "For today, we initiate our newest healer into the Gom clan." She continues with the preamble before inviting Mrs. Kim, the Gumiho elder, to take over.

"Now let's get this initiation started." Mrs. Kim steps forward and rubs her wrists together. As her gifted mark glows silver, she chants a spell under her breath. Before our very eyes, a young man materializes in front of the altar, clutching his stomach in pain. He looks so real, it's hard to believe he's just a Gumiho illusion.

"Please help me," he gurgles to Hattie. "There's something wrong with me."

Hattie immediately springs into action and goes to the

man's side. She assesses him thoroughly while calming him with reassuring words. Then she announces, "This patient is suffering from internal bleeding. I will now perform a blood-clotting spell."

Eomma lets out a relieved sigh beside me as Hattie rubs her wrists and casts the spell with familiar ease. All those practice sessions between them have paid off—Hattie looks calm and composed; her lisp is hardly noticeable as she pronounces the difficult Korean consonants.

One down, two to go!

Mrs. Kim reveals the second test, and it's obvious to everyone what this patient's ailment is. She is missing big chunks of flesh from her legs, and the other clans, who aren't used to seeing so much blood, cover their eyes.

I, on the other hand, do a small fist pump. This one's easy. Hattie needs to do a muscle-grafting spell, followed by a flesh-replenishing spell. And I know she can perform both. "She's got this!" I whisper to my parents, and they nod back in agreement.

Hattie rubs her wrists again, and when her gifted mark glows gold, she holds her palms over the patient's legs. As Hattie's chanting grows in volume, the patient's wasted limbs begin to transform, the hollowed cavities of sinew and bone filling with muscle and flesh.

"Another pass!" Auntie Okja announces. "Only one more spell to go."

Hattie grins, and I clutch my hands. She's almost there!

Mrs. Kim reveals her final test, and a frail old man appears where the woman was lying a moment before. He's in the fetal position and unusually still. I lean forward, trying to figure out what he's suffering from.

Hattie crouches down and assesses him from head to toe. She pauses at his face and then again at his neck and at his wrist. She frowns, and I look to Eomma and Appa. "What is it? What's wrong with him?"

Appa's forehead creases. "I think it's a trick question."

Eomma nods, swallowing hard. "I think so, too."

I look back at the man and rack my brain for possible ailments. He's not bleeding, and none of his bones look obviously broken. He doesn't seem to be in pain, and he's so still it looks like he's not breathing.

Then it dawns on me.

"Oh my Mago." I breathe out.

I look to Hattie just as she rechecks the man's pulse a third time. She takes a moment to gather her thoughts. Then she stands confidently and announces to the council, "This man is not alive. And while there are certain spells that can bring mortals back to life, it is against the council's code of conduct to do so, as it would break the sacred covenant the clans have with the Spiritrealm. For this reason, I will refrain from casting any spells to revive this patient."

"Wise answer, initiate," Auntie Okja declares, her voice booming with pride. "And you are correct. You have officially passed all three tests, and your Gi is now yours to keep and use at your will. Please come to the cauldron to receive your blessing from the Cave Bear Goddess."

As cheers and applause fill the sanctuary, Hattie walks over to the cauldron and holds her wrist over its mouth. The cauldron trembles into action, and with it, the food and drink offerings on the altar start levitating out of their bowls. It looks like we're in outer space and experiencing zero gravity.

A deep guttural wail escapes from the cauldron as Hattie's Gi and gifted mark glow Gom gold. The glow spreads from her wrist up her arm, through her torso, and down her legs until she is completely bathed in warm light. Then, with a loud, thunderous *boom*, a bolt of blinding white light hits Hattie.

When the light subsides and we can see again, all the food and drink have disappeared to the Godrealm, and Hattie is grinning widely.

The crowd breaks into another round of applause, and Eomma bursts into tears. Appa claps furiously, and I jump out of my seat to cheer at the top of my lungs. "She did it! You did it, Hattie!"

Hattie completes her vows, and as she nears the final words, the blood starts pumping through my body in double time. *Are we going to do this? We're actually going to do this. We shouldn't do this. No, we* definitely *should* not *be doing this.* At one point, I even contemplate leaving Hattie there and running away while I still can. This is officially the worst plan ever.

But then Hattie looks over at me and makes a subtle drinking motion, and my nerves ignite like flint. I can't run away now. My sister is doing this for me. We're doing this together, and it's going to work, darn it! The line *Sometimes you gotta burn your fingers to enjoy the s'more* rings in my ears.

Hattie and I exchange one final look. One determined nod. And then I take a deep breath and count to three.

"Now, Riley!" Hattie calls out.

I rip the potion out of my pocket and throw back half the liquid before I can change my mind. It burns slightly as it makes its way down my throat. But there's no turning back now. I have to commit.

Eomma and Appa stare in shock, frozen in their seats, as we start the incantations.

"*Jega gajingeon, dangsinege jumnida,*" Hattie chants. *That which I have, I give to you.*

I respond in earnest, my voice shaking like a leaf. "*Dangsini gajingeon, jega gajyeogamnida.*" *That which you have, I take from you.*

I start making my way to Hattie and the cauldron.

The motion brings Appa back to his senses, and he grabs my arm. "Riley, what are you doing? Sit back down!"

I give him a guilty look and hope my eyes are apology enough as I continue to chant. "*Dangsini gajingeon, jega gajyeogamnida.*" I break away from his grip and continue toward Hattie.

We're doing the right thing, I tell myself. *Everyone will come around, and they will eventually understand. Everything is going to be all right.*

Eomma is up on her feet now, pleading with us to stop. "Girls, please. Don't do this!"

It pains me to ignore her, but I keep walking. I focus my eyes on Hattie, and we both look at the cauldron. We're so close now. All we need to do is pour the second half of our vials into the cauldron and the spell will be complete.

Sweat beads on my forehead as I finally reach Hattie and we both lift our potions over the cauldron's mouth. This is our moment. I am finally going to become a witch, and the adrenaline is like a living thing pinballing inside me.

"Stop, girls, STOP!" Auntie Okja screams, running toward us. "You can't!"

Something about the frenzy in her voice makes me halt dead in my tracks. I have never heard her sound like this before.

"It's okay, Auntie O," Hattie assures her, beginning to tip her vial into the cauldron. "We know what we're doing."

Auntie Okja shakes her head so hard her perfectly coiffed hair frizzes around her head. She slaps the vial out of Hattie's hand with one swift movement. "No, you don't understand. It could kill you!"

My vial has started to tip slowly into the cauldron, but I flip it upright even before Auntie Okja makes it to my side. "What do you mean? It's only a temporary spell. We've done our research. The spellbook said it'd only be risky if cast between witches."

Auntie Okja cups my face in her hands. My eyes flit to my parents, who are both standing midway between the pews and the cauldron, holding on to each other. They look like they've seen a gwisin.

"It's dangerous," Auntie Okja blurts out in a rush, "because you're not a saram, Riley."

There is a confused murmur from the onlookers, and Hattie's jaw drops to the ground. I stay frozen, unable to comprehend her words.

"Whoa, whoa, whoa," Hattie says, her palms raised up. "Back up the bus. Are you trying to say that Riley has been a

Gom *all along?*" She shakes her head and glances at me with a disoriented look on her face. "Rye, what's going on?"

"No, not a Gom." Auntie Okja tightens her grip on my face. "You, my sweet child," she whispers hoarsely, "are a Horangi."

6.
The Tiger Is Out of the Bag

 I PULL AWAY FROM MY AUNTIE'S grip and rub my ears, because what I just heard cannot be true.

"Sorry, come again?" I splutter. "I thought you just said I was a *Horangi*." The clan name tastes bitter in my mouth.

The congregation lets out a shocked gasp. I'm pretty sure I hear Mr. Pyo using some colorful words that, according to Appa, only drunken sailors and politicians use.

Eomma and Appa have clambered up to the cauldron and are now looking at me as if I've grown a Haetae horn on my forehead.

"Tell her," I say to my parents confidently. "Tell Auntie O she's got her wires crossed. I'm a saram. You adopted me because my birth parents were teenagers who were too young to raise me. Go on, tell her."

The sanctuary goes so quiet I'm pretty sure the congregation can hear my heart thumping in my chest.

Eomma takes a big breath and steps toward me. All the color has drained from her cheeks. "Riley, my aegi-ya..."

Hattie squeezes my hand, but the muscles in my face freeze. *Aegi-ya?* Eomma only calls me *baby* when she's about to deliver really bad news.

"We'll talk about this later, okay? This isn't the time or place—"

"No!" I interrupt. "Tell Auntie O she's wrong." It goes against everything I know about myself to make a scene, especially in front of the entire congregation. But this can't wait. After all, how hard could it be to say the words *You are not a Horangi?*

Eomma winces. She starts to talk, but it's so quiet I have to lean in to hear her. "I'm so sorry, aegi-ya, but I'm afraid what your auntie says is true. Your birth parents were scholars from the Horangi clan. You're not a saram. You're just as gifted as the rest of us."

I guess she wasn't as quiet as I thought she was, because another wave of appalled gasps ricochets through the congregation. Out of the corner of my eye, I see the other elders gathering and whispering conspiratorially to one another.

"No, that's not right," I mutter. "I can't be... It's not possible!" My legs give out under me and I crumple to the ground. Hattie squats down to hold me, and I bury my head in her shoulder. This must be as much of a shock for her as it is for me.

Eomma and Appa approach to pull me into their arms, too, but I cower away. Everything I have ever known about me, about my identity, about my heritage . . . it was all just a made-up story. And of all the clans to be a part of, why did it have to be *that* one? They are power-hungry heretics who were banished from our community. They were cursed to never wield the power of the goddesses again. They killed Emmett's mom. Being a Horangi is a thousand million gazillion times worse than being a saram.

"Were you ever going to tell me?" I dare to ask.

Eomma drops her head into her hands, and Appa takes over, his voice all shaky. "We never meant to hurt you, Riley. We were just protecting you—"

"Protecting me, or yourselves?" I blurt out. "Admit it. You were just ashamed of your cursed daughter and what people would say if they knew. That's why you kept it from me."

"We could never be ashamed of you," Appa assures me.

"We love you more than anything," Eomma says.

"I wish I'd never been adopted!"

A flash of pain marks their faces, and my chest momentarily wrenches. "I didn't mean . . ." I trail off, feeling my face get damp. "But you *lied* to me. You knew how much I wanted to be gifted, and you made me believe I was a saram." Just thinking about it makes the anger return to the surface. "Were Hattie and I the only ones who didn't know?!"

Eomma and Appa lower their eyes, and it's obvious there's something else they're hiding. Auntie Okja glances nervously at the other elders, but then she exhales deeply and turns toward me. "It was me. I made them keep it a secret."

The elders narrow their eyes at her, and the congregation is now openly shaking their heads and muttering to one another. I suddenly realize Auntie Okja is going to be in a *lot* of trouble. And we're going to be the talk of the community for years to come.

"But why?" I whisper. "Why did I have to be a secret?"

"The plain truth is this, Riley," Auntie Okja says, her voice calm and soft. "When the Horangi staged that attack against the clans all those years ago, many innocent lives were lost. But the Horangi lost some of their own, too. Your parents were two of the scholars who died that day, and you . . ." She takes a deep breath. "You were still in your mother's womb when she died. I was there, and I felt you fighting for life. So I saved you. And I brought you to Eunha and James."

Hattie gasps next to me, and I hold on to her tighter as the world blurs.

"We knew you'd be banished with the rest of the clan if the council found out," Appa explains. "And we knew the future for the Horangi was bleak and lonely at best. What wrong had you committed but be born to foolish parents? We had to do everything in our power to protect you."

Eomma wipes her eyes. "We couldn't let anyone find out about you. So we decided to raise you as our own. And we have never looked back. Not once."

I don't get the chance to digest what has just been explained to me. Before I can even stand up and get my bearings, Mr. Pyo, the Samjogo elder, has convened with his fellow elders and begins addressing the congregation.

"All these confessions, as you can imagine, are a great shock to the council. Not only have these two children attempted to perform an illegal spell today, but also it is clear in our code of conduct, as stipulated by the Godrealm, that anyone seen colluding with the excommunicated clan must have their gifts stripped, too. Even if that someone is an elder."

Auntie Okja lowers her gaze, but my parents nudge her and the three adults cluster together with a mixture of pride and fear in their eyes.

"We stand by our decision to protect and love our daughter," Appa declares.

Mr. Pyo ignores him and continues. "We will put the girls' transgression aside and revisit it at a later date. As for these three adults, harboring a cursed fugitive—and for almost thirteen years, no less—is the very definition of colluding with the cursed clan." A sea of approving murmurs comes from the Samjogo pews. "But my other council members are of the opinion that the crime here is not so black-and-white. We have therefore decided—albeit reluctantly on my part—to exercise a degree of mercy."

He turns to my auntie and my parents. "We will allow you to choose a punishment you feel is commensurate to your crime. If you continue to claim innocence, we will report your act to the Godrealm, and the full curse will be enacted against you. The three of you will henceforth be stripped of your powers."

Hattie and I look at each other, and my fear is mirrored as plain as day on my sister's face.

"On the other hand, if you wish to retain your powers and continue being part of this sacred community, you must do two things. One, admit your crime publicly. And, two, excommunicate Riley from the gifted clans as all Horangi should be, including cutting off all future contact. We will give you seven days to make a decision. This is the final ruling of the council."

Eomma faints on the spot, and Appa catches and holds her in his arms while Auntie Okja chants her back to consciousness. The congregation is on its feet, and Hattie is squeezing my hand so hard I can't feel it anymore.

Today was supposed to be the best day of our lives.

Hattie was supposed to become an initiated witch, and I was supposed to become a healer alongside her. I was going to channel the power of the divine, and my sister and I were going to start our futures as healers together, side by side.

Instead, I learned that I am cursed, and that I come from a line of heretics and murderers. My birth clan killed my best friend's mother, and my adoptive parents will have to give up their divine callings if they want to keep me in the community.

No matter what happens, I will never belong.

As this realization dawns on me, I understand there is only one thing to do. Before I can change my mind, I turn and run, past Hattie, past my parents, past Auntie Okja, past the elders, and past the congregants who are now more than ever questioning my place in this society.

With sharp grief puncturing my chest, I charge out of the room, stopping only for a second when Mr. Pyo grabs my arm with his bony hand.

I shake him off and turn away. But not before I hear him whisper in my ear, "Don't do anything foolish, cursed child. We will be watching you."

7.
Where There's a Will, There's a Way

I RUN ALL THE WAY HOME. I run until my lungs feel like they're going to explode, but it still doesn't hurt as much as what just happened at Hattie's ceremony. I was outed as a Horangi in front of the entire congregation, and now my parents have seven days to choose between me and their gifts. I can't let them make the worst decision of their lives.

"Thank you for keeping the bugs out, door-sin," I whisper, and it unlocks itself for me.

I go straight to my room, and it's like the house knows the decision I've made. The floors creak and the walls stretch and whine, as if they're trying to stop me.

"You've been an amazing home," I say as I trace my fingers along the squirming wall. "But I can't stay. I can't let my parents sacrifice their divine calling for me. I just can't."

The house groans as if it's in pain, but I start putting clothes into my suitcase anyway. If I leave, my parents won't need to make an impossible choice. I go to pack my onyx stone but realize it's a reminder of my cursed heritage. I shove it into my bedside drawer instead.

Mong runs into my room and jumps into the open suitcase, still in his Haetae outfit. His eyes are round and watery as if he knows exactly what I'm planning, too.

"I'm gonna miss you, boy." I sigh. "Even your stinky breath."

"You don't have to miss him. Because you aren't going anywhere."

I swivel around to see Hattie standing at the door, with Emmett at her side. He's carrying a Tupperware container of freshly baked cookies. I can smell their warm yumminess from across the room.

"What are you guys doing here?" I demand, wiping my damp eyes. "I'd like to be alone."

"I ran after you and stopped to get Emmett. I told Eomma and Appa that I'd try talking to you. This is *not* the time for you to be by yourself."

Emmett walks over and upends my suitcase, dumping all my clothes on the floor. "This is what we think of your plan, by the way."

"Yeah, it stinks, Rye," Hattie agrees.

"Since when have you been one to run away from your problems?" Emmett asks. "You know that's more my jam."

I put my hands on my hips, feeling my face get hot. "Do you think I *want* to run away? But what choice do I have? I can't stay and let Eomma and Appa lose everything they've ever worked for. What kind of daughter would I be?"

Emmett closes the empty suitcase and sits on top of it. "On the way over here, Hattie filled me in on what happened."

I immediately shoot Hattie a look. Surely she didn't tell him I'm a Horangi. She wouldn't have!

"I told him," Hattie quickly says, "about how, after our spell failed, Eomma and Appa created a huge scene, demanding you be allowed to initiate into the clan. And when they wouldn't let up, the elders charged them with contempt of the code of conduct. As punishment, they have been given seven days to choose between disowning you or losing their gifts."

I breathe a sigh of relief. Emmett doesn't know. He still thinks I'm a saram.

Emmett shakes his head. "What did I tell you? Magic is *bad news*. If you hadn't tried to do that spell today, none of this would have happened. That goes for you, too, Hattie—you're an enabler."

He gives Hattie the side eye, and she looks sheepish. I lower my own eyes, mostly because I'm scared he'll be able to read in them what *really* occurred. But also because he's right. None of this would have happened if I hadn't agreed to do the spell. I mumble some random sounds just to fill the silence.

"But you didn't listen to me, and now look at you." He scowls. "It's pathetic seeing you like this, packing your bags and running away from parents who love you. You do realize some people don't have moms to run away from?"

That hits me like a punch in the chest. "You're right, Em."

"I know I am."

"I'm sorry . . ." I murmur.

"I know you are." He sighs and passes me a salted-caramel cookie. My favorite. "But it's happened now, so the only thing we can do is stay focused on the future and find a solution. And luckily for you, your best friend is a genius."

Hattie nods. "I have to agree with Emmett. His idea is genius."

I finally look up at him. "What do you mean?"

"Well, Hattie says the only reason the council can charge your parents for being in contempt is because you're a saram. So what if there was a way we could turn you into something else? What if we could literally turn you into a Gom—not with some temporary spell, but permanently, from the inside out? Then the basis for your parents' crime would disappear."

My heart drops. "No offense, Em, but if that were possible, wouldn't Eomma and Appa have done it to me years ago?"

Emmett takes a seat next to me on the bed. "I was thinking about it the other day. Remember that story you told me about how the Cave Bear Goddess came to be?"

I nod. Before becoming divine, our patron goddess was a mortal bear who wanted more than anything to be reborn in Mago Halmi's image. She prayed to Mago Halmi for her wish to be heard, and the mother of all creation entrusted her with a challenge. If the bear could survive a hundred days in a dark cave with only a bundle of mugwort and garlic to eat, her wish would be granted. The story goes that our bear ancestor was so devoted that, on the twenty-first day, Mago Halmi turned her into a beautiful goddess. That's how she became the patron of service and sacrifice.

"So," Emmett concludes, "why don't you do the same?"

"Wait, you want me to sit in a cave and eat mugwort and garlic?" I ask, genuinely perplexed.

He groans. "No, you dummy. I'm saying you should pray to Mago Halmi and see if she'll grant you your wish to become a Gom. I may not approve of magic, but I don't deny it exists. If Mago Halmi did it for the bear, maybe she'll do it for you, too."

"Even better than that," Hattie says, with a spark in her eye, "we don't just pray—we summon her."

"*Whoa!*" Emmett stares at Hattie. "Trust you to always take it a step too far."

I snort. "Em's right. You can't *summon* the mother of all creation. That's impossible."

"It *is* possible. There's a specific summoning spell. Noah told me about it." Hattie does this weird face twitch I've never seen before. "It's prohibited magic, so, technically, we need council approval before casting it, but desperate times, right?" She shrugs. "Anyway, Noah said the Miru protect one of the things needed for the spell. They keep it at his dad's Taegwondo dojang."

"Just because Noah said it's true doesn't mean it's true," I point out.

Emmett coughs. "Also, you just said yourself, it's *illegal*. Haven't we all learned our lesson about breaking laws today?"

Hattie doesn't say anything, so I continue. "Emmett has a point. Besides, people say things all the time without meaning them. Noah seems nice and all, but how do we know he's trustworthy?"

"Noah wouldn't lie to me, okay?" Hattie snaps.

I clamp my mouth shut. What was *that* about?

"Holy shirtballs!" Emmett bursts out. "Hattie Oh, do you have a crush on this guy?"

Her face turns as red as a monkey's butt, and suddenly the weird vibe between Hattie, Cosette, and Noah at Saturday School makes sense. Emmett's nunchi (basically, his ability to pick up what's going on without being told) is seriously next-level.

"Wait, the same Noah Noh who wears hipster glasses and has hipster hair?" I ask. "Oh my Mago, you *totally* have a crush on him!"

"What? No, I don't." Her voice is so high-pitched it sounds like Alvin the Chipmunk.

"Yes, you do."

"No, I don't."

"Yes, you *do*!"

"No, I *don't*!"

I crack up and slap my thigh so hard it stings. "You know what this means, right?"

Hattie frowns. "No, what?"

"If you guys get married and hyphenate your last names, you'll be Hattie Oh-Noh."

Hattie groans loudly, but Emmett cackles like a hyena, and even Mong seems to appreciate my comedic genius. He runs in circles a few times trying to chase his tail.

"Oh-Noh. *Oh no!* Get it?" I curl over myself and almost wet my pants. "It's too good. Just *too, too* good."

Hattie crosses her arms and harrumphs, but I see the ends

of her lips curl upward eventually. "I realize it's at my expense, but it's nice to know you still have a few laughs in you. Especially when so much has gone wrong today."

The reminder of today's events sobers me up. My eyes glance down at the mess of clothes strewn across the floor. Summoning the mother of all creation and asking for a wish is a radical plan, if ever there was one. But it's got to be better than running away from home. I'm not even thirteen, I don't have any money, and I don't have anywhere to go. At least this way I have a minuscule chance of saving my parents' gifts *and* remaining a part of this family.

I turn to my sister. "Okay, let's do it. I mean, at this point, what have we got to lose?"

"Uh…" Emmett raises his eyebrows and gives Mong an exasperated look. "Am I the only one with an amygdala in this room, boy?" Mong barks and wags his tail.

Hattie ignores Emmett's nerdy comment and smiles at me. "Good, we've got this! I'll text Noah and let him know we're coming. Also, the adults are gonna be home any minute, so we need to get out of here fast. They'd never let us try this. We can leave them a note so they don't worry."

She grabs a pen and paper from my bedside cabinet. "Dear Eomma and Appa," she says aloud as she writes. "We're sorry about the gift-sharing spell today. We didn't mean to get you in trouble with the council. But don't worry, we have a plan, and we're going to fix everything. We'll be back as soon as we can. (And no, we haven't run away or anything, so please don't call the police.) Lots of love, Hattie and Riley. P.S. We borrowed the money from the swear jar, just in case. Sorry!" She picks up the paper and scans it. "There. That should do the trick."

I take the note from her and add the words *really, reaaally* between *We're* and *sorry*. Because I really am *that* sorry. Although I'm still a teensy bit mad at them for lying to me for all these years. Maybe they deserve to stew for a *little* while....

Emmett fiddles with his ring, and suddenly I remember the big elephant in the room.

"Em," I start slowly, "you said yourself that magic got me into this mess in the first place. And I know your dad hates you getting involved with any clan stuff." I glance down at his ring. "And understandably, too. So thank you for your genius idea about praying to Mago Halmi. But I think you should go home now. Leave this to us. Hattie and I will do the summoning."

He jumps to his feet and puts his hands on his hips. "Are you serious? Look what happened when I let you two take charge at the ceremony." He stares down at me with laser eyes so intense I shrink back. Even Hattie takes a step away. "No way. Not in a million years. I am not leaving you to ruin your life any more than you already have. If you're gonna summon the mother of all creation, you're gonna need me around to keep you alive. Let's face it—I'm the only one here with their head screwed on straight."

He takes a long moment before speaking again. "Besides, I lost my mom once to magic. I'm not gonna lose you to it, too."

I swallow hard and look at Hattie. I have to tell Emmett everything. He needs to know I come from the clan that killed his mom. What kind of best friend would I be to keep that from him when he's willing to put everything on the line for me?

Hattie's eyes are sympathetic, but she doesn't give me a sign either way.

"Stop dawdling," he says. "Let's go."

And just like that, the moment is gone. I know at some point I'll need to tell him. And I mean, I *will*.

But not now.

Not today.

Because right now, we have the mother of all creation to summon. And I need all the help I can get.

8.
Noah Noh and the Dojang

 AFTER WE MEET NOAH OUTSIDE the dojang, he sneakily leads us past his mom's bodega on the ground floor and then up the back stairs. Hattie and Noah are acting super awkward with each other, and I can't believe I hadn't picked up on their lovey-dovey vibes before. Now that I know, I kind of feel bad that I didn't notice earlier. Sisters should notice these things.

"Hattie says you're a b-boy as well as a martial artist," Emmett says to Noah, looking at him curiously. "Are you as good as she says you are?"

Noah stops at the top of the stairs and French-tucks his shirt into the front of his trendy whitewashed jeans. He smiles freely, revealing two dimples at the ends of his mouth. "Sure, I love break-dancing. But it's easy when you've got Miru blood in your veins. Half the work is already done for you."

Most protector-clan witches are born with either super-human speed or strength. But Noah was blessed with both. Definitely a case of good genes (and also, good jeans).

"As for martial arts, I get by."

Hattie coughs. "Humble, much? He's only the undefeated national Taegwondo champion for his age group, not to mention he also does Capoeira, Hapkido, *and* Zumba."

Noah blushes slightly at Hattie's praise but grins. "Zumba is by far the hardest. Never realized how hard it was to do a shimmy while shaking your hips. You guys should come to a class one day. It's an awesome workout."

Emmett tries to hide it, but I see the smile creeping up his face. This is the first time he's met Noah, but it's clear even Emmett isn't immune to his charm. There's something about Noah's quiet confidence that screams *I'm cool.* The cute glasses and fauxhawk don't hurt, either.

"Seriously, though, it's nothing special," Noah explains. "Martial arts kinda comes with the territory."

Noah's dad is a Taegwondo grandmaster and comes from one of the most well-known protector families in the Miru clan. His dojang in the heart of Koreatown is famous for churning out Olympic-level martial artists, but you wouldn't know it by walking in there.

We enter through the staff-only back door. The training studio is drab and outdated, with peeling wallpaper and way-too-bright lights. The sound of voices chanting Taegwondo commands reverberates through the walls.

"Just keep your voices down," says Noah. "My appa is teaching a class in the front studio, but we should have five minutes before the session finishes." He leads us down a hallway to what I assume is his dad's office.

My first thought when we enter the room is *Whoa, if Taegwondo were a goddess, this room would be her shrine.* The place is littered with trophies of all shapes and sizes—on the desk, on the shelves, on top of a stack of pressed white uniforms, and even on the floor. It's obvious the dojang has won its fair share of competitions.

Noah closes the door behind him and rests his back against it. He nudges his glasses up on his nose. "Hey, I'm sorry about what happened earlier, at temple," he says to me. "That was pretty rough. I can only imagine what you must be going through right—"

"Thanks," I quickly interrupt before he can say anything else to raise Emmett's suspicions. "I understand you know how to summon Mago Halmi," I say instead, looking at Hattie for confirmation.

"I can't say I've ever done it before or know anyone who's tried," Noah responds. "From what I've heard, none of the gifted councils in the country have approved a summoning-spell application for years. But I *have* seen it in our family spellbook. I even memorized it, because it looked so badass."

"I told you so," Hattie says to me, looking smug.

"Would you be willing to teach it to us?" I ask.

Noah pauses and glances over at Hattie.

"We know it's illegal," I quickly add, "but we wouldn't ask if it wasn't important. And we wouldn't tell anyone about your involvement, of course."

Hattie nods. "It's the only way we can think of to save our family."

Noah runs his hand through his hair before answering. "Okay, I'll teach you. Anything to provide and protect—it is our clan motto, after all."

Emmett and I raise our eyebrows at each other. That's an excuse if I ever heard one. We both know the real reason Noah is helping us is because he likes Hattie. Not that I'm complaining.

Noah rummages through the mess on his dad's desk and somehow finds a pen and some paper. "I'll write down the incantations for you, but you'll also need to find some ashes of death and the elixir of life to complete the spell. That, and a willing initiated witch."

Hattie raises her hand. "Willing witch present and accounted for."

"Any chance you have access to some ashes of death?" Noah asks.

We all go quiet. They're not exactly something you can find on the shelves of a supermarket, and I've never seen them stocked at our clinic.

Emmett clears his throat and slowly raises his finger—the one with his silver band on it. "Could this work? It contains some of my mom's ashes." He coughs uncomfortably. "There's only a tiny bit in there, though, and I'm not sure how much you'd need. . . ."

"You'd only need a pinch," Noah confirms, "so that could work, if you're willing."

"No!" I shake my head furiously. "Absolutely not. Not your ring, Em. It's your most prized possession."

"But I'd get the ring back, wouldn't I?" Emmett asks Noah. Noah nods. "We only need the ashes."

"In that case, I'll offer it up. The sooner we get this done, the quicker we can go back to our normal lives. All this magic stuff gives me indigestion."

I frown and study Emmett's face. "Are you *sure*? Like, swear-on-your-salted-caramel-cookie-recipe sure?"

He shrugs. "It's fine. The rest of the urn is at home. And besides, the ashes aren't what's important."

The ring used to be his mom's wedding band before it was refashioned for Emmett. He once told me, in a rare moment of candor, that the ring was special to him because it represented his parents' love—and their love created him.

I pull Emmett in for a hug. "Thank you."

He scowls and pushes me away. "You've heard me before—emotions give you wrinkles. Simple cause and effect."

Noah passes the handwritten incantations to Hattie. "So, that just leaves the elixir of life."

"That's here somewhere, right?" I ask, remembering what Hattie had said. The Miru had one of the things needed for the spell.

He frowns. "Well, not exactly. The Joseon Chalice is kept here at the dojang, yes. It's the sacred chalice of King Sejong the Great from the Joseon dynasty. Did you guys know he was gifted? Anyway, the artifact itself is not the elixir of life. The witch has to collect the elixir *in* the chalice along with the ashes for the spell to work."

"So what *is* the elixir, then?" I ask, my stomach dropping.

"Do we have to find an infuser or something? David Kim is the only Tokki I sort of know, and he lives on the other side of the city."

Noah pauses cautiously before answering. "The elixir of life is blood. Blood must be drawn from the witch and collected in the chalice."

I freeze. Did he just say *blood?*

I turn to Hattie. "You knew, didn't you?" I feel bubbles of anger rising in my throat. "And you purposely didn't tell me."

She looks sheepish. "I knew you'd try to stop me if I did."

"Of *course* I'd stop you!" I shout. "I can't make you *bleed* for me!" It's enough that Emmett is giving up his mom's ashes without my sister having to hurt herself, too.

Hattie comes over and grips me by the shoulders. "Riley, I know you're just looking out for me, but I'm doing this for me, too, okay? They're also my parents, and the last thing I want is for them to lose their gifts. And you know what else I don't want? I don't want to lose my only sister. A few drops of blood to prevent that from happening is a price I will happily pay. Besides, Eomma or Appa can heal me later."

I take a big breath. I still feel nauseated at the thought of Hattie having to bleed for this spell to work. But she's not wrong. We're in deep now, and this is our only way out.

"Fine." I squeeze her so tight, her eyes start to bulge out of her head. "I owe you. Big-time."

Noah walks across the room and bends over to pick up a dusty trophy hiding behind a photo of some people in Taegwondo whites. It's a small, unassuming cup that's been sitting there so long the metal has dulled to a tawny brown.

"The chalice has been enchanted to automatically return to this position within four hours, so you'll need to be quick." He polishes the trophy's face with the bottom of his T-shirt, and a golden sheen emerges.

"Wait, *that's* the Joseon Chalice?" I ask. The six-hundred-year-old sacred artifact is a tacky-looking trophy gathering dust in his dad's messy office?

Emmett gawks. "It wasn't even inside a glass cabinet."

Noah runs his hand through his hair in that carefree way of his. "Sometimes putting a thing in plain sight is the best hiding place of all."

"Genius!" Hattie beams, and Noah grins back at her so hard his two dimples look like sinkholes on his face.

"Holy shirtballs, get a room, lovebirds," Emmett says with a snicker.

Hattie throws us a death glare before turning back to Noah. "Thank you so much for helping us. And for lending us the chalice. But we better go. It's already dark outside, and we need to find a quiet place to do the spell."

He hands her the chalice, and when their fingers touch, they jolt away from each other as if they've been electrocuted.

Noah rubs the back of his neck shyly. "You're gonna need all the power you can get for the spell. How about I take you through the Saturday School portal to Santa Monica Pier? My brother is on guard duty there tonight, so I can sneak you in. The spell will work best if you go into the ocean at high tide and get the full strength of the moon's pull behind you."

"We share the same sky as the Godrealm," I explain to Emmett, who is looking confused at the mention of the ocean, "so our moon is part of the divine. It gives spells more *oomph*, if you know what I mean."

Emmett shrugs. "Whatever you say."

Hattie nods gratefully. "You're a gem, Noah. Thank you so much!"

Emmett makes kissy noises and whispers in my ear, "Oh yes, you're such a *gem*, Mr. Oh-Noh. You can bling me up *anytime*."

Noah's eyes widen behind his glasses, while Hattie throws up her hands in exasperation. "Dude, what does that even *mean*?"

I laugh heartily. I know that we're about to summon the mother of all creation and that Hattie will have to sacrifice her own blood to make it work. But the truth is, I can't think of any two people I'd rather be with right now. One thing is for sure—I would be utterly and overwhelmingly lost without my sister and best friend.

9.
Um, Mago Halmi, Is That You?

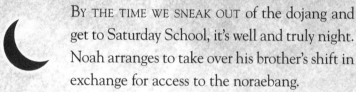 By the time we sneak out of the dojang and get to Saturday School, it's well and truly night. Noah arranges to take over his brother's shift in exchange for access to the noraebang.

We enter room 18, and as the glamour-reveal song loads, I stand there, trying to ignore the phone vibrating in my pocket. It's been buzzing for ages now, but I can't bear to look at the increasing number of missed calls showing on my screen, much less actually answer it. My parents will have seen our note by now, and I imagine Eomma's glasses fogging up in panic as Appa reads it out loud, his forehead creasing with worry. The guilt bubbles inside me like trapped air, and a bout of hiccups escapes my mouth.

Hattie takes my hand reassuringly. She knows hiccups are my tell when I'm nervous. "Everything is gonna be okay. The sooner we get this summoning over and done with, the sooner you'll become a Gom. And the sooner that happens, the sooner our parents' crime will be pardoned. We're doing the right thing."

The Gumiho glamour on the noraebang room dissolves as we sing "Fake Love" for the second time this week, and I survey the classroom. The wall mural of Santa Monica Pier is just as impressive as when I first saw it. The Ferris wheel and roller coaster are bright and inviting, and the waves lapping against the wooden poles look as fresh and foamy as an ice-cream soda.

"All right, stand back," Noah says, stepping toward the mural and rubbing his wrists together. As his gifted mark glows blue, he starts chanting.

> *"Nae nunape inneungeot,*
> *Geurimsoge inneungeot.*
> *Nuneul keuge tteugo boseyo,*
> *Muni jamsi yeollyeoyo."*

"What's he saying?" Emmett whispers in my ear. His dad doesn't speak Korean, so the only words he knows are the ones he's picked up from hanging out at our house over the years.

I listen hard as Noah repeats the chant, and I translate it for Emmett.

> *"The thing that is in front of me,*
> *Inside the picture that I see.*
> *Use your eyes, look carefully,*
> *A door opens momentarily."*

The next thing I know, the sound of crashing waves fills my eardrums. My lips tingle, and when I lick them, I taste the salt of the sea.

"Sorry I can't come with you," Noah says, rubbing the back of his neck. "My brother is about to leave his post, and I can't leave the portal unguarded." He unfolds a weird kid's scooter he's been carrying since the dojang and gives it a little nudge, forward and back. "But I thought this might help for the trip home."

We all stare at it, unsure what to say. First of all, it's tiny. It looks the perfect size for a six-year-old kid, not for three teenagers. Second, the trip from Santa Monica to our house can take an hour by car. I can only imagine how long it would take by scooter—and none of us have helmets, either. Third and most important, it looks all types of strange. It's covered in shiny blue scales, and two webbed ears poke out from the handle bars. Little wings are attached to either side of the front wheel, and a pointy tail sticks out from the back. It looks like the spawn of a dragon mom and scooter dad.

"Uh, what *is* that?" Emmett asks.

"He's a dragon-on-wheels. We Miru use them before our gifts kick in—when our parents want us to practice moving at super speed, but within safe parameters. I guess you could call them training wheels for protectors." He pats the handlebars affectionately.

"Ahh!" I point at the back. "His tail just wagged!"

Noah tickles the scooter behind the ears. "My man Boris and I go way back. Ever since I got him for my sixth birthday.

A real firecracker, this one. He might be getting a bit rusty, but he's still got a few trips left in him. Don't ya, buddy?"

Boris's little wings flutter happily in response, but then he splutters and wheezes like an old man.

Noah looks a little embarrassed, but he quickly hides it with one of his easy smiles. "Sorry. I know he's not perfect, but hopefully he'll be better than nothing. Use him for as long as you need." He pushes the dragon-on-wheels toward Hattie.

"Thanks," she says, though I can't imagine what we're going to do with it.

"Oh, and one more thing," says Noah. He takes a Swiss Army knife from his pocket and extends it to her. "Here. You'll need this, too, for the . . ."

The cutting, I silently finish for him, wincing.

"Thank you," Hattie says. "This would've been impossible without you."

"And please be careful, won't you? I won't forgive myself if something bad happens to you."

Noah's declaration of feelings toward my sister is so open and honest that even Emmett doesn't dare to crack a joke.

Hattie pockets the knife and nods. "We will."

And with that, she folds Boris, tucks him under her arm, and strides through the wall. As she passes through the mural, her body pixelates as if she's a digital image in the middle of loading. Then she simply disappears.

"*Whoa.*" Emmett tries to hide his reaction, but I see the momentary look of awe on his face. "Are you sure it's safe for a saram and a halfie to pass through?" He points to me and himself, reminding me that I'm keeping the biggest secret of my life from my BFF.

Noah nods. "Totally safe. Good luck, guys."

We hurry in after Hattie, and the barrier feels cool and almost liquid, as if we're passing through a wall of Jell-O.

Once we're on the other side, we find ourselves standing on the beach underneath the Santa Monica Pier, and the gentle night breeze is blowing wisps of hair onto my face. Hattie's a few feet away, but there isn't another soul out for miles. From the damp outline on the sand, it looks like high tide has just passed, but I hope the spell will still work the way it's supposed to. I take off my shoes and feel the soft sand squish between my toes. It's still warm from a day of soaking up the summer sun, and it feels so good that I dig my feet in.

My eyes move up to the sky and I freeze. The moon is as red as a tomato.

"Guys," I call out. "Look up. The moon is bleeding."

Emmett wolf-whistles. "Wow, yeah, that's a blood moon, all right. It's the sign of a lunar eclipse. What a beauty."

Hattie joins us in studying the sky. "That's funny—I was just reading about a solar eclipse that happened in New Zealand today. You know, when the sun goes completely black, not red. What are the chances . . . ?"

Emmett shakes his head. "You must have read it wrong. You can't have both a lunar eclipse and a solar eclipse on the same day. It's impossible."

Hattie frowns. "But I'm sure it was in today's news."

Emmett crosses his arms. "Dude, do you know how much *Battle Galactic* I play? Our squad is the best in the galaxy, and I know space like the back of my hand."

Hattie raises her eyebrows.

"Em's obsessed with that game," I explain. "You know, the one that's like *Fortnite Battle Royale* but set in space? It's turned Emmett into a total astronomy geek."

I leave Hattie and Emmett to argue it out, and I walk toward the water, mesmerized by the way the moon paints a crimson glow over the Pacific. This is going to sound odd, but sometimes the sky makes me feel a bit . . . well, *sad*. Like when you forget something you know was important, but no matter how hard you try, you can't remember it.

"Anyway," Hattie says, coming over. She holds up the chalice and Noah's knife. "Back to the plan. This is how we're gonna do this. I'll take Emmett's ring and—"

"You won't forget what I showed you, right?" Emmett asks from behind us. He twists the ring nervously around his finger. "How you have to open the compartment gently so it doesn't break?"

"I'll be careful," Hattie assures him. "I know how important it is to you."

Emmett nods but looks nervous. He takes a cookie out of his backpack and nibbles on it to calm himself.

"Like I was saying," said Hattie, "I'll take Emmett's ring, and once I'm in the water, I'll activate my Gi, cut my palm, collect the blood in the chalice, sprinkle in the ashes, and then recite the incantations. Sound like a plan?"

I swallow the lump in my throat. It basically sounds like

Hattie is doing everything while Emmett and I sit around and watch. This should not be a spectator sport.

"I'll go into the water with you," I offer. "You don't even like the ocean, and you might get caught in a riptide. I'm a better swimmer than you."

She nods gratefully and passes me the chalice. "Thanks, Rye."

Emmett passes his ring to Hattie. "Protect it with your life."

She puts it on her finger. Then, holding hands, my sister and I step into the surf.

The water is freezing, which shouldn't surprise me, since I've grown up swimming in the Pacific (it's always colder than you think). But it's not every day I go for a dip in the middle of the night, and we both shiver as we wade in up to our knees. By the time we get chest-deep, the current picks up, and my sweater billows around me as if it's desperately trying to swim. If I'd known ahead of time we'd have to go into the ocean, I would've made us wear wet suits. Hattie's gorgeous ceremony dress is going to get trashed. I check the shoreline, and Emmett is looking at us nervously. He's standing a safe distance from Boris.

We've got this, I tell myself.

Hattie takes a big breath and rubs her wrists together. As her gifted mark activates, she flips open the Swiss knife and holds it in front of her open palm. "I can do this," she says confidently.

I'm sure she can—Hattie is the bravest person I know. But it still doesn't make it any easier seeing her hurt herself for a spell *I* need.

"I can do this," she says again. But this time, she doesn't sound as confident. She remains still and stares intently at her hands. Then I hear her say something so quietly, I'm not sure if I imagined it. "How do I do this?"

"If you want," I say softly, "I could help you."

She doesn't answer for a while, but eventually she whispers, "Yes, I think that would be best." She hands me the knife and takes the chalice. "You don't have to be scared of hurting me, okay? Just do it, and do it fast." Her voice is steady, but I can see fear in her eyes now.

I turn the knife in my hand a few times to make sure I have good control over it. "How about we count down together from five?"

She nods. "Okay."

"Five. Four. Thr—"

Before she can register what's happening, I quickly run the knife across her palm. She lets out a yelp, and I drop the knife in the water. I cup my hands around her palm and help pool the blood into the chalice.

"You did it," I whisper.

"Thank you," Hattie says, still wincing from the pain.

As her blood drips into the chalice, I slip Emmett's ring from Hattie's finger. Under the eerie red moonlight, I can just make out the secret compartment on the inside.

"There's a little tab you twist to open it," Hattie explains. "Don't turn it too far."

It's finicky work, but I manage to empty the ring's contents into the chalice before returning it to Hattie's finger.

"It's showtime," she says.

She closes her eyes and starts reciting the incantations Noah taught her.

Immediately, there is a change in the atmosphere and a suffocating thickness to the air. I clutch at my chest, trying to catch my breath. A fierce gust blows in from the Pacific, splashing sea spray into my eyes. I cover my face. When I can see again, my sister is floating facedown in the water in front of me.

"Hattie? *Hattie!*"

In a frenzy, I wade to her, and turn her over. She looks unconscious. I grab her by the armpits and start pulling her back toward shore. The wild waves try to swallow us, but I body-block them with all my strength. Emmett runs into the water, and somehow, together, we carry Hattie's limp body to the beach. We lay her on the sand, and I drop to my knees over her soaked, still form. I put my hand on the side of her neck, feeling for a pulse. I *think* it's there....

This wasn't supposed to happen.

This wasn't part of the plan.

"Rye, she's not breathing!" Emmett cries. "We need a healer!"

Never in my life have I been so helpless. I'm not a Gom! What's the point of knowing all the words to the spells when I can't use them to save Hattie? It feels like someone is punching my chest, over and over again, and I can't remember how to breathe.

"Stuff it!" Emmett screams, taking out his phone. "I'm calling nine-one-one!"

The prospect of explaining this disaster to a saram police

officer breaks me out of my daze. I crouch down over Hattie's face and start giving her mouth-to-mouth. Last summer, when Appa suggested I take a first-aid course, I'd sulked for a week. Who wants to learn modern medicine when you can learn magic? But right now, as I pinch Hattie's nose and breathe into her mouth, I'm so grateful I did.

"Ugh, my phone's dead!" Emmett cries, repeatedly hitting the blank screen with his finger. He eventually gives up and drops onto the sand next to me. "Please tell me the CPR is working."

I shake my head as a dam of tears explodes behind my eyes. I know my technique is right, but Hattie's eyes remain closed and her body is still. "It's no use!" I cry hysterically.

"Oh, bother. Where did my kitchen go?" I hear someone say.

My eyes flit up toward the voice, and my eyebrows furrow together. I don't know where she came from, but a frumpy middle-aged woman with frizzy hair has appeared on the beach in front of us. Her knitted vest looks dated, and—I won't lie—she smells a little like mothballs. But she has a soft, kindly face, and she's carrying a soup ladle covered with an oily red sauce. There's a picture of Winnie the Pooh on her apron with the line I'M SO RUMBLY IN MY TUMBLY, which is also covered in red stains.

"Who are you?" Emmett splutters.

My mind reels. "Ma...Mago Halmi, is that you?" Did the summoning spell actually work? Could this Korean Mrs. Weasley really be the mother of all creation?

The woman laughs heartily, and the red moon pulsates in

the sky, as if chortling with her. "By golly, no. I'm old, but I'm not *that* old." She waves her saucy ladle in the air. "I was just whipping up a low-calorie spicy tofu stew." She pats her stomach. "I'm on a diet, you see—too many indulgent initiation ceremonies of late. But then I heard one of my baby subjects summon me, so here I am, ladle and all."

I study the woman again from head to toe. If Hattie didn't summon Mago Halmi, then who *did* she summon?

"I do love those honey-drizzled rice cakes, though," she muses. "And I am partial to a good vintage rice wine on occasion." She looks dreamily into the distance.

Indulgent initiation ceremonies. Honey-drizzled rice cakes. Rice wine. It all reminds me of Hattie's ceremony, when the delicious food offerings disappeared into the Godrealm.

Suddenly, it dawns on me.

"Cave Bear Goddess?" I whisper.

The woman smiles warmly and tips her head. "At your service."

I let out a series of loud hiccups, and I clamp my mouth shut with both hands. *Whoa.* The patron goddess of service and sacrifice—the divine ancestor of my clan—is *here*, breathing the same air as me. I picture her golden statue at the temple, with its long neck, silken hair, and youthful glow....

"You're not how I imagined you," I blurt out. The shimmery golden hue to her skin is the only thing that looks familiar.

She chuckles and her soft belly jiggles with the movement. "I presume you mean the statue?" She winks at me. "The good thing about art, my dearie, is that it does not have to be accurate."

As the initial shock of seeing our patron goddess wears off, I realize this is not the time for small talk. "Benevolent goddess," I say urgently, "we need your help." I put my hand on Hattie's unmoving arm. "We were trying to summon Mago Halmi, but something went wrong, and my sister...She... She's not..." I break into another bout of tears.

"*Shh*, be calm, my child. I am here. Dry your tears. There's no reason to cry." The goddess drops her ladle, wipes her hands on her apron, and places one hand on my head. Suddenly, a calmness washes over me. It's as if she has physically lifted the prickly weight that was pressing on my chest.

"Goddess," I try again, "I will do anything you ask. Please, will you use your divine power to heal my sister? She was only trying to help me, and now she's...she's..." I trail off.

The goddess crouches down next to me and cracks her knuckles. "Well, now, let's see what we've got here." She places her hand on Hattie's heart, then lets out a loud sigh. "*Tsk-tsk*, she overexerted herself, I see. A baby witch shouldn't be performing such demanding spells. And prohibited ones, at that." She raises her eyebrow at Emmett and me, and we both look away.

"Will she be okay?" I ask, the heaviness returning to my chest. "You can heal her, right?"

The goddess looks from Hattie to Emmett to me. She pauses thoughtfully. Then she scratches her chin and speaks. "First, my dearies, do me a favor, won't you? Tell me why you were wanting an audience with the Mother."

I think on my feet. If I tell her the truth, Emmett will find out about my Horangi heritage, and that's the last thing I can deal with right now. Not when we need to save Hattie. My lying streak is just going to have to continue for the time being.

"The truth is, Goddess, my adoptive parents are being charged with the crime of protecting me because I am a saram. I wanted to summon Mago Halmi so I could ask her—like you did once—to be reborn, but as a Gom." I wipe my eyes and get on my knees. "But now, none of that matters. All that matters is that my sister be okay again. Please, Goddess, I beg of you, please help us save her. I'll do anything you ask. *Anything.*"

The goddess pats my back. "What a burden you have been carrying, child. I'm sorry you are hurting. But I admire your honesty. It's not an easy currency to come by in these troubled times."

I wince. Honesty is not a virtue I can claim today.

"Unfortunately, I am not allowed to interfere in issues of the Mortalrealm. Mother Mago's rules." She looks sadly at Hattie. "As much of a shame as it would be to lose a baby witch—"

"But you *must!*" I plead, the hysteria building inside me again. "This is all my fault. She wasn't supposed to get—"

She holds up her open hand. "Let me finish."

I snap my mouth shut.

"I am moved by your love for your sister. I also have sisters—five of them, in fact. And I, too, would stop at nothing to protect their interests." She affectionately traces Hattie's face with her fingers before addressing me again. "Like I said, I'm not allowed to interfere. But since I was summoned, I can offer you a job. And jobs, my dearie, must be compensated, even under Godrealm law. Would you be interested in doing a wee task for me?"

"Yes!" I shout. "Whatever you need!"

The goddess claps, and the moon flickers bright like a ruby. "Wonderful! All you need to do is find me the Godrealm's last fallen star. It's a piece of my world that doesn't belong here. While it can only enhance beauty in the Godrealm, on Earth it can grant its user divine power. That power has driven humans mad with greed and wrought only destruction and despair. I want to remove this evil from your world. If you bring the star to me, I will reward you." She smiles at me. "You, my child, will be reborn in my image—as a Gom and a healer. And I will restore your sister's life. This I promise you."

Emmett squeezes my hand, and I squeeze back with all my might. I have no idea what the Godrealm's fallen stars are, what they look like, or how we'd go about finding the last one. We are completely out of our depth, and I am *terrified*. But right now, all that matters is Hattie. And if we have a chance to save her, we *must* take it.

"I accept!" I blurt out, figuring the goddess will supply more details. "I will find the Godrealm's last fallen star and bring it to you."

The goddess grabs her ladle and jumps up to her feet. "Well, isn't that delightful news!"

"But how will we find you once we have it?" Emmett asks. His voice is trembling, but I'm glad he had the guts to ask, because it's a good question. Without Hattie, we won't be able to summon the goddess again.

"Don't you worry your pretty little heads about that," says the Cave Bear Goddess. "I will find *you.*"

She lifts her sand-covered ladle to the sky, and Hattie's limp body rises from the ground and levitates. "I will take your witch with me for now, for safekeeping, but leave you with a memento of her. However, you should know, the Godrealm is no place for a wee mortal, even if she is a witch. She won't last long there. When your time is up, the memento will help me locate you."

The goddess snaps her fingers, and suddenly Hattie's body disappears into the night air. Emmett and I gasp and leap to our feet.

"Wait . . . How long—?" I start.

"Well, I'd better be going now," she says. And, as if on cue, her stomach rumbles. "My stew awaits. But it was a treat meeting you today. I really mean that. And I will see you two very soon." She gives us a little wave of her ladle, and then just like that, she vanishes, too.

"But you didn't . . ." I look at where she was standing a moment ago, and my mind reels. "Em, can you believe—"

But Emmett's eyes are locked on a spot on the beach.

I follow his gaze and drop to my knees. Something under the sand is glowing.

"What is it?" I dig inside Hattie's still-fresh outline.

Emmett picks up a small, dark object. "My ring's here, but I don't know what that is."

I keep digging. My fingers land on something hard. I brush off the sand and hold it up to the moonlight. It's a glass vial, small enough to fit in my palm.

It's warm, and casting a red light.

And whatever is inside is *beating.*

I gasp, nearly dropping it back onto the sand. Floating inside the clear glass is a miniature human organ, veined and bloody and pumping steadily.

"What *is* it?" Emmett bites his lip so hard, a drop of blood blooms on it. "It looks like—"

"A heart. It looks like a *heart,*" I whisper, the words sticking in my throat.

"Ugh!" Emmett shrieks. "But *how? Why?*"

"The goddess said she'd leave a memento of Hattie with us. This must be it."

Emmett undoes his black cord necklace and throws it at me. "Here, use this."

I tie the cord around the contoured nape of the vial and put it around my neck. Hattie's shrunken heart hangs like a pendulum next to my own, and suddenly it all hits me like a ton of bricks.

"Em," I whisper, my voice hard and jagged, "if we can't find the last fallen star, and *fast,* Hattie will be gone forever." I pause. "And it will be all my fault."

A gull squawks in the distance as it flies across the blood moon, and I look up at the sky, terrified.

What in the three realms have we gotten ourselves into?

10.
The Dark Sun and Dark Moon

 "WE HAVE TO TELL YOUR PARENTS," Emmett says, gripping my shoulders tight. "This is officially too big for us to handle by ourselves. We need help."

"No!"

He raises his eyebrows at my sudden outburst. "But why? Even you have to admit we're out of our depth here."

I look down at my hands. He doesn't know I come from the cursed clan. If the adults found out Hattie had been carted off to another realm after illegally trying to summon Mago Halmi on my behalf, it would just prove everything the council has been saying about me. I have to show them I'm not a rebel. I'm the opposite—I want to fit in. If we can find the last fallen star, not only will we get Hattie back, I will be turned into a real Gom, too.

"We can solve this on our own. My parents have enough on their plates as it is. I got us into this mess, and I will get us out. I can do this. I *will* do this."

He frowns, and I can tell there's a lot more he wants to say.

"Just *one* more day," he finally says. "One day, and then we get the adults involved."

"Five." My heart is racing.

"Two. And that's my final offer."

"Fine," I say, relenting. "Two days."

He squirms, but nods. "Then tell me, Sherlock. Where do we start?"

I think of Hattie. What would she do in this situation?

"When Hattie and I do jigsaw puzzles, she always starts with the edge pieces," I say. "We need to do the same thing now—start with the edges, or what we know, and work our way in."

Emmett rubs his temples. "Okay, Emmett Harrison, think. *Think.* You've conquered fifty planets on *Battle Galactic*—you've got this. What do you know about stars?"

He closes his eyes for a moment, and then turns to me. "For starters, I know there's no such thing as a fallen star. There are fall*ing* stars, but they're just streaks of light you can see from the Earth when meteoroids enter our atmosphere and burn up. They're not really stars at all."

He closes his eyes again, then bites his lip. "Man, if only we could get into the Griffith Observatory. There are some amazing resources there." He looks up at the sky, where the sun has only just started to rise. "But it won't be open yet. It's too early."

A small flicker of hope kindles inside me. "Em, I overheard Cosette Chung, one of the girls at Saturday School, say she was going to be at the Griffith Observatory all week. Some type of sleepover summer program for budding astronomers. Maybe she'll let us in."

Emmett's eyes brighten. "Now you're talking. Can you text her and double-check?"

I reach into my damp pocket to DM Cosette on Instagram, only to realize my mistake. "Darn it!" I say, pulling out my phone. It's dripping like a tap. "I . . . I guess I forgot to leave my phone behind when I went into the ocean."

"Sorry," says Emmett. "I'd offer you a bag of rice to dry it in, but I'm fresh out."

I press the phone's power button, already knowing it won't turn on. "It's ruined." I want to collapse on the sand and cry.

"And mine is out of juice," Emmett reminds me.

"What are we going to do?" I ask, on the verge of panic.

"We'll just have to turn up and hope this girl lets us in."

"But how are we going to get there? Without a phone, we can't get a ride. . . ."

I look over at the small scooter, still lying in the sand where Hattie left him. "I guess we'll have to take the dragon-on-wheels."

Emmett makes a face. "But he's so creepy. We could walk?"

I pull Hattie's heart vial from under my sweater and dangle it in Emmett's face. "Do you think we have time to *walk* right now? It'll take us half a day just to get there."

He swallows. "You're right. But I'm not touching him. You drive, and I'll hold on to you."

"Wimp."

I carefully unfold Boris and turn the handlebars left and right to get a feel for him. He's kind of slimy to the touch, and I wonder how we're both going to stay on. "Sorry in advance for being so heavy," I say to the scooter. "You probably aren't used to carrying two people, but we need to get to the Griffith Observatory as fast as we can."

Boris's tail wags in response, and with that encouragement, I gingerly step aboard. Emmett quickly gets on after me and wraps his arms around my waist like a baby koala. Boris lets out a groan but stays upright. Then he bounces slightly, as if testing the new weight.

"Here goes nothing." I go to lower my right foot to push off, only to realize that it's stuck on the scooter. "What the—?" I look down to see Boris's blue scales spreading over my feet. They unfurl like a second skin, until the cold sliminess has swallowed me right up to the calves. It feels like I'm encased in wet concrete. But at the same time it seems secure, as if I've been strapped on tight to a snowboard.

"Ahh!" Emmett shrieks, hopping from one foot to the other. "He's *eating* you alive!"

Boris's ears and wings start to flap, and I grip the handlebars. "Hold on tight, Em!" I yell. "I don't think I'm the one driving!"

And sure enough, as soon as the words escape my mouth, we start to move. *Fast.* So fast I don't even get a chance to close my mouth. The world blurs past us in dark blues and greens, and I'm glad it's too early for any saram to see us. I'm pretty sure I swallow at least three flies.

We make excellent time and, thanks to the whooshing

air, our clothes are now mostly dry and sand-free. I really can't complain, but I wish we hadn't left my stomach back at the beach.

When we eventually come to a stop at the pointy obelisk outside the Griffith Observatory, the sun has almost fully risen. It's hard to tell without our phones, but I'm guessing it's almost six a.m. I hope Cosette is an early riser.

The blue scales retract from my skin, and Boris lets go of my feet. And it's a good thing, too, because as soon as Emmett and I stumble off him, we both hurl the contents of our stomachs onto the monument. I guess I didn't leave mine at the beach after all.

Emmett groans and looks up apologetically at one of the faces carved into the Astronomers Monument. "Sorry, Galileo. But you'll be happy to know the Earth still orbits the sun."

With Boris tucked under my arm, Emmett and I make our way to the entrance of the cream-colored domed building. As we'd guessed, the main doors are shut tight. But taped to one of them is a poster advertising the Summer Camp for Future Astronomers program.

I study the building and grounds. "Let's go around," I say. "Maybe there's a back entrance."

We walk the perimeter of the structure, trying every door in sight, but each one is bolted shut. Eventually, there's only one left to try.

"Here goes nothing." I give the handle a slight tug, only to find that this door, like the others, is locked. "Nooo!" I cry, banging my head against the glass.

"Um, *Riley?*" a female voice calls out. "Riley Oh?"

I look up, startled.

A beautiful K-pop apparition has appeared on the other side of the glass door, already dressed for the day in a navy camp polo over pressed khakis. She looks at me with wide eyes. "What are you doing here?"

I squeal. "Cosette!" I point to the door handle. "What are the chances! Let us in, please. We need your help!"

Cosette looks behind her, as if checking that the coast is clear. Then she cautiously opens the door but doesn't invite us in. She narrows her eyes, and all I see are her ridiculously long eyelashes. "You're not allowed in here," she says, giving a quirk of the eyebrow when she sees Boris. "Everyone's going to be awake soon."

"Please!" I say. "We won't tell anyone we saw you. We just need to get inside."

"But why? Just come back after noon, when it opens to the public." She gives Emmett a look as if to say *And who the heck are you?* before glancing back at me. Her forehead suddenly creases as if she's just remembered something. "Besides, my parents will kill me if they find out I talked to you."

Wow, news travels fast around here. I don't think I saw Cosette at Hattie's ceremony, but it's obvious she knows I'm one of the cursed clan.

She goes to shut the door, but I wedge my foot into the gap before she can close it completely. I open my mouth to quickly change the subject....

But Emmett talks first. "Hey, where did you get that?" He points to the shiny silver badge on Cosette's shirt that reads

SPACE PIR8S RULE THE GALAXY. "How do you know about the Space Pirates?"

Her frown transforms into a proud grin. "Because it's my squad. We've conquered fifty planets in the galaxy, and we might even get external sponsorship this year. We're *that* good. Why? Do you play *Battle Galactic*, too?"

Emmett's jaw drops open. "No. Way. No freaking way!"

Cosette scowls. "Hey, don't knock it before you try it. It's an amazing game."

His eyebrows twitch in concentration. "Cosette... Cosette..." he mumbles under his breath. Then he freezes. "Cosette as in CasetteTape99?!"

She puts her hands on her hips. "Wait, how do you know my username? Are you some kind of spy for the Darth Invaders? Because we *will* destroy you."

"It's me!" Emmett exclaims, waving his hands in excitement. "I'm BakersDelight. My real name is Emmett."

This time it's Cosette's jaw that drops. "No. Freaking. Way. Are you serious right now?! I can't believe we're finally meeting in real life! And like this!"

They high-ten and grin at each other like clowns.

"Uh, care to explain?" I ask Emmett.

He slaps me on the shoulder. "She's the captain of our spaceship, Rye! We're on the same squad!"

Cosette jumps up and down. "Your friend Emmett is my chief commanding officer." She tosses her hair and flashes a perfect-toothed smile. "Wow, what a small world!"

"I know, right?!" They give each other another round

of high tens and I genuinely can't recall the last time I saw Emmett so pumped. I feel a weird pang of jealousy.

I elbow Emmett in the side. "We're kinda in a hurry right now," I remind him, tapping the vial underneath my top.

That sobers him right up. "Yes, of course, totally. I've got this." He turns to Cosette, all business. "Captain, remember the time the Darth Invaders ambushed us on Planet Kangshee and we had to risk everything to go on a rescue mission to save Cadet PJO4eva?"

She nods solemnly. "That's a day I will never forget, Commander."

"Well, Riley and I are on a similar rescue mission. One of our crew is in grave danger, and we need to save her. We are willing to do whatever it takes, and we need your help."

Cosette listens, then looks over at me contemplatively. She frowns slightly, but eventually, she offers Emmett her hand. "I will do everything in my power to help you, Commander BakersDelight. You have my word. Fly or die."

Emmett shakes her hand and grins. "Fly or die."

She opens the door wider and invites us in, putting a finger to her lips. She leads us on tiptoe past an exhibit with a large pendulum ball hanging over a hole and then ushers us into a small meeting room. "We should be left alone in here." She takes a seat and leans her elbows on the table. "So how can I help, team?"

"We're looking for some information," I start, resting an exhausted-looking Boris against the wall. "About . . . stars."

Cosette nods. "Well, you've definitely come to the best place for that. What do you want to know?"

"Have you ever heard of the Godrealm's last fallen star?" I ask.

"Hmm." She cocks her head. "Can't say that I have. But you're not going to find anything about the Godrealm here. It's strictly saram stuff."

"You're sure?" I press. "Nothing about falling stars?"

She taps her fingers on the table. "It does kind of remind me of something my sister performed in the Saturday School talent quest last year."

"What was it?" Emmett asks.

"One of the old legends. About back when there were two suns and two moons in the sky. I'm pretty sure it mentioned something about the Godrealm's stars."

Emmett and I look at each other.

"You don't happen to remember the story, do you?" I ask. "Any part of it at all?"

She takes out her phone and puts it on the table. "No, but I have something even better. Adeline uploaded it to a private Vimeo so the family could watch it."

Emmett and I wait eagerly as Cosette searches for the link.

"Bingo!" She props up her phone at an angle so we can all see, and we huddle around the screen as the video loads.

Adeline looks just like Cosette but a few years older and taller, with wavy dark hair flowing down to her waist and that same creamy, flawless complexion. She's dressed in a beautiful long robe of Gumiho silver that shimmers and sparkles as if made of stardust. In the clip, Adeline walks onto the stage and then waves at someone off-camera. She closes her eyes and takes a big breath before beginning her performance.

"Our legends tell of a time when two suns and two moons adorned the sky. There were no days, no nights, no passage of time. They called this the Age of the Godrealm."

Adeline's voice is deep and velvety, and I'm immediately drawn in.

"One day, upon considering the luminous sky, the six goddesses asked the mother a question. 'Mago Halmi, why are there two suns and two moons?'

"The mother of all creation responded, 'They are each a pair—a dark sun for a light sun, a dark moon for a light moon. They represent a balanced set of scales, like the eum and yang, built in perfect equilibrium, as you are.'"

Adeline uses her glamour magic to turn the stage into the night sky, and then creates the illusion of the two suns and two moons floating majestically above her. The backdrop makes her look ethereal, and my eyes are glued to the sight. I've always known about this legend—it's where the gifted mark originated, after all—but I've never heard the end of the story, and how we got the sky we have today.

The performance continues.

"But the goddesses did not understand, and so Mago Halmi thus explained, 'There is light within us all, as there is darkness within us all. These two absolutes make us whole. This is the way of the universe.'"

I lean in even closer toward the small phone screen.

"This revelation, however, distressed the six goddesses. They could not accept that divine beings such as themselves could be flawed. They deemed the dark sun and dark moon—symbols of their inner darkness—an unsightly reminder of their weakness. So they hatched a plan. *They commanded Mago Halmi's guardian pet, the Haetae, to leap into the sky and devour the dark sun and dark moon."*

Adeline waves her hand, and suddenly the dark sun and moon floating above her explode, sending a shower of light falling down onto her shoulders.

"*When the uni-horned lion beast bit into the dark sun and dark moon, shards ricocheted to all corners of the sky, peppering the wide expanse with twinkling pockets of light. Some smaller fragments fell to the Mortalrealm—our Earth—to be lost to the Godrealm forever."*

Emmett breathes out, and I look over to see his eyes all wide and curious. I know he'd never admit it, but he's enjoying this gifted legend as much as I am.

"*Mago Halmi was saddened by the goddesses' actions, because their selfish vanity led them to destroy her precious creations. So the Mother punished them by closing the doors between the realms, thereby preventing the goddesses from entering the Mortalrealm at their will. This is why the gifted clans came to be, to do the will of the goddesses on Earth."*

Adeline turns to the audience and raises her arms in a final flourish.

"*And so Mago Halmi left the twinkling shards of the dark sun and dark moon in the sky—what we now call the stars—to serve as a reminder of what the world had lost."*

The clip ends, and Cosette leans back in her chair. "She's good, right?"

"That's pretty epic." Emmett gives Cosette an approving look. "Your sister's really talented."

As they excitedly discuss whether or not Adeline should get an agent, one line from the monologue keeps playing in my head.

Some smaller fragments fell to the Mortalrealm—our Earth—to be lost to the Godrealm forever.

I slap my palm on the table. "Oh my Mago! *That's* what we have to find. The last fallen fragment of a dark sun or moon!"

The color drains from Emmett's face. "Holy shirtballs, how are we supposed to find *that?*"

Cosette puts her phone in her pocket and swivels in her chair a few times. "I'm getting the sense that this is a need-to-know mission, and I respect that." She stops spinning and faces us. "But if *I* wanted to know more about the star, I'd try the gifted library. According to my mom, it's a treasure trove of info. I know no one's been able to activate the sacred texts since the Horangi left, but I dunno—maybe *you* could figure it out?" She glances meaningfully at me and I quickly look away before Emmett can pick up on the subtext. "That is, if you can get in. It's still restricted entry."

I swallow. It's actually not a bad idea. But the library's inside the temple, and Emmett isn't allowed to enter—not since his dad had the council ban him from the grounds. Plus, after what happened at Hattie's initiation, I won't be welcome there, either.

Then there's what Jennie said at Saturday School. The strongest Miru are guarding the entrance. Even if we managed to enter the temple, there's no guarantee we could get past the protectors.

Emmett and I both grimace, and Cosette pauses, reading our expressions.

She pushes back her chair and rises to her feet. "I shouldn't be doing this, but"—she puts her hand over her Space Pirates badge—"I promised I'd do everything in my power to help. So, if you want, I'll glamour you both as Gumiho so you can get into the temple. The effect will only last an hour or so, though, so you'll have to be quick. And once you're there, I won't be able to help you access the library. For that part, you're on your own."

I'm rendered speechless. I'd always kept my distance from Cosette because of her closeness with Jennie. But maybe I'd misjudged her. If she's willing to go this far for Emmett—and all the while knowing I'm Horangi—then she's definitely a good egg.

"Thanks, Captain CasetteTape99," Emmett says, rising to his feet, too. "Space Pirates forever."

"Space Pirates forever." Cosette rubs her Gi against her skin. "Are you guys ready? This might feel kinda weird at first, but I promise it won't hurt." She closes her eyes and starts chanting.

Suddenly, my body feels strange. "Are there ants crawling on me?" I whine, scratching at every inch of my skin.

Emmett is squirming and scratching himself, too. Then he starts to change in front of my eyes. His body stretches like one of his homemade pizza doughs, being pulled from top to toe. His hair grows out and flows down his back in luscious dark curls, his legs lengthen, and his face starts to look like another I've seen before. Like, *just* before.

"Whoa, Em, you are the spitting image of Adeline!" I exclaim.

He looks down his body and then yelps. "Holy shirtballs, I have boobs!"

I stare at him in awe. Even his voice sounds just like Adeline's.

He fumbles with his hands, not knowing where to put them. He reaches over his shoulder and feels for his backpack, which is still on his—well, Adeline's—back. "Oh *phew*! My cookies are safe."

He then turns to me and gasps. "Whoa, and you look *just* like Cosette!" His eyes shift between me and real Cosette, and he shakes his head. "So trippy. I'm seeing double."

Cosette laughs. "Sorry. Hope you guys don't mind looking like my sister and me. It's much easier to glamour you into people I know well."

Emmett and I shrug. "I'm not complaining," Emmett says.

"Just don't do anything I wouldn't, okay?" She points to me. "Especially you."

"Hey—" I start, but then we hear the chatter of other young astronomers coming from down the hall.

"C'mon," says Cosette. "Time for you to get a move on." She quickly sneaks us out the way we entered.

When we leave, Emmett gives her a Space Pirate salute while I check out my reflection in the glass door. I can't help but stare. That girl definitely looks like Cosette, with Boris tucked under her arm.

I shake my head in disbelief and put my hand over Hattie's heart vial.

Just hang on a bit longer, sis.

I promise I'll bring you back home, if it's the last thing I do.

11.
The Cheollima and His Cookies

DESPITE EMMETT'S RELUCTANCE, WE RIDE BORIS all the way to Koreatown. Every second counts when Hattie's life is on the line, and he's the fastest form of transport we've got. I'll even admit that his wagging tail is starting to grow on me. He's kind of cute—for a scooter, anyway.

I'm not sure what time it is, but as we approach the H-Mart, the streets are full of people grabbing their morning coffee on the way to work. I squirm inside, thinking of how worried Eomma and Appa must be by now....I wonder if they even got any sleep.

The image of their tired, red-rimmed eyes lights a fire under my butt. We rush to the Korean fried chicken counter in the H-Mart, and I hold my breath as the Miru guard checks our gifted marks. Cosette's glamour works like a charm, though, and as the symbols glow silver on our wrists, the protector gives us entry.

The temple lobby is lively today. Clan witches are busily

going about their business, entering and exiting the elevators. By the number of people dressed in green robes, I'm guessing there's some kind of event happening for the infusers today.

"Wow," breathes Emmett, looking around. "I knew this place existed, but seeing it with my own eyes is something else. Can't believe all this is inside that walk-in fridge."

"You haven't seen anything yet." I feel a small flower of pride bloom in my chest as I show Emmett this part of my world. I want him to know how amazing it is, to understand why it's so important for me to be accepted here.

I lead him to the elevators and we jump into the first one that opens. Thankfully, no one else is waiting to use it. We don't know who might recognize Cosette and Adeline, so we need to keep our distance from everyone and keep moving. I press the button for the basement floor and hold my breath. I remember Auntie Okja once telling my eomma that it was fitting the gifted library was in the basement, since the Horangi clan were "beneath us."

I jab the CLOSE DOOR button over and over again in a vain attempt to make the elevator shut faster. Eventually, the doors begin to slide together. I'm about to let out a sigh of relief when a loud (and frustratingly familiar) voice calls out.

"Hold that elevator!" A hand slides between the doors, which causes them to open.

I immediately groan and make a face at Emmett before hiding Boris behind my back. Two people walk in, and it's just our luck that one of them happens to be my *favorite* person in the entire world. *Not.*

I force a smile. "Hi, Jennie," I say with fake cheer. "Hi, David."

"Hi, Cosette," David Kim, the Tokki infuser from Saturday School says. His cheeks are as round and ruddy as usual, but he's got a queasy look about him that makes me worry he's going to puke. His hand shakes a little as he pushes the button for level 88, and I plaster my back against the elevator wall.

"Cosette?" Jennie raises her eyebrows. "I thought you couldn't make it to David's initiation because of space camp."

I suddenly realize why there are so many infusers at the temple, and why David is looking so nervous.

"Oh, um..." I try an upward inflection to come across as Cosette-like as I can. "The camp got canceled? So Adeline gave me a lift. Surprise!"

"You should have told me. We could have picked you up." She pauses and studies me as if I'm one of those *spot-the-difference* puzzles. "Hey, are you feeling all right?"

I giggle nervously. "Of course. Great. Never better!" My voice is an octave too high.

The elevator stops at the basement. "That's weird," I say, way louder than I need to. "I wonder why we went down. We're obviously going to the sanctuary like you, right, Em—I mean, Adeline?"

Emmett nods awkwardly and Jennie studies me suspiciously. "You sure you're feeling all right? You seem a bit... off."

"Of course I'm fine." I quickly change the subject as the doors close and the elevator starts moving back up again. "So, David, you all ready for the initiation?"

He wipes the sweat off his forehead. "Not really. I mean, I hope so."

"Dude, no offense, but you're not looking too hot," Emmett/ Adeline points out.

Jennie reaches into David's backpack as if it's her own and takes out a small glass vial from the inside pocket. When she opens it, the scent of omija berries, passionflowers, and lemon balm fills the elevator. I immediately recognize it as a calming tonic Eomma and Appa get from David's mom to use at the clinic.

"I told you to take this ages ago, you dummy." Jennie hands it to David, who gratefully downs it in one gulp. "You're hella useless, you know that?"

It strikes me as odd that someone as sweet and gentle as David would be friends with someone as harsh and prickly as Jennie. But if I've learned anything from talking to Cosette earlier, it's that people aren't always as they seem on the surface. Still, though . . . *Jennie?*

The elevator finally reaches level 88 and the doors start to open. I quickly tug on Emmett's hand to keep him with me, and instead of getting out, I say, "Oh, sticks! I totally forgot my bag down in the lobby. You guys go ahead—we'll see you in there."

Jennie gives me another side-eye of suspicion but eventually relents and steps out of the elevator with David. And when the doors finally close again, Emmett and I both breathe out the biggest sighs of relief. That was *hella awkward*, as Jennie would say.

Thankfully, the second time around, we manage to get to the basement without being caught. "That was close," I whisper to Emmett as the doors open.

I haven't forgotten what Jennie said—about there being Miru guards patrolling the library's entrance. We'll need to be super stealthy. I also haven't forgotten that our disguises won't last much longer. Cosette said we'd only have an hour or so. We'll have to move fast.

But as we step out of the elevator and survey our surroundings, a wave of confusion washes over me.

"I thought you said the gifted library was on this floor," Emmett says, scratching his head. "This just looks like a laundromat."

I frown. It's bigger than any laundromat I've ever seen, with rows and rows of humongous washers and driers. But it's definitely a laundromat. It even has, at the end of each row, those funny ironing contraptions that look like standing coatracks with vacuum hoses. A brightly lit vending machine selling single-use boxes of detergent and fabric softener is tucked into one corner, and next to the familiar brands is a detergent I've never seen before called Pure and Divine. Its slogan says it's *tough enough for even the holiest of stains* and the price is an astronomical twenty dollars per box. What a rip-off!

"Maybe the guests from the Godrealm need somewhere to do their washing?" I say. "But I'm sure Auntie Okja said it was on this floor...." I'd assumed the library's entrance would be protected somehow—perhaps with a Gumiho glamour or something. But this is the last thing I was expecting. The only good news is that there are no Miru guards around. In fact, there's no one here at all.

Emmett walks over to one of the washers. "Aw, look, Rye! It's a cute little horsey statue." He reaches up and pats the head of a small black stone horse that's sitting on top of the machine. "And wow, it's nice being tall for a change," he says, stretching Adeline's long arm as high as it can go. "I can reach everything."

"Hey, that's a sculpture of a cheollima!" I walk over to get a closer look. The stallion is the size of a Chihuahua, and his angel-like wings are spread wide, as if he's about to take flight.

"What's a cheollima?"

"They're winged horses known for being too big, too swift, and too majestic to be mounted by any mortal being. They're supposed to be the goddesses' preferred mode of transport in the Godrealm. I even heard all horses on Earth are descendants of a cheollima that lost his wings and fell to Earth."

Emmett studies the figure and grins. "But this one's so *smol!*"

"I know, right?!"

Emmett pats the cheollima's smooth stone back and coos at him like he's a cute puppy. "Who's a good little horsey? And what are you doing here all by your lonesome?"

The statue suddenly splinters and cracks under Emmett's hand, and little pieces of debris fall on the machine and the ground.

"Shirtballs!" Emmett jumps back in horror. "I think I broke him!"

Little by little, patches of glossy hair are revealed underneath the stone, until a teeny-weeny black winged horse emerges from his shell. He shakes off the last bits with a flutter of his mini wings.

"Who *dares* disturb my slumber?" He has a high-pitched, nasal voice, and for some reason, he speaks with a British accent. "You have disrupted my rest, and now you will pay with your lives. Say your final good-byes, mortals, and prepare to *die*."

Oh no. . . . What have we awoken?

I hiccup and jump back, only to collide with Emmett. He yelps and falls down, and his container of cookies tumbles out of his backpack.

The cheollima clicks his little hooves on the washing machine and holds his head high. He pauses with his wings outstretched as if he's about to Hulk out at any minute. I quickly glance behind us, wondering if we'll be able to get back to the elevators before he makes his next move.

Then out of the blue, he grins. It's a million-dollar smile, revealing every single one of his tiny perfect equine teeth.

"Did I get you? Were you scared?" He neighs with glee. "Oh, I've been wanting to try that out for *so* long. It's been a while since I've had any visitors."

Emmett and I look at each other and then back at the cheollima, stunned. Is he for real?

"Is this the entrance to the gifted library?" I tentatively ask, taking another step away from the cheollima, just in case.

He nods, and I feel a rush of relief. Auntie Okja *was* right, after all.

"This is indeed the protected entrance to the gifted library, my cherry cupcakes." He jumps up onto his two hind legs, and suddenly, a tiny clipboard with a piece of paper appears in his front hooves. "Your names, please?" he asks, looking from his paper back to us.

"Why do you need our names?" Emmett asks, narrowing his eyes.

"To see if you're on the list, of course! I can't ask you the verification questions if you're not an authorized council member, now, can I?"

I let out another hiccup. Even glamoured as the Chung sisters, we couldn't pass as council members. We're doomed.

"Why are *you* protecting the entrance, anyway?" Emmett asks. "Aren't the Miru guards supposed to be watching it?"

The cheollima drops his clipboard and stomps his hooves. "I *am* a guard, thank you very much."

Emmett raises an eyebrow. "Are you, though? I thought cheollimas normally lived in the Godrealm?"

The winged horse sighs dramatically. "Indeed they do, my sweet sausage. But look at me." He spins once so we get a sense of his full size. "Do you know how difficult it is for a runt to find stable employment in the Godrealm? No divine being wants to ride a cheollima who only comes up to their calves! It's tough pickings up there, I tell you."

"So you got a job working as security for the Miru," I say. "Good for you."

"Yeah, you do you, dude," Emmett echoes. "It sucks to be small."

The cheollima smiles his pearly whites. "Shucks, thanks,

ladies. But, enough about me. As nice as this wee chat has been, if your names aren't on the list, I will have no choice but to end your lives, right here, right now. I may be small, but I am deadly."

We laugh uncomfortably at his second attempt at the killing-us joke, but this time he doesn't smile. His poker face is next-level. He's either got a really dry sense of humor, or we might not make it out of here alive.

Emmett slowly picks his fallen cookie container off the ground, sensing that we may have to make a run for it very soon.

"Wait a bloomin' minute!" the cheollima shouts, his eyes widening. "What do you have there?"

"Cookies," Emmett says, prying open the Tupperware. "Salted caramel. Baked fresh yesterday."

The cheollima gasps and hops up and down on his back legs. "My favorite! What do I have to do to get my hooves on one of those, sugar plum?"

Emmett and I look at each other, and the same lightbulb goes on in both our heads.

"If you let us into the library, I'll happily give you a cookie," Emmett says.

"His—I mean, *her* cookies are the *best*," I add. "I can definitely vouch for them."

The cheollima taps his front hoof on the washing machine, considering the offer. Eventually, he stops and turns to us. "*Hmm*. Well, I *could* waive the authorized-personnel requirement in exchange for a cookie. But the portal still won't open if you don't pass the verification process."

"What does that involve?" I ask.

"You have to answer my three riddles correctly. The people on the list know the correct answers." He glances at Emmett's cookies and licks his horsey lips. "Although, if you were willing to part with two of those, I might let you get away with just one correct answer out of three."

"We'll do it," Emmett says.

The cheollima flaps his wings. "Deal!" He clears his throat and puts on one of those fake game-show-host voices. "All right, contestants, let's get this party started. Verification question attempt number one: Who's the more powerful of the two, the ant or the elephant?"

I shoot my hand into the air. "Ooh, ooh, that's way too easy," I squeal. "It's the elephant. They're the largest land animal on Earth."

I hold up my palm for a high-five from Emmett, but a loud neigh escapes from the cheollima's mouth.

"Incorrect!" he announces. "While the elephant is indeed very powerful, the humble ant is able to lift up to one thousand times its own body weight. The correct answer is *ant!*"

I lower my palm. "Sorry, Em," I say sheepishly. "I should have checked with you before answering."

"It's okay," Emmett says, a determined-to-win look on his face. "He said we have three tries."

The cheollima shakes out his wings. "Better luck next round, contestants. And remember, two minds are better than one. Verification question attempt number two: Which is stronger, steel or silk?"

This time, I keep my mouth shut and look to Emmett. "What do you think?"

He pouts in thought. "I mean, steel seems like the obvious answer. But the obvious answer was wrong before. So maybe it's silk?"

I nod. "That logic makes sense. There'll be some kind of technicality that makes silk stronger. Let's go with that."

Emmett puts his hands on his hips. "Our answer is silk."

We look hopefully at the cheollima, but he bleats out another incorrect-buzzer sound and looks disappointed. "Wrong again, my delicate macarons. Everyone knows steel is stronger than silk. I thought I'd throw in an easy one to help you out, but it looks like you threw it down the loo!"

My hands start to sweat, and Emmett lowers his head. "Sorry, Rye. That was my bad."

I put my hand on his shoulder. "We're in this together, Em. No need to apologize."

The cheollima does a final twirl on his right hind leg and clears his throat. "So, contestants, this is the moment of truth. The moment we've all been waiting for. My last chance to obtain those cookies, and your last chance to gain passage into the gifted library or face certain death. Are you ready to hear the question for your final verification attempt?"

We both nod, swallowing hard. I really hope he's joking about the certain death part. . . .

"Third and final attempt: Which is the mightier of the two, the sun or the wind?"

Emmett and I take our time working this one out.

"The answer that first comes to mind is the wind," Emmett muses. "I mean, the sun just shines, but the wind can be strong and blustery, right? It can create hurricanes, destroy entire houses, that kinda thing."

I nod, thinking hard. "That's what I was gonna say, too. The wind is the obvious choice." But then I remember the story Auntie Okja used to tell me about the power of empathy over brute force. "Wait, do you know the old Aesop's fable about the wind and the sun?"

Emmett shakes his head.

"Essentially, the north wind wanted to prove he was mightier than anyone else in the universe. So one day, he challenged the sleepy sun to a duel. If he could remove the jacket from a human faster than the sun could, there would be no doubt that he was the mightiest of all."

Emmett is listening carefully, so I continue. "So the north wind went first, and he huffed and puffed, blowing on the man as hard as he could. He thought it was going to be easy, since he was so powerful, but the more wind he created, the colder the man felt, and the tighter he held on to his jacket. Eventually, the wind ran out of breath and fell into a heap, exhausted."

"And the sun?" Emmett asks.

"Well, then the sun shone her gentle warm rays on the man. The man started relaxing, and yawning, and eventually he got too warm from all the heat. Before long—*bam!*—he took off his jacket."

Emmett slaps his thigh. "That's gotta be it, Rye. It's the sun."

The cheollima flaps his wings and clips his hooves on

the washing machine. "Righto, time's up, cinnamon creams! What's your final answer? The sun or the wind?"

"The sun!" Emmett and I call out together.

The cheollima pauses. "Are you *sure*?"

For a second, I waver. Maybe it's the wind?

But Emmett's confident expression erases my doubt. "Our final answer is the sun," he says. "Lock it in, thanks."

The cheollima takes flight and does a few 360s in the air. "Hooray!" he cries. "The cookies are mine!"

Emmett and I high-five each other and fist-pump the air. We did it!

"You have earned passage into the gifted library, my sweet dumplings! But remember, you don't have all day. My shift ends this afternoon, and after that the next guard will eventually notice you're in there."

Emmett lifts off the lid of the Tupperware container to take out two cookies. Then he changes his mind. He walks over to the cheollima and places the entire thing on top of the washing machine.

"You know what? Why don't you have all of them," he says. "You've been really good to us, and we're grateful for your help."

I smile at the gesture. It's a very sweet, very Emmett-like thing to do.

"Oh boy, oh boy, how *kind* of you!" coos the cheollima. He flaps his wings excitedly. "And to reward your utmost generosity, my little cheesecakes, I will offer you a piece of advice about the place you are about to enter."

We lean in, listening eagerly.

"The library may not be what you expect. But books have a way of finding their rightful owners. So trust in their wisdom and you'll have a hoot."

And with that, the cheollima presses the red button on the washing machine, and the round door on the front opens with a satisfying *click.* "Jump in whenever you're ready!"

"You want us to go in *there?*" I ask, horrified. I look down at Cosette's long limbs, and then at Emmett's even longer Adeline limbs, not to mention Boris the dragon scooter. Suddenly, the washer doesn't seem so big anymore.

The cheollima looks at me, confused. "You *do* want to enter the library, don't you?"

"Ugh. Of course that's the entrance." Emmett shakes his head. "Why do I even bother acting surprised anymore? Magic is wack."

"It's just a quick spin," assures the cheollima, "one at a time, with no water. You'll be there in a jiffy."

Emmett takes a big breath. "Here goes nothing." He extends a long Adeline leg and starts climbing into the open mouth of the machine. The angle doesn't work, though, so he then backtracks and tries to enter butt-first. This time, he manages to squeeze himself in there—just barely—but it doesn't look comfortable by any means. This would be so much easier if we were in our own shorter bodies and not these gazelle-like supermodel disguises....

Emmett waves at me awkwardly, his arm wedged between the machine and Adeline's boob. "See you on the other side, Rye."

The cheollima closes the door and pushes the START CYCLE

button on the washer. As the machine whirs into action, Emmett/Adeline's surprised face begins to spin—slowly at first, then faster and faster, until he's nothing but a blur of colors. Eventually, there's a sharp *bing!*, and when I look inside the barrel again, Emmett is gone.

"Your turn!" the cheollima says to me. He chuckles and glances happily at his container of cookies. "Get it? Your *turn*? This is *turning* out to be such a great workday."

I clasp Hattie's heart vial around my neck and send her a mental message. *We're getting close, Hat. Just be patient—we're going to save you, I promise.*

And I hope, wherever she is, she can hear me.

After picking up Boris and wedging him in before me, I somehow defy physics and squeeze us both inside the washing machine. I poke my head out to bid the mini cheollima good-bye. "Thank you for all your help," I say. "The Godrealm should appreciate you more."

The cheollima dips his head in a grateful bow and then he looks me right in the eye. "Don't forget to smile!"

He pushes the door closed with a click of his hoof. And two seconds later, the world starts to spin.

12.
Don't Forget to Smile

 ONCE I'M EJECTED FROM the spin cycle and my brain stops whirling, my first thought is: Why is it so hot and stuffy in here?

My second thought is: Why is my skin so itchy?

I open my eyes and have to shield them from the glare. Light is pouring in through glass walls, and I realize I've landed on my butt in some sort of huge conservatory. Ferns, palms, and other lush, leafy greens fill every inch of the space, and the air is so thick and humid, it's like I'm in a tropical rain forest.

"Emmett, where are you?" I call, getting to my feet by using Boris as a crutch. At least the dragon-on-wheels doesn't look any worse for having been tossed like a salad.

I wander around and finally find Emmett sitting by a small pond in what looks like the heart of the greenhouse. Although, to be honest, I can't be sure about that. This place is *seriously big*. It stretches so far to my left and right, I can't see where it ends.

"You okay, Em?"

He's scratching his thigh furiously with one hand, and poking a water lily with the other. He looks like his normal self again.

"Rye, did we just get punked by the cheollima?" Emmett wipes sweat off his brow. "This does *not* look like a library. Also, they need some AC in here."

"I mean, he did say the library wouldn't be what we expect...."

I lean over the pond to check out my reflection. My familiar angled features look up at me, and I frown back. Ah, I get it now. The itchiness must be from Cosette's glamour wearing off. We're going to have to find our way out of here as our real selves.

"Cosette said no one's been able to activate the sacred texts since *they* left, right?" he says. "So maybe we need to figure that out to reveal the real library?"

My image in the water gives me a wide, welcoming smile, and I let out a yelp. "Em! Did you see that? My reflection just smiled at me."

He looks at me as if I've grown cheollima wings. "Are you feeling okay? I thought I just heard you say that your reflection *smiled* at you."

I steal a glance at the water again. Sure enough, my reflection is grinning like it's won the Powerball. Without thinking, I reach out to touch the surface of the pond. The water ripples under my fingers, and my reflection blurs. But as soon as the image clears again, water-me winks.

I frown even harder.

The words of the cheollima echo in my ears. *Don't forget to smile.* Is this what the horse was talking about?

Tentatively, I move my face muscles. It feels weird to smile at a reflection that isn't actually mine, but I force myself to do it anyway.

As soon as my cheeks stretch and my expression mirrors the one in the pond's surface, the water begins to swirl as if someone's flipped a switch. A red glow emanates from below, and I take a sharp breath. "Em, look at the wat—"

"Rye, turn around! Now!"

The tone of Emmett's voice throws me off guard, and I swivel around in a hurry. My jaw drops open.

The conservatory has become overpopulated by birds. Fowl of every shape and size are perched in the greenery side by side, stacked on each branch like colorful book spines on a shelf. There are orange-beaked toucans sitting in the palms, kingfishers balanced on the ferns, and even tricolored scarlet macaws rustling their tail feathers on the lily pads.

And they're all staring at *us*.

Emmett gawks. "Where did they come from?" He shudders. "So many eyes . . . Just. So. Many. Eyes."

I study the birds carefully and realize there's a certain order to them. Each one is different, but they're organized by color, size, shape, and plumage.

"It's weird," I think out loud. "It's like they're waiting for something."

I walk toward the closest flock and tentatively extend my

hand toward a bright hornbill. It has a heart-shaped mark on its head, and it squawks at me before nipping my finger. But as soon as I touch its feathers, the bird vanishes. Instead, it is replaced with a heavy tome entitled *The Art of Infusing: Love Tonics, Part II*. It floats in the air above the tree branch, spine up, flapping its pages like wings.

I gasp and pull it toward me. "Em! They're not birds— they're *books*!"

The sacred texts had been lost to the witches ever since the scholar clan was banished. But I had somehow managed to awaken the books simply by smiling at my reflection in the pond water. Was it because I was of Horangi blood? That might explain why Emmett's reflection hadn't smiled at him. . . .

My mind reels. It strikes me that I could've had access to a whole world of magic if history had gone differently and I had been raised Horangi. The thought leaves a bitter taste in my mouth.

"The birds are *books*? Shut up right now." Emmett walks toward a blue parrot and gingerly reaches out to touch its tail feather. Immediately, the parrot disappears and is replaced by a blue hand-bound book about the Spiritrealm and its numerous boroughs. He grabs the flapping book from the air and shakes his head in disbelief. "This is so cray."

Hope surges through me. "There *has* to be a book about fallen stars in here, Em. Keep looking. We have to find it!"

We transform birds into books for what feels like hours, all the while growing more and more worried about the cheollima's shift ending and the new guard discovering us.

As we discard the books, they fly in a flock above our heads. And though we find loads of volumes I'd die to read, none of them have anything to do with the Godrealm's fallen stars, or even the dark sun and dark moon.

Exhausted, we fall onto a bench, startling a nearby stack of books and sending them flapping to the ceiling.

"We're never gonna find anything," Emmett whines, rubbing his bird-pecked fingers. "There are just too many, and we're pushing our luck with time. We need to get out of here, like, *now.*"

I look down at Hattie's heart vial and bite the inside of my cheek. "We can't give up. Hattie wouldn't lose faith. We just need to be smarter about it." I scan the next section of birds and think hard. "What else did the cheollima say when you gave him your cookies?"

Emmett thinks. "He said something about books finding their rightful owner. Oh, and if we trust in their wisdom, we'll have a hoot."

"Wait, *hoot?*" I say.

Emmett's eyes widen. "Holy shirtballs, we need to find an owl."

Propelled by a second wind, we run up and down the conservatory, until, eventually, we find the owl section behind the giant Venus flytraps.

Emmett rubs his palms down his face and groans. "Who knew there were so many owls?"

There are countless types of them, all similar and yet distinctly different in color, markings, and shape. Some with black spectacles around their eyes, some with spotted orange tails, and even some that look like they're covered in white fluff.

I study their big eyes. The last thing I want to do is get in touch with my cursed Horangi side, but for a moment, I wish I could channel the part of me that summoned the birds in the first place. Maybe if I could, I would somehow know which owl to touch.

Emmett and I roll up our sleeves and get started on the lowest row of owls. I'm just about to tap the third one when something bangs into my head.

"Ouch!" I yelp, as the claws of an owl dig into my hair. "Argh, get it off me!"

Emmett swats at the pointy-eared owl and manages to chase it off for a second. But as soon as it regains its balance, it swoops in and lands on my crown again. It hoots loudly.

I freeze. *Books have a way of finding their rightful owners*, the cheollima had said.

I get a rush of adrenaline. "Em, wait—I think this might be the one."

I try to stay as still as possible. And when the bird stops flapping and scratching, I quickly reach up and pat its side. The owl immediately transforms into a book, falling with a heavy thump onto my shoulder.

"Ow! Why couldn't they have just made this a normal library, darn it!" I rub my shoulder and pick up the brown leather-bound book. The cover reads *The Loyal Tales of the Haetae*.

Emmett and I open the book and skim the contents, hoping for clues. But instead, the pages are full of old stories about

Mago Halmi's guardian lion-beast using his time-manipulation powers to help her. I sigh and close the cover.

"Hey, what's this?" Emmett picks up a piece of paper that dropped out of the book.

It's a letter, dated almost thirteen years ago and signed by someone named Sora. It reads:

Dear H,

If you are reading this, we have already lost the battle.

We will continue to keep the seventh artifact hidden, but I worry it may already be too late. Something is brewing, and I fear the elders may have figured out our secret.

Please let us know what we should do. Our safety is in your hands.

In Knowledge and Truth,
Sora

On the back of the letter, there are additional scribbles:

Fifth artifact: sword—presumed destroyed
Sixth artifact: midnight bow—presumed destroyed
Seventh artifact: sunstone ax
Eighth artifact: unknown—a celestial object?

I rub my eyes. My mind feels like mush. I don't understand what this letter is, or why it was in the book. And why did this owl choose *me*?

"Who do you think H was?" Emmett asks. "And what about Sora?"

I swallow. "Well, *Knowledge and Truth* is the Horangi clan motto—it's written on their statue's plaque in the Gi sanctuary. So maybe they were two scholars writing to each other?"

He clenches his jaw. "This Sora person says that they're keeping the seventh artifact hidden. But why would they write down what it is when the note could fall into the wrong hands?"

I shake my head, feeling despondent. "I wish I knew. Maybe it wasn't Sora who wrote that stuff on the back."

He pauses. "Do you think the artifacts have something to do with what we're looking for?"

It's my turn to pause. I study the list and read the words *eighth artifact: unknown—a celestial object?* over and over again. "Well, a star is a celestial object. So the eighth artifact could be the Godrealm's last fallen star, couldn't it?"

Back at Santa Monica Pier, the goddess had told us that the fallen piece of her world could grant divine power here in the Mortalrealm, and it had driven humans mad with greed, leaving only destruction and despair in its wake. She had called it evil. Maybe the sunstone ax had the same effect on people, and the power-hungry Horangi had been keeping it for themselves. Then the council discovered their secret. . . .

I shake my head again, too confused to articulate my thoughts. "I'm not sure yet, Em. But something tells me we've stumbled across something big. Something *much* bigger than us." I fold the letter and put it in my pocket. "And we're gonna have to get to the bottom of it if we want to save Hattie."

I hear a weird *clonk*, as if something small and hard has fallen on the ground. I look down to see a cloud of smoky purples and midnight blues mushrooming from a tiny round stone.

"What the . . . ?"

Fear creeps into my bones. Did the new guard figure out we were in here?

The weird fog keeps growing until it has swallowed me up to my chest. I try to cover my mouth and nose, but my head is starting to feel a bit woozy.

"Em!" I manage to cry out. "Don't breathe the—"

Emmett drops to the ground like a rag doll.

My body suddenly feels so heavy, like it's tied to an anchor. And the next thing I know, everything goes dark.

13.
Where Does the Bearded Man Buy His Suits?

ONCE CONSCIOUSNESS RETURNS to me, I realize I'm lying on a cold stone floor. I turn my head to the left and right, looking for Emmett. Where is he? Is he okay?

Groaning loudly, I try to get up, but I can only manage a sitting position. My head feels like it was removed and then surgically reattached by Mong's fluffy paws. What was in that weird blue-and-purple fog?

I blink a few times. I seem to be back in the basement laundromat, but some of the lights are flickering and others are completely out, making it hard to see. There's a dark figure standing in front of me with his hands behind his back.

"Who . . . Who are you?" I instinctively scoot away a little.

A man steps out of the shadow. He's tall and statuesque with wide-set shoulders. I estimate he's about Appa's age, but he's less well-groomed—he has a mop of thick, unruly hair and an impressively bushy beard falling from his chin. He's dressed in a full three-piece suit, and he's even holding one of those old-school pocket watches attached to his vest by a chain. As he slips the watch back into his front pocket, I steal a glance behind him. The winged horse isn't on the washing machine anymore. This must be the Miru guard who took over the cheollima's shift. I *knew* we were wasting too much time with those owls!

The man narrows his eyes as he takes me in. "I'm the one who should be asking *you* that question."

I look for Emmett again, but he's nowhere to be seen. The image of him falling to the ground like a rag doll plays back in my mind, and panic rises in my throat. "Where's . . . Where's my friend? What have you done to him?"

"He is unhurt. But I will not release him or you until you answer my question. You must be well aware that the gifted library is prohibited, and yet you ignored the rules and broke in. How did you get through security? And what reason do you have for this indiscretion?"

My heart is racing and, though I don't want the council to put another X next to my name, I don't respond. No way am I going to rat out the cheollima. It would be too hard to explain everything anyway, and I don't trust this man's word that Emmett is unhurt. The guy gassed us, for crying out loud.

The man frowns and continues. "For over ten years the sacred texts have been inaccessible without the Horangi. And yet somehow you were able to activate the library." He holds up the copy of *The Loyal Tales of the Haetae* we'd found. "Are you working with the cursed clan?"

"No," I quickly say, wincing at the allegation. "I'm not working with them. I was just—"

A glint of glass in his other hand catches my eye and the blood drains from my face. I grab at my neck—no cord necklace. "Hey, that's mine—give it back!"

He opens his palm to reveal the vial containing Hattie's bloody shrunken heart. "Tell me what this is."

A sudden feeling of desperation washes over me. Emmett once told me that baking is the art of balance and restraint. Unlike cooking, baking is an exact science that requires the perfect mix of ingredients. If you use too little baking soda, your cake won't rise. But add too much and you get a bitter, inedible result. The key is to always stay in control—never let the ingredients get out of balance.

Now I realize what he meant. I've always been a cautious person, never one to attract attention to myself or stick my nose where it's not wanted. I knew my place, even if things weren't fair. It was only after we found out about the gift-sharing spell that the balance started tipping. I started wanting more. *Needing* more.

Even when that spell went wrong, I told myself it was okay, because we had a plan. And then, when the summoning spell went wrong too, I told myself there was still hope, because we had a way of saving Hattie. But now, with my parents' gifts at risk, Emmett's life in danger, and Hattie's heart dangling in a stranger's hand, I realize I have lost all control. I let the imbalance of ingredients get the best of me. And I wonder if this is how the Horangi started on *their* path to self-destruction.

By being too greedy, and losing the things most dear to them as a result.

I really am cursed like them.

"I will not ask you again," the man threatens, dangling the glass vial by the black cord. "Tell me what this is."

I grit my teeth. I have done my loved ones enough harm. It's time to take control, even if it scares the Mago out of me. I have to do *whatever* it takes.

The task in front of me is clear. Tackle the man, grab Hattie's heart, find Emmett, and get out of here. And do it *pronto*. As adrenaline burns through my body, I let out a Xena-esque battle cry and spring up, lunging headfirst at the man.

"Ow!" My head bonks into something cold and hard, and I fall back onto my butt with a heavy thud.

The man stands unfazed.

I look around me, confused. There's nothing to be seen in the air, and yet I could have sworn my head hit something solid. I tentatively raise my hand, only for my fingers to feel long vertical bars in front of my face. I frantically follow the invisible beams and find they surround me on all four sides and a few feet above me, too. I'm boxed in.

"Why have you trapped me in here? Magically imprisoning a minor without parental consent is against the gifted council's code of conduct," I warn, pushing through the quiver in my voice. "If you don't let me go this instant and tell me where you're holding my friend, I *will* report you—and I'll have you know, my auntie is an elder on the council!" I really wish I could stand up to make these threats.

The man cocks his head slightly as he studies me. Then one side of his mouth quirks upward.

"You think this is *funny?*" I spit out the words, feeling my emotions unravel like a ball of yarn. "This is a matter of life and death! That heart you're holding belongs to my sister, and if I don't find what I've promised to find, I will lose her forever. Do you understand what I'm saying?"

A weird heat flares in my gut. And for a moment, I feel like I've caught on fire. As if my four elemental fires have been switched on. "I'm not messing around, Mr. Fancy Suit. I'm going to ask you *one last time*. Release me, and tell me where you're holding my friend, or else!"

Something changes in the man's face. His features soften, and he looks at me with an expression that seems kind of like recognition, or maybe even . . . respect. As the heart vial hangs down from his fingers, he opens the copy of *The Loyal Tales of the Haetae*.

"Have you read the story about how the Haetae came to wield time-manipulation powers?"

I stare at him in disbelief. Does he really think this is the time to be making small talk?

He continues. "The Haetae once helped the six goddesses commit a crime. He then became so guilt-ridden that he condemned himself to relive his mistake over and over again, because he believed that was the punishment he deserved. Although he was never able to rewrite history, his return to the past granted him the ability to manipulate time. And with his new power, he was able to help many people in need." He strokes his beard and looks me right in the eye. "To find that which you seek, you must also turn back your clock. You must return to the very beginning—to where you first started. Because, like a coin, there are always two sides to every story. Without the two sides, it cannot be whole."

I scowl like I've never scowled before. "I didn't ask for a lecture," I start, channeling my inner Boss Hattie. "I asked you to let me go!"

He nods simply. "As you wish."

The bearded man carefully places Hattie's heart vial on the floor between his feet. Then he removes a marble from his pants pocket and throws it down in front of me. He starts chanting, and clouds of blue and purple smoke start rising from the ground.

I cover my face. Ugh, I will *not* be knocked unconscious twice.

I hold my breath for as long as I can, and when I feel myself getting light-headed, I sneak a peek between my fingers. The man is gone. And with him, the strange fog.

I take the opportunity to reach for Hattie's heart, still on the ground in front of me. Thank Mago, the invisible bars are gone. I grab the vial with a triumphant grunt, only to break into a frown. The glass feels colder to the touch now. I'm not sure if I'm imagining it, but I think the heart is pumping slower than it was before, too.

I pick myself up and loop the black cord over my head. This isn't good. We need to move faster. "Emmett! Where are you?"

I turn toward the elevator, prepared to search every floor of this temple if that's what it'll take to find my best friend. But as I'm moving, I see something out of the corner of my eye. I swivel around to find Emmett's body curled up on the floor next to the detergent vending machine. Boris is there too, folded neatly next to him.

"Em!" I scream, and I run over and fall to my knees. His chest is moving up and down, and it doesn't look like he's bleeding or has broken any bones. But he remains unconscious. "Wake up, Em. Get up!"

His face is pale, his lips blue. He looks so little lying there, and suddenly I flash back to when we were in elementary school.

Emmett was way smaller than the other boys, and he got teased a lot for it. When we had parent visiting days, he would pretend his absent mom was a wildlife photographer on assignment in Africa, and kids would write LIAR on his locker. The worse the bullying got, the more he raised walls around himself and retreated within them. Sometimes I think he likes the fact that his dad is so strict. It's easier to lay low when there are rules to hide behind.

But he was different with me. One time in third grade, I was in the library, eating lunch by myself. Jennie Byun had told me I couldn't come to her birthday party—it was for "real" gifted kids only—and as usual, I'd burst into tears and run away. I was sitting in the corner, trying to hide my red face behind a book, when someone dropped a Ziploc bag of chocolate-chip cookies into my lap. I looked up to see Emmett quietly taking a seat next to me. He didn't say a word that first day—I don't think he even looked at me—but from then on, we ate lunch together every noon, like it was an unspoken rule. He was always there for me, making sure I never felt alone.

Not much has changed since then. When everything went pear-shaped after Hattie's ceremony, Emmett stepped up without hesitation. He put his own beliefs about magic and the gifted community aside to help me get what I wanted. He put himself in danger for me. Because that's the type of friend he is.

Before I even know what's happening, tears are running freely down my cheeks and dripping onto Emmett's face. I dragged him into this mess. I am a horrible best friend.

"Seriously, what is *with* you and your leaky-bladder eyeballs? Repeat after me—emotions are bad for your health." Emmett rubs his eyes and tries to sit up. "Holy shirtballs, did you sit on my head with your big butt? My brain feels like it's about to explode."

"You're alive!" I hug him and kiss him and rub my happy snot all over him.

"Ew! You're disgusting, Rye. Get off me!"

I wipe my nose with the bottom of my sweater and give Emmett a big, toothy grin. My BFF is back, and I couldn't be happier.

"Wait, how did we end up in the laundromat again?" he asks. "What happened?"

I help him to his feet. "I'll explain everything later, but first, we need to get out of here," I say. "The bearded man might come back for us."

"The bearded man? Who's he?" Emmett mumbles. "And where are we gonna go next?"

I shake my head. "I don't know," I admit. "But for now, I need to get you to safety, and it's not safe in here. So stop asking questions and move your butt. Let's go!"

He raises his eyebrows at me, surprised by my new assertive vibe. But he doesn't argue. Instead, he picks up Boris—with only a slight shudder—and rises to his feet. "Lead the way, boss."

We run to the elevators, only to find that they're out of order.

"You've got to be kidding me!" I cry.

Emmett points to the fire exit to our right. "I guess we're walking."

We hurry to the door, and Emmett pushes on the bar. "Ugh, it's jammed!"

I join in, and we ram the door over and over until it starts opening, inch by inch.

"Again," Emmett says, breathing heavily. "Push together in one, two, three!"

As we fight with the door, there is a low and deep growl behind us. I freeze in my tracks. "Did you hear that?"

Emmett continues pushing as if he hasn't noticed anything out of the ordinary. But the hairs on my arms stand tall as the rumble sounds again. "Em," I whisper. "Can't you hear that?"

I wrap my hand around Hattie's heart vial and turn slowly. My eyes land on a creature that is at once familiar and unlike anything I've ever seen.

He's the size of an elephant, but he kind of looks like a mastiff. Well, except for the iridescent scales all over him, the lion's mane, the single blunt horn, and the red eyes that shine like rubies. His back twitches as he takes a step toward me, and his scales glisten as though they're wet. A bell tinkles on his collar. And when his nostrils flare, I can't help but pee a little. "Em, turn around!"

He looks over his shoulder and I wait for his jaw to drop. Instead, his eyebrows furrow. "Why are you just standing there like a dodo? This door isn't going to open itself. Come on, help me push." He turns back to the door and gives it another thrust.

I blink and rub my eyes, expecting the apparition to have disappeared. But as certain as the hairs on my arms, the Haetae—the *real* Haetae—is still standing in front of me. Had our finding his book in the library somehow called upon him to appear in the flesh?

I know I should be *very* careful. His teeth are sharp enough to bite the sun and the moon, after all. But in that moment, I stop thinking altogether. Instead, I reach out to touch him.

The Haetae sniffs my hand, and just when I think I've made a big mistake, he leans in to nuzzle his cheek against my palm. His scales are warm and hard and smooth, like heated marble. I exhale slowly, trying not to freak out. I just touched Mago Halmi's guardian pet!

He growls again, but this time it sounds more like a deep purr, and he lifts his head in pleasure, revealing the brass bell tied around his neck. In its shiny surface a scene appears, like on a miniature TV screen.

I peer closer.

At first the image is cloudy and hard to make out, but as the fog clears, I see a group of people dressed in red hanboks gathered protectively around a glowing ax. A number of unmoving bodies lie sprawled on the ground. A woman stands apart from them, chanting incantations, until the ax leaps into the air and flies into her hand. I squint and study the woman's face. She seems so familiar. . . .

I look over my shoulder at Emmett, glance down at his silver ring, and turn back to the vision in the bell. Yes. I've seen pictures of her, at Emmett's house and at Auntie Okja's. It's definitely her. *Emmett's mom.*

Before I can react, the scene changes. Now Emmett's mom is lying on the ground, still and unmoving. A tall black-haired man with angular features looms above her with a dark expression on his face. I don't know who he is, but I notice something in his hand. It looks like . . . like my onyx teardrop stone. I cover my mouth with my hand. It can't be. . . .

The vision flickers again. And this time, it shows Emmett and me. We're at the zoo, standing in front of the tiger enclosure. We're drinking what looks like . . . *boba tea?*

"What in the name of Mago—?"

But I don't get to say more. Emmett grabs my wrist just as the fire-exit door swings wide, and he pulls me into the stairwell. He drags me up the stairs, and in a rush, we burst into the temple lobby. We run through the secret portal, emerge from the walk-in fridge, and hurry past the surprised man at the Korean fried chicken counter. Finally, we find ourselves back on a busy street in the heart of Koreatown. While catching our breath, we look up at the H-Mart.

"I can't believe we made it out of there without being caught," I say, my chest heaving.

Emmett lets go of my wrist. But instead of answering, he just stares at me. And there's a strange look in his eyes.

"What?" I say.

He points to my chest.

For a second, I panic. Did I lose Hattie's heart again?

My hands search around my neck for the second time today, and I'm relieved to find the vial still hanging from its cord. I grasp it and look down at my sister's tiny heart, only to see why Emmett is wearing a horrified expression.

A corner of the heart has started to blacken, slowly shriveling like a dying flower inside its glass prison. Now I know I'm not imagining it. Hattie's heart is changing. It's not as *alive* as it was before.

My breath catches in my throat as I look up at my partner in crime. "Em, we need to hurry. Hattie's running out of time."

14.
The Best Boba Teas in Town

 "WHAT DO WE DO NOW, RYE?" Emmett asks, massaging his temples. "We're fresh out of clues and Hattie's heart is...you know..."

"Actually," I start, choosing my words cautiously, "we do have a new lead."

"We do?"

"When you were unconscious, a bearded man came to speak to me."

His eyes widen. "Was he the one who gassed us? What did he want?"

"He said that in order to find what I seek, I need to return to the very beginning. To where I first started."

He facepalms. "Another riddle? Ugh, I'm sick of puzzles."

"And right before we left, I saw the Haetae. The real one."

"The *Haetae*?" He shakes his head. "I don't even know what you're saying anymore. I thought things were cray-cray enough when the goddess turned up with her ladle. But then came the little horse dude with an inferiority complex, and the pecking bird-books, and now a uni-horned lion beast? I mean, I knew magic was *real*, but all this is literally breaking my brain."

I put an arm around his shoulders. "It's a lot, I know. But stay with me. Because the Haetae showed me some visions, and I think they could be our next clue."

I lead him over to a nearby bench. "Let's sit a minute. You can check to make sure Boris is okay while I gather my thoughts."

I have to be careful about how much to share with Emmett. The first scene I saw in the Haetae's bell floods my mind. The Horangi clan were standing protectively over a glowing ax, and Emmett's mom spelled it away from them. That had to be the seventh artifact—the sunstone ax.

The Cave Bear Goddess had told us that the fallen star would grant divine power. I also remember Auntie Okja telling me that the Horangi had figured out a way for witches to become as powerful as the goddesses. And when the other five clans tried to stop them, the scholars attacked. They'd left a path of destruction and despair, just as the Cave Bear Goddess had said.

These things could not be a coincidence. Maybe *all* the artifacts were fallen stars . . . which means that, if the letter is correct, she wants us to find the eighth, and seemingly last, one—whatever and wherever it might be.

Then I think of the second scene in the Haetae's bell, in which a man with an onyx teardrop stone just like mine stood above Mrs. Harrison's dead body. A man with angular features . . . just like mine. Emmett's mom must have been killed for trying to keep the seventh artifact out of the Horangi's clutches. By my biological appa, no less.

There's no way I can reveal my true identity to Emmett now. But the lies are stacking up like pancakes, and I don't know how much longer I can keep this up.

Emmett is folding Boris, signaling that I'd better be ready to talk again, when a shiver of realization goes down my spine.

If the Horangi were trying to use the seventh artifact for their own benefit, chances are they'd want the eighth one, too. They may well have found it by now. And the bearded man had told me to return to the very beginning, to where I first started. He and the Haetae's visions were both telling me the same thing.

I swallow hard. "I...I think I've figured it out, Em. But you're not gonna like the answer...."

He crosses his arms. "Try me."

I force out the words. "We need to find the Horangi clan."

Emmett cracks up. "Good one, Rye. You almost had me there."

I stay silent, and he abruptly stops laughing. "You're kidding, right?"

I shake my head.

"The bearded man and the Haetae said we need to go to the cursed scholars to find the last fallen star?"

I nod. "You saw it in the letter, too. The Horangi were keeping track of the artifacts, and hiding the seventh one. I think they wanted to use it to become divine. If we want to find the eighth artifact, we need to find the scholars."

"But you *know* what they did to my mom."

I swallow the lump in my throat and nod, focusing on a spot on his forehead. "I know."

"They're *dangerous.*"

"I know."

"And *cursed!*"

I cringe. "I know."

Emmett throws his head back and starts cackling maniacally. "You can't be serious right now." Spit gathers at the edges of his mouth. "You're basing this on the words of a giant scaly lion, who was probably a hallucination, and a bearded man who tried to kill us. Who even was he? Why would we trust him? There must be another way. There *has* to be!"

He looks down at his ring, then stuffs his hands in his pockets. "I can't, Riley, I just can't. . . ."

I pinch my thigh. "I know, Em. I know." I take a big breath. "Which is why I've decided to go on alone."

He screws up his face but doesn't say anything. So I continue.

"I don't want to go there, either." *For more reasons than you know.* "But I *have* to. I promised Hattie I would save her. But I can't ask you to come with me. No—I don't *want* you to come with me. You need to go home now."

Emmett covers his face with his hands and kicks the pavement with his foot. "All of this scares me, Rye," he finally says. "It scares the freaking jelly beans out of me."

I nod. I know how hard it was for him to say those words. If Emmett founded a clan, its motto would be Emotions Are Evil. I pat him on the back. "Me too, Em. Me too." And it's the most honest thing I've said to him in a long time.

He drops his hands and sighs. "But I'm not a quitter. And I'm not about to leave my best friend to walk into a clan of murderers by herself."

My eyes well up with tears. "But you can't possibly go there," I mutter. "Not after what they did—"

He unfolds Boris with a decisive snap. "My mind's made up. Like you said, Hattie is counting on us, and I'm not gonna let her down, either." He steps onto the scooter and holds his breath as the blue scales creep up his feet. "Besides, my mom deserves justice. And I'm gonna get it for her."

He waves me over. "What are you waiting for? Jump on."

Stunned by this new gutsy Emmett, I climb on behind him without another word.

"Although, uh," he says, testing Boris's handlebars, "where exactly do we go to find these mother killers?"

I recall the third scene that played in the Haetae's vision. The one in which Emmett and I were at the zoo, drinking boba tea. "This is going to sound weird, but you'll have to trust me," I say. "We've got to go have some tea with the tigers."

Boris dutifully delivers us to the Los Angeles Zoo. We're becoming a lot more confident on him now, and by the time we get off, not only are our stomachs intact, but Emmett's feelings toward the dragon-on-wheels have done a complete 180.

"Aren't you just the cutest," he coos, rubbing Boris behind the ears. "And the way you do that invisibility thing—full of surprises, aren't you!"

On the way over, we'd gotten some gobsmacked looks from saram pedestrians who couldn't figure out how we were moving so fast. Boris kept pointing an ear toward a toggle on his handlebars until Emmett gave in to curiosity and pressed it. Turns out it put us into stealth mode, which kept us conveniently hidden from suspicious saram eyes. Genius.

After folding up Boris once more, we rush over to the posted directory to find the tiger enclosure.

"There," Emmett says, pointing at the signboard. "Right next to the bears and the Desert Garden. It's really close."

It only takes us a few minutes to walk there. And just as the scene in the Haetae's bell showed, there's a food truck parked nearby.

"I don't know why," I explain to Emmett, "but the Haetae told me we need to get boba tea."

Emmett's eyes sparkle. "Hey, I'll make the sacrifice if we must!"

We walk up to the window, and a young woman hands over a laminated menu. She has piercings in her ears, eyebrows, and nose, and her hair is dyed in four different colors, like a shaved-ice cone. She is the definition of cool. "Hey, dudes, let me know what you want when you're ready."

We nod and study the list, which looks pretty standard. How is ordering one of these drinks going to get us to the Horangi?

I glance inside the food truck to see if there are any clues, and that's when I spot the poster on the wall. It's bright red, showing a tiger sitting in a library, drinking boba tea while reading a book. The words YOU NEED A SWEET TOOTH TO KNOW THE TRUTH are written in cursive letters underneath. It looks like a cute hipster ad for drinking boba tea.

The Horangi's clan color is red, and their motto is Knowledge and Truth. Plus, the tiger is in a library. The poster has to be some kind of secret message.

Emmett has already changed his mind three times about his order, and he's now wondering whether his mango green tea slushy should have boba, or coconut jelly, or both.

As the woman patiently listens to him, I notice there is water sloshing inside a glass charm on her wrist. *Ah,* she's gifted. And she's selling tea, so she's probably a Tokki infuser.

She sees me looking at her and smiles. "And you? Have you decided what you want?"

I take a stab in the dark. "I have a real sweet tooth, and I want to *know* the *truth.*" I cock my head toward the poster on the wall, hoping I don't look like an idiot.

She freezes like a rabbit caught in headlights. I must be onto something. She looks down at my empty wrist and narrows her eyes. "Who's asking?"

I clear my throat and improvise. "Sora sent for us." I'm starting to become an expert liar, and I don't know how I feel about that.

The woman breathes out a sigh of relief. She smiles. "Well, I do have a house special, if you're into *forbidden* fruit. I'm sure you'll like it if you're into the truth. It's a real *trip.*"

Forbidden fruit? I *have* to be on the right track. "That sounds great," I say. "We'll get two of those, please."

Emmett opens his mouth to disagree, but I nudge him in the side. "Trust me, Em, that's definitely what you want."

He mumbles under his breath but doesn't argue.

"Coming right up." The woman disappears from the

window, and when she returns a few minutes later, she's holding two large boba teas. They're more expensive than the rest of the teas, but luckily, I have the money Hattie grabbed from the swear jar. We pay, and she passes the drinks over to us with a wink. "And if you speak a word of this to the council, I *will* hunt you down."

The woman gives us a beaming smile and we scurry away with our teas. Who knew infusers were working with the Horangi and selling illegal potions on the black market? And in broad daylight, no less.

We carry our drinks over to the tiger enclosure and stand there taking long sips of the creamy goodness. Mine tastes like taro milk tea mixed with the sweet banana milk you can get from the H-Mart. Yum. We chew happily on the sweet little balls of tapioca, enjoying the momentary respite from the Cave Bear Goddess's assignment.

"So what now?" Emmett asks.

"I'm not sure. I—"

I frown. Something is off. I scan Emmett's body from top to toe. And that's when I see it. Or in this case, *don't* see it.

Emmett's right foot is gone.

"Ahh, your foot!" I shout, pointing at the empty space between his shin and the ground.

Then, before my eyes, more of Emmett starts disappearing. It's as if someone has taken an eraser and started to rub him out. His other foot goes *poof!* and then the invisibility spreads up his legs and torso, engulfing poor Boris along the way. Soon, Emmett is nothing more than a floating head.

"OMG, it's happening to you, too!" Emmett shrieks. I look

down to see my limbs have gone AWOL, and my boba tea is floating in midair.

As Emmett turns from a weird bobbing head into nothing at all, I find my eyes blurring until the tiger enclosure and the zoo have faded to black.

When my vision clears again, dense forest surrounds me on all sides, and the sounds of cicadas and birdsong fill my ears. The sun is drooping in the sky, painting a warm golden hue over the trees, and the smell of pine is strong in the air. We aren't in the zoo anymore—we're in the *mountains*. It reminds me of where my family went on a camping trip in the Angeles National Forest a few years ago.

Emmett appears next to me, looking stunned. "I know she said it'd be a *trip*, but I didn't think she meant it literally."

I shake out my limbs, grateful I can see them again. "Be on guard, Em. We don't know where the Horangi might be hiding."

"Or what they might do to us," he mumbles.

Judging by how low the sun is, it's already late afternoon. If we don't find the scholars in the next few hours, we'll have to find somewhere to camp out for the night.

I think of our family trip again and smile when I remember how stubborn Hattie was about putting up the tent by herself. It took her two hours, but she somehow managed to do it before sundown. Which was great, because my blood was half-drained by mosquitos by that point. Eomma and Appa let us roast s'mores on the campfire, and afterward Mong slept with Hattie and me, tucked in tight between our sleeping bags.

A vision of Eomma's and Appa's worried faces pops into

my mind, and I wonder how they're dealing with our disappearance. Have they told the police? Will anyone in the gifted community (besides Auntie Okja) help them when they're in so much trouble with the council?

I sigh. I miss them so much. I miss Mong. I miss our house. I even miss the toilet-sin.

"Let's start walking," I suggest to Emmett, heading toward the pine trees. "The quicker we complete this job, the sooner we can go home. Maybe the scholars will be—"

"Riley, help!"

I turn around and stop dead in my tracks. A giant hand made of soil has reached out and started to engulf Emmett in its grasp. It's like one of those claw machines at the arcade, but upside down; Emmett is the plushie, and I don't know who's controlling the game.

"Emmett!" I scream. I try to run to him, but my legs are bolted to the spot.

I look down to see the roots of a pine tree wrapping themselves around my feet.

I wriggle and writhe, trying to free myself. But the more I struggle, the tighter the tree's hold becomes. Its limbs wind up my legs, and soon my entire body is trapped in its embrace. As black spots appear in my vision and my breath gets shallow, my blood turns cold.

We're never going to get out of these mountains alive.

15.
Potato Sacks and Truth Bombs

WHEN I COME TO, THERE'S A sack over my head. At least I think it's a sack. It's heavy and rough and smells like rotten potatoes. I try to rip it off, but my arms are tied behind me. And my hands feel . . . wet? When I move my feet, I realize they're also bound and wet. *Huh?* I try to stand, but I find my butt is stuck firmly to a chair. I'm completely immobilized.

"Let me go!" I scream. But the sound gets absorbed by the stinky sack. Instead, I get a big mouthful of l'eau de potato.

Footsteps sound behind me, and the sack is wrenched off my head. I take a huge gulp of air, and it feels so fresh and satisfying it almost tastes sweet. I glance down at my feet and realize why they feel wet. They're submerged in water. And what I thought were ropes tying my legs to the white wicker chair are ribbons of water. Wait, *water*?!

"Riley!" Emmett cries out.

I turn my head to discover him in a chair to the left of me. His is also made of wicker, which makes me feel like we should be on a porch drinking iced tea. Instead, Emmett's legs are tied to the chair with the mysterious water ropes, and his wrists are bound in the same way. I've never seen magic like this.

"Riley, are you okay?" Emmett's eyes are so full of terror that, in that moment, I know we've achieved our goal.

We've found the Horangi.

"Are *you* okay?" I ask. His eyes are bloodshot and his lips purple. I wish I could reach out and squeeze his hand. I can only imagine what he's feeling right now.

He trembles a little, but he nods. "I'm okay."

I scan his face and body to make sure he isn't injured. And when I'm sure they haven't hurt him, I take stock of our surroundings.

From what I can see in front of me, we are sitting smack-bang in the center of a windowless room that is flooded with water up to our ankles. I'm relieved to see Boris is propped up against the wall, next to the door, which is raised slightly above the water. The room isn't big, and it's devoid of any furnishings besides our two chairs. The walls and ceiling are completely white—*so* white, in fact, that it's hard to see where the wall ends and the ceiling starts. It feels like we're inside a picnic cooler.

A tall, lean woman my eomma's age, with a long neck and intelligent eyes, reveals herself from behind us. "Who are you?" she asks, in a deep, authoritative voice. "And how did you know about the boba-tea portal?"

Her hair is swept up into a French twist, and she's wearing a black turtleneck and jeans. She looks like a Korean female version of Steve Jobs, but with more hair. She's the first Horangi

I've ever met. Well, aside from my birth parents, that is, but they don't count.

A man and boy walk out from behind us, too. The man is wearing jeans and a turtleneck like the woman, but he also has on a leather biker's jacket studded with metal stars. The boy—who looks about my age—is dressed in bright-red chinos, an orange-checked shirt, and a red bow tie. He stands out like a beacon against the stark white walls.

The woman studies my face, and for a split second, her eyes widen, as if she's taken by surprise. "You look *just* like . . ."

Her reaction makes my insides wobble. Mostly in a bad way, but a little bit in a good way, too. Does she see my biological eomma or appa in me? Do I have any of their characteristics or traits? What kind of people were they? There are so many questions I want to ask.

But then I remember what they did, and the good feeling vanishes. I don't care who they were. I already know who my real parents are.

The woman shakes her head and clears her throat. "What brings you here?"

"Untie us, and then we'll talk," I demand. "Who kidnaps innocent kids, anyway? No wonder you were disowned by your goddess."

I have no idea where all this bravado is coming from, but thinking of what these cursed witches did to Emmett's mom is enough to light a fire in my gut.

She scowls at me. "I'm sure you don't need me to remind you that *you're* the one who has trespassed on *our* property, and *you're* the one being held prisoner. Are you sure you want to keep talking to me that way?"

"Riley," Emmett warns, "be careful. You know what they're capable of."

I bite my lip. He's right. We need their help to find the last fallen star, and we can't do that if we're dead.

"Let me ask you again," the woman says. "Why have you come here?"

When I don't answer immediately, the man rubs his wrists together until his gifted mark glows red. He holds his hands over the metal stars that adorn his leather jacket. With a flick of his wrists he sends the studs flying like tiny ninja weapons straight toward Emmett's face. When they're an arm's length away, they stop and hover in midair, as if awaiting their final command.

Emmett blanches and I scream, "No!"

The thing is, this scene disturbs me for two reasons. The obvious one being that my best friend is yet again in peril because of me. The other is that this man does not have a Gi on his wrist.

"How are you *doing* that?" I ask, incredulous. Hasn't the Mountain Tiger Goddess cursed them never again to wield magic? And what kind of magic *is* this?

The woman crouches in front of me and looks me square in the eye. "I will *not* ask you the same question three times. If you do not answer, I will have Austin complete the task he has started." She looks to Emmett. "And that would be a shame for your poor friend, now, wouldn't it?"

I nod frantically. "Yes, yes, of course. Please, just lower the blades."

The woman nods, and the man, Austin, makes a swift cupping motion with his hands. The weapons fly back to him and reattach themselves to his jacket. Judging by the way Austin obeys the woman, I'm guessing she's some kind of senior figure here.

I stare in awe as I try to find the right words. "The truth is, we've come to ask for your help."

The woman frowns, and both Austin and the boy look curiously at me.

"You just said we were disowned by our goddess and banished from the gifted community," says the woman. "What makes you think you're in need of our assistance?"

I feel the hard glass of Hattie's heart vial next to my skin. *Because I have to save my sister.* "Because we're looking for something, and we believe you know where it is."

"And what might that be?"

I look at Emmett, and he nods at me to continue.

"We are looking for the Godrealm's last fallen star—what we believe to be the eighth and last artifact. And we need your help in locating it."

Austin's eyes widen and he puts a hand in front of the boy protectively. "Sora, how do they know of the artifacts?" His voice is strained.

My ears perk up at her name. *Sora.* The boba-tea woman sent us to the right person! Could this be the same Sora who wrote the letter? It has to be!

Emmett must have come to the same realization, because

he speaks up. "It doesn't matter how we know about them. What's important is whether you know where the last one is. Do you? Do you know where we can find it?"

Sora studies us carefully. "And if we *did* know where it was, what makes you think we would help you?"

I glance over at Emmett, knowing that this is, without a sliver of doubt, the worst time to come out with the truth.

But I also know what's at stake. Even if Emmett is mad at me for the rest of my life, we have to save Hattie. And if he doesn't forgive me, it will be my fault and my fault only.

"Well?" Sora asks.

I take a big breath. "You see this black cord around my neck? Take a look at what's hanging from it."

Sora walks over and pulls out the vial from under my collar. She exhales sharply.

I puff up my chest and channel the courage that can only come from loving your sister and your best friend more than anything else in the world. "This is my sister's heart, and you're going to help me save her."

Sora doesn't answer for a while. She just stares at the blackening heart and then at me with a weird look that makes me feel sad inside.

When she finally speaks, her deep voice is surprisingly gentle. "And why, pray tell, would I do that?"

I avoid Emmett's gaze and clench my hands together behind my back in prayer. "Because," I say, "you believe in knowledge and truth. And the truth is, I am one of you. I'm a Horangi."

16.
Of Course There's a Prophecy

 I'M NOT SURE WHAT I thought would happen after I dropped the ultimate truth bomb on Emmett. I guess I expected him to scream and shout. Maybe even throw out some colorful words that would land a few bucks in the swear jar. But in reality, he doesn't even look at me. It's like he *can't* look at me.

"Em...?"

The three Horangi scholars are staring at me with plate-size eyes, so I know everyone in this room has heard the truth. But instead of responding, Emmett shrinks into his chair. He keeps his eyes down and blinks blankly like a robot. It's like the news is so outrageous and unbelievable that all he can do is retreat into his shell and pretend it was never uttered.

"Em," I try again, not knowing what I want to say. "I only found out at Hattie's ceremony. It's why we couldn't do the gift-sharing spell. I was going to tell you, I promise. I was waiting for the right time. I... It's just that I..." I trail off. What words could I possibly find to tell him how sorry I am for keeping the biggest secret of my life? How must he feel knowing that I come from the clan that killed his mom?

My eyes start stinging, and I don't know if it's from the blinding whiteness of this room or my blinding guilt. "Em, I'm sorry," I manage to whisper before a hard lump forms in my throat.

Sora coughs as if to bring herself back into the present. Then she signals to the Horangi boy and nods to Emmett. The boy rubs his wrists together. I notice that, like Austin, the boy doesn't have a Gi. He closes his eyes and clasps his hands into a ball. Then, in one swift motion, he releases them and brings them down as if imitating a lava flow. Immediately, the water ropes binding Emmett release and splash around his feet.

I gasp. The man could control the metal stars on his jacket, and this boy can wield water. . . . And neither of them used Gi or incantations. How is that possible?

But I don't get to ponder the question for long. As soon as he is free from his watery shackles, Emmett makes a mad dash for the exit, taking Boris with him. He doesn't give me a second thought, much less a glance. He just pulls the door open and runs away, away from *me*, and something withers inside my chest.

I strain against my liquid ropes, wanting to go after him. But Sora shakes her head. "Let him go. He won't get far. And we need to talk."

I bite my lip but don't argue. It's probably best if I give Emmett a bit of time to cool off anyway.

Sora crouches in front of me so we're at eye level. "I don't believe we got your name," she says. "You know my name is Sora. I'm the clan leader of the LA Horangi."

She points to the man. "This is Austin, and this," she says, nodding to the boy, "is Taeyo."

The boy adjusts the red bow tie around his neck. He stares at me curiously but doesn't say anything. I glance at him and at the two adults and wonder if they're his parents. Aside from Taeyo's very different fashion choices, they look like they could be a family.

"I'm Riley Oh," I say hesitantly. The last thing I want to do is make small talk with these people.

Austin whispers something in Sora's ear, and she nods sadly. "Yes, that's what I thought, too."

She turns to me. "Riley, I think I know your parents. You are the spitting image of your mother. I believe you are the daughter of Mina and Yoon Seo."

I'm momentarily stunned. My birth parents are still alive? "Are they . . . Are they *here*?"

Her face looks pained. "Sorry, I should've been clearer. I *knew* your parents. They were valiant and loyal scholars who passed away protecting our clan. I'm sorry you didn't get to meet them."

My gut wrenches. And then I feel stupid. It's not like I knew of them before today, and I have loving parents who raised me. I shouldn't care what happened to the Seos, let alone be disappointed they're not here.

"Where have you been living all this time?" Sora asks.

"*Who* have you been living with? And how are you even ... alive?"

When I think of the horrible things the Horangi have done, both to Emmett and the gifted community, my first reaction is to shut down. She doesn't have the right to ask me any questions.

But I see genuine concern in her eyes. She must have been close to Mina and Yoon. And if I want these scholars to help me, I need them to trust me.

So I hunker down and give her the highlight reel of my life. Right up until coming here with my best friend to save my sister's life. And when it's all off my chest, I feel a weird sense of relief. As if the burden is lighter for having shared it.

The three of them listen intently. No one says anything after I finish. Instead, Taeyo silently releases my water shackles, while Sora swings open the white wooden door with a flick of her hand. With that, the three of them walk toward the exit, and Sora says, "Follow me."

The door leads straight out into fresh air, and to my surprise, I'm in the upper branches of a tree. The room is suspended up here. It's a windowless rectangular tree house with a wooden staircase spiraling down to the forest floor.

When my feet land on the soil and I look back up, I frown. All I see is a leafy canopy.

"Wait, where did the building go?" I ask, confused.

"All the campus structures have camouflaging mirrors on the outside," explains Austin, "so they blend in with the forest."

"The campus? Is this a school?"

Austin nods. "That and more. The campus is what we call our entire network of tree houses. The water-training room is merely one of the buildings. We have offices, dorms, cafés, restaurants—everything you need to live, study, and work here."

I raise my eyebrows. I don't want to admit it, but I'm low-key impressed. I wish Emmett could be learning this, too. I look around for him, but he's nowhere to be seen. Sora had said he wouldn't get far. What did that mean? I hope he's okay, wherever he is.

"I have some business to attend to," Austin says, turning to leave in the opposite direction. "But Sora and Taeyo will give you the grand tour."

He hurries off, and Taeyo smiles at me shyly. "Come on, we'll show you around."

Sora and Taeyo lead me through the trees until we get to a sparser part of the forest that opens onto a lake. Sora rubs her wrists and chants some incantations, and a nearby fig tree stretches and morphs until it transforms into a staircase up to the canopy.

"Can you see the building?" Taeyo asks, his eyes sparkling.

I squint and look up. Now that I know the walls are covered in mirrors, I can just make out the edges of a structure above us. This one is *much* larger than the one we were in earlier.

Sora twists her wrist, and leafy green vines wrap around the staircase's banister, weaving themselves all the way to the top. I admit it's a nice finishing touch, giving it a fairy-tale look.

"When the council excommunicated us, we had to reestablish ourselves from the ground up," Sora explains, as we climb the newly built stairs. "We and all the other Horangi clan chapters around the world lost our Gi, our access to the temple, and with it, our library and source of knowledge. So we had to adapt. It was the only way to survive."

When we get to the top of the stairs and walk into the building, my jaw drops. This one doesn't look like the inside of a cooler. It looks like Google's headquarters.

"Welcome to the campus HQ. This is one of our main office blocks." Sora waves at a few people who walk past and greet her.

I look around curiously. There are people sitting at shared desks, typing on laptops; others lounging on beanbag chairs while drinking coffee from reusable cups; and kids playing with dogs in the designated playground areas. I spy two huge gumball machines—one full of Skittles and the other with M&M's—and a big vending machine with the largest variety of Pepero sticks I've ever seen. The walls seem to double as whiteboards, and people have scribbled notes, spells, and illustrations all over them. One section has *Knowledge and Truth* spelled out in impressive graffiti.

Taeyo sees my expression and grins. "Sora says we started using tech to strengthen our spellwork way before we were cut off from the community. And afterward, even though we lost access to our sacred texts, we figured out a way to upload as much of the knowledge as we had left to the Cloud." He holds up his phone. "My spellbook's in here now." He then waves to the space around us. "Who needs a temple when you have all this, amirite?"

Sora smiles and puts her hand around Taeyo's shoulders. "By relying on the Horangi hive mind around the world, we also managed to hack the five sacred elements on Earth so we can do magic without a Gi."

I stare wide-eyed at them and down at their Gi-less wrists. "Is that how you were controlling water before?" I ask Taeyo. "And you, wood?" I say to Sora.

Taeyo proudly holds up his wrist. "Some of our best scholars programmed a biochip that can be inserted into the wrist and do the job of a Gi. *Without* the need for divine intervention."

I frown, not following.

Sora explains. "In a traditional Gi ceremony, the cauldron reveals the element you're *not* born with. The focus is on what you lack. And then the goddesses channel their divine power through the witch's Gi for the witch to do magic."

"Yeah," I say. "That's how it's always been, for thousands of years."

"But we posed the question: What if there's another way— one that doesn't require the divine? What if, instead of focusing on what we lack, we focus on what we already possess?"

I think of the four fires revealed at my Gi ceremony and cringe. I didn't lack just one element—I lacked almost all of them.

"The goddesses require us to have a perfect balance of all five elements in order to channel their powers. But we found that tapping into our dominant element—the thing we already have in abundance—is enough. It not only works like a Gi, it also allows us to *wield* that element. Like you saw when Austin controlled metal, or when Taeyo manipulated water."

My mouth gapes. Does that mean I could wield fire? The thought blows my mind. I grew up thinking I didn't have a drop of magic in my blood. Now I find out there's a way I could control the thing I've always been ashamed of. No, not just control—*master*.

My first gut reaction is to ask Sora if I could learn this skill, too. I want to know how it feels to have magic at my fingertips. But then Hattie's face pops into my mind, reminding me of my priorities. This is not the time to be picking up party tricks. I have a job to do.

Instead, I ask another question. "But how does it work? Where does the power come from if not the goddesses?"

Taeyo points to the water cooler near us, and then to a running tap a man has turned on in the kitchenette across the room. "The five sacred elements are all around us. The Earth was made by Mago Halmi herself, and we were all created in her image, which means we and the elements are all divine in our own right. We don't need the Godrealm to access our gifts. Magic is inside each of us."

I immediately think of Auntie Okja. She'd told me the Horangi had become obsessed with power because they'd figured out a way for witches to become as potent as the goddesses. That's why the scholars had been cursed by their goddess to never wield magic again. It was also the reason Emmett's mom had been stuck in the cross fire keeping the seventh artifact out of their hands.

A bubble of anger pops inside me. They can adapt all they

want—it doesn't erase the horrible things they've done. At the end of the day, they killed Emmett's mom, and there is *no* excuse for taking a life.

"Is that why you did it?" I ask quietly. "Is that why you staged an attack against the gifted community? Why you *killed* people? For . . . for *power*?" I consider the life I could have had if the Horangi hadn't become corrupt. All the things I don't even know I missed out on. "Why couldn't you just have been happy being the keepers of the sacred texts? Why did you have to be so greedy?"

"You don't know the full picture," Sora starts. "There are always tw—"

"Don't lie," I say. I slip the letter out of my pocket and show it to Sora. "I know you were hiding the seventh artifact for your own use."

She reads it, and her eyebrows arch in surprise. "How did you come to have this?"

When I don't respond, she grabs a Swiss ball and invites me to sit on it. "You were honest with us about what brought you here. So let me now repay you in kind."

Out of principle, I refuse the Swiss ball and sit on a nearby chair instead. I don't want her to think she's won me over. I cross my arms. This had better be good.

She takes a big breath. "People know the Horangi as keepers of the sacred texts because we looked after the gifted library. But that was only one of our duties. For generations upon generations, we have also been the keepers of the sacred artifacts—divine but dark objects that represent the goddesses' original sin."

Original sin . . . I remember Adeline's monologue about the goddesses believing that the dark sun and moon represented their inner darkness. When the goddesses commanded the Haetae to devour the sun and moon, they committed a sin against their mother. As a result, Mago Halmi locked them out of the Mortalrealm. It makes sense that the fallen shards, or artifacts, are physical representations of the daughters' crime.

"But our ancestors were sworn to secrecy," Sora continues. "We had a duty to protect the artifacts, even from people in our own community. If they fell into the wrong hands, these powerful dark relics could break the equilibrium between the three realms."

Now I understand the real reason why the Cave Bear Goddess wants the last fallen star destroyed. "Okay," I say, trying to see where this is going, "and . . . ?"

"But we failed to adequately protect the sunstone ax. The council found it, and they, like so many others, became infected by its power. They became corrupt. We had no choice but to destroy the artifact before the members kept it for themselves."

I snort. "No, that's wrong. The council was trying to stop *you* from using it. The elders aren't corrupt."

A dark shadow passes over Sora's face. "We believe they were. And when we tried to reveal the truth, they framed us and banished us from the gifted community." She shakes her head. "Because of the council, many innocent people were killed. Including your parents."

I swallow. This is all a lie. A big, elaborate invention. Emmett's mom had been an elder on the council. And in the vision around the Haetae's bell, I'd seen her taking the sun-stone ax from the Horangi.

Suddenly, the blood freezes in my veins. Could Emmett's mom have been taking it from the Horangi to use for *herself*? I shake my head. *Impossible.*

"How do you know all this, anyway?" I ask, starting to feel sweaty and uncomfortable.

Taeyo sits on the Swiss ball that Sora offered me earlier. "Sora was the Horangi elder on the council at the time. She knows because it happened on her watch."

Wait, Sora used to be on the council? I shake my head. So this woman standing in front of me is the infamous Ms. Kwon—the one the council accused of masterminding the Horangi attack against the gifted community all those years ago.

Hiccups start erupting from my throat, and I sound like a gurgling drain. The council couldn't be corrupt—*no way*. But what Sora and Taeyo are saying doesn't seem illogical.

Taeyo bounces gently on the ball. "We've been searching for the eighth artifact for years. None of the Horangi clans around the world have it, and we think the only way to keep the Mortalrealm safe is to destroy it. Like we did with the seventh one."

It's all too much. I pinch my thigh for even entertaining the idea of believing them. "You guys just want to find the last artifact for yourselves! This is all a big story to cover up what you really want—to take the power of the last fallen star for your own gain. Admit it!"

Taeyo looks super offended and starts talking really fast. "It's *not* a story. It's the *truth*! You're too blinded by what the council has told you to see it. You've been brainwashed!"

Sora goes to borrow one of the scholars' laptops. She brings it over and opens it in front of me. "I know it's hard to question everything you've ever been taught, but let me show you something."

She opens an app that looks a lot like Google Drive but is called Campus Drive, and selects a folder called Project Prophecy. She scrolls down the files and clicks on a JPEG.

The photo that opens shows me the man I'd seen in the Haetae's vision—the man who'd had the onyx stone. Here he's gazing at the woman next to him with utter admiration. She's smiling broadly at the camera, her hand draped lovingly over her pregnant belly. When I see her face, my heart stops. We have the same eyes, the same angled cheekbones, the same sprinkling of sesame-seed freckles across the nose. I know without a semblance of doubt who she is.

"It's them," I whisper, reaching out to touch the screen. "My birth parents."

"Yes," Sora says softly. "It is."

Tears well in my eyes, and suddenly I don't care that they were cursed or that they were power-obsessed or that they were outcast from the community. For a moment, I just miss them with all my heart. I know it sounds weird to miss people I don't remember, but right now, I wish for nothing more than to be held in their arms.

Taeyo hands me a tissue, and Sora opens another photo.

This one is of Mina and Yoon sitting side by side in front of their computers, working intently. Lines of concentration mask their faces.

"Your biological parents were some of the first scholars to use complex algorithms to decrypt our oldest, most indecipherable sacred texts," she explains. "And before they died, they made an incredible discovery."

I lean into the photo, wishing I could jump into the scene and ask them about their discovery myself.

"They decrypted one of our oldest prophecies," Sora continues. "One that we believe predicts a frightening future."

She opens a third document—this time an encrypted file that she runs through a program called Decryptonite. The loading bar boots into action, and when it reaches 100 percent, a simple text file opens with the following words:

When the blood moon and black sun appear to the gaze
To mark the start of the end of all days,
In the one last divine, a weapon shall rise;
Unless the gold-destroyer ends the soul who lies.

I read the prophecy over and over and feel my head go light as I digest the first two lines.

"A lunar and solar eclipse recently happened on the same day," I say, frowning hard. "Do you think that was the blood moon and black sun?"

Sora's mouth tightens as she nods. "We don't know what the second couplet means yet. But if we don't locate the eighth artifact—which we believe is the one last divine weapon—and destroy it, our days may be numbered."

My heart races. Were Sora and Taeyo telling the truth about the council, my biological parents, and this prophecy? Could the entire Mortalrealm actually be at risk if I don't find this star?

I grip Hattie's heart vial through my top. Maybe the Horangi aren't the villainous clan I always believed them to be. Maybe the bearded man at the temple was right and there really *are* two sides to every story.

There's a thundering crash down the hall, and I jolt out of my chair and out of my thoughts. "What was that?!"

Taeyo and Sora look at each other with worried expressions.

"Was it you? Did you kill my mom?" I hear someone scream in the distance.

"Emmett," I explain in a rush. "We need to get to him *now*."

17.
Why Is There Always a Catch?

When Sora, Taeyo, and I rush over to where the sound came from, my worst fears are realized. Emmett has cornered a bunch of scholars and is having a one-sided screaming match with them. Broken cups and dismembered laptops litter the floor next to Boris, and Emmett is holding a jar of multicolored jelly beans over his head.

"Why won't any of you *talk*?! Tell me, which one of you killed my mom?!"

The scholars are holding out their wrists, ready to attack if provoked. But Emmett's clearly not scared of them. I see sheer desperation in his eyes, and it's like something in him has snapped. As if he's decided he's got nothing to lose.

"Em, please, stop!" I cry, taking the jar from him before he smashes that on the ground, too. "I know you're mad, but this is not the way to deal with it."

He swivels around to face me, and there is venom in his eyes. "And why should I listen to *you*? You're just as bad as them. Power-hungry and magic-obsessed, using your loved ones for your own gain."

The accusation cuts through me like a knife. He's right. I dragged him to the clan that made him motherless, only for him to find out I'm one of them. . . . I'm the definition of selfish.

Emmett turns toward the scholars again. "Which one of you killed my mom?"

"What are you talking about?" Sora asks. She disarms the scholars and sends them away. "Why would you think we killed your mother? We don't even know who she is."

Emmett storms up to Sora and points his finger in her face. "But you *did* know her! And yet, you killed her anyway. Do you know how much my dad is still hurting? You stole the love of his life from him! You ruined both our lives, and you don't even know it."

With that he bursts into tears, and I immediately feel tears welling in my eyes, too. Emmett never cries. But today, his carefully built shell is cracking.

Sora and Taeyo look at me for answers. "Emmett's mom used to be the Gom elder on the LA council," I explain. "She died in the attack you guys orchestrated."

Sora gasps. "Sookhee Harrison was your mother?"

Emmett nods and clutches his head in his hands. I run over to him and hug him hard, and he must be exhausted, because he doesn't push me away. He just sniffles into my shoulder.

Sora sighs deeply and holds her chest. "I'm sorry for your loss, Emmett. And I'm sorry I didn't recognize you. Sookhee was a good colleague and friend of mine."

He angrily wipes his eyes with the back of his hand. "Then why did you do it? *Why?*"

She massages her temples and pauses as if trying to choose her words carefully. "Sookhee wasn't . . . *herself* near the end. She was obsessed with the sunstone ax, and when we tried to protect her from it, she turned violent. It was almost like she became someone else. She fought anyone who stood in her way, and innocent lives were lost at her hands." She glances at me and at Taeyo, and something in her eyes makes me feel uneasy. "So we had no choice but to defend ourselves. I'm sorry, Emmett. I really am."

Emmett sobs harder, and I pull him closer to me. Could the person who gave birth to my best friend really have been corrupted by an artifact and driven mad with greed? I don't know what to believe anymore.

Sora comes over and puts a hand on Emmett's shoulder. "But the thing is, I don't believe Sookhee meant for any of that to happen. I've been thinking about that day for a long time now, and something she said before she passed has stayed with me."

"What was it?" I ask, and Emmett looks up, too.

"She said, 'She made me do it—I thought she was my friend.'" Sora pauses thoughtfully. "The council pulled the strings—there's no doubt about that. But I believe someone else was involved. Someone close to her, whom she thought she could trust."

A shiver runs through my body. Emmett's mom and Auntie Okja used to be best friends. And Auntie Okja took over as Gom elder after Mrs. Harrison died. . . .

I quickly push the thought away. This is my auntie, the gracious, selfless healer we're talking about. She would *never*. Not in a million years!

Eventually, Emmett pulls himself together. "I've heard enough. The only person who could clear this up is my mom, and she's not here anymore. That leaves us with one option: Find the last artifact and destroy it ourselves." He wipes his face and sniffles away his last tears. "Regardless of whether your story or the council's is true, a fallen star is the reason for my mom's death. So I will destroy the last one before it can ruin anyone else's life. I won't let her death be in vain."

I squeeze his shoulder. *Yes.* Finding and destroying the last fallen star is our solution to everything. The Cave Bear Goddess will be pleased, we'll get Hattie back, and Emmett will have avenged his mother's death. And if the prophecy's to be believed, we'll have saved the entire world from the end of days.

"He's right," I declare to Sora and Taeyo. "Let's work together. Let's find the eighth artifact so we can destroy it."

A part of me still wonders if the Horangi have fabricated this entire story in order to get their own hands on the last artifact. But time is running out. We have to take the risk.

Emmett turns to me. "I don't know if I can ever forgive you—you realize that, right?"

I lower my eyes and nod.

He clenches his jaw. "But Hattie needs us, and this is finally something I can do to make my mom's death meaningful. So for now I'm gonna pretend things are okay. For them."

I nod again. It's a start, and I'm willing to work with that.

Emmett turns to Sora. "How do we find the last artifact? What do you know?"

Sora considers her words carefully. "I respect your bravery in coming here for answers, and your courage in telling me your truth. We Horangi uphold knowledge and truth above all else." She raises her wrist to me. "But we have suffered too much to enter into new partnerships lightly. Unless you are willing to officially initiate into our clan, Riley, I am afraid we will not be joining hands with you or your friend."

"Me?" I point to my chest.

"You are of Horangi blood, and you were taken from us," says Sora. "It is time for you to return to your rightful clan."

I am stunned into disbelief. "But we're after the same thing!" I say. "We both want to find the last artifact and destroy it. You don't need me to become a scholar to do that."

Sora shakes her head. "Oh, but we do. We lost too many of our own during the last conflict. We can't take any more chances. You are either one of us and we work together as a team, or you're on your own."

Emmett fidgets with the hem of his black T-shirt. "And what exactly would she have to do? To initiate into the clan?"

I glare at Emmett, but he avoids my gaze. I think of Hattie's initiation and how long she had to train for it. There's no way I'd be able to prepare for one in a short amount of time. Especially without a Gi.

"When we were excommunicated, we lost our ability to initiate our witches in the traditional way," Sora says. "But we have adapted. In fact, with our biochip discovery, we've found that a successful initiation isn't about the magic—we already have that. What we're looking for is commitment and loyalty."

"Okay..." I say, feeling uneasy. "And what does that mean?"

"It means that, if you were to accept the challenge, you would agree to have a biochip inserted into your wrist. Then we will give you a specific task of our choosing. If we deem your conduct in the task worthy of initiation, we will invite you to pledge your allegiance to the Horangi clan. If you accept, you will leave your old clan behind and officially become a scholar—for now, and for all time."

As Sora's words sink in, I touch my wrist. I think of Mina and Yoon. And for a moment, I admit I am tempted by the prospect. In another life, I could have been raised in this clan. And having seen Sora, Austin, and Taeyo wield the sacred elements, I am curious about my own potential. For once, I could have magic at my fingertips. I could belong.

But then I remember who I am. I think of the parents who raised me, and the sister who put herself at risk so I could earn my gift. I recall our clinic, my healer clan, and the promise the goddess made to turn me into a Gom when I complete my job. I remember where my loyalties lie.

I am not a Horangi, despite what my blood may say.

"No way," I say. "Nope, never, won't do it. Not in a million years. I know who I am. And I am not one of you."

Taeyo's face falls, but Sora simply nods. "We may be firm, but we are fair. If that is your wish, we will respect it."

18.
It's Time to (Rescue) Party

 IT'S ONLY BEEN TWENTY-FOUR HOURS since the summoning spell went south, but it feels like years have passed since this madness started. I am *so* tired.

Sora lets us sleep in the dorms for the night so Emmett and I can recharge before we go off on our own. And I'm grateful for it. I still don't trust her, but when the night passes without a hitch, I do start to wonder if there's some truth to her stories. If they really were the dangerous and power-crazed people I was told they were, wouldn't they try to keep us hostage and use us to get back at the council or something?

The bed is super comfortable, but my sleep is plagued by nightmares, and I toss and turn all night. In some, I'm lost and looking for my family, but I have no facial features, so no one knows who I am. In others, my parents find me, but they don't want me anymore. I wake several times hiccuping and drenched in sweat. I do eventually find sleep, but it feels like only five sweet minutes before it's morning and we have to get up.

As Emmett and I walk to the campus HQ to find Sora, I consider our options. There's only one day left before, as I agreed, Emmett will get the adults involved. But a part of me wonders if we should go to them sooner. They won't understand why we had to seek out the Horangi clan, but at least we learned about the prophecy. Maybe my parents and Auntie Okja will know what we should do next? Then again, if what Sora said was true, the council might not be as trustworthy as I once thought. . . .

Our farewell to the scholars is short—Taeyo doesn't even show up. Sora offers us two black-market boba teas before seeing us off. She looks a little disappointed, but she doesn't try to convince me to stay.

When Emmett and I rematerialize at the zoo, I take a nervous glance at my necklace. A quarter of Hattie's heart has now shriveled, and I grip the vial hard. At this rate, we're going to run out of time in two days. Maybe less.

"I don't see why you couldn't at least *consider* taking up Sora's offer," Emmett says, as we start walking away from the tiger enclosure. "I mean, beggars can't be choosers, and we're not exactly flush with leads."

Heat alights in my gut and I feel like shouting at him, *Don't you understand? It doesn't work like that! You can't just choose a new family like choosing a new outfit. I'm a Gom. My entire family are healers. I can't just betray them and join another clan. You can't be both!*

But of course, I keep my mouth shut. After everything I've put Emmett through, who am I to talk? Instead, I bite my tongue and rack my brain trying to figure out what to do next.

Emmett reads my mind. "So where do we go now?" He studies me, then looks down at my empty hands. "Wait, where's Boris? I thought you had him!"

The last time I saw the dragon scooter was last night, lying next to my bed in the dorm. I groan loudly. "I must have totally forgotten him this morning. There was just so much on my mind. . . ."

"How are we gonna get anywhere now?" Emmett moans. "And just when I was starting to bond with the dude . . ."

"Looking for something?" says a voice from behind us.

I get such a fright, I almost trip over my own feet. We swivel around to see Taeyo materializing from out of nowhere. He's wearing yellow chinos, a bright pink shirt, and a purple blazer. Like yesterday, he's sporting a bow tie, but today it's purple to match his blazer. He looks like a human rainbow.

"Argh!" Emmett cries, shielding his face. "My poor eyes! It's blinding!"

Taeyo looks up at the sky. "Is the sun too bright? Sorry, Emmett. I should have brought my sunglasses for you. I have two pairs, so I definitely could have given you one of them!"

He is completely oblivious to Emmett's sarcasm, and for some reason, that makes me warm to him. Sure, Taeyo's vibrant color palette is a world away from Emmett's all-black uniform, but there's an earnestness about the guy that makes him easy to be around. And anyway, I actually think his outfit's kind of cool—even if he is a bit overdressed for the zoo.

He holds up what looks like Boris but also doesn't *quite* look like Boris. "I think you guys forgot your friend."

He unfolds the scooter and wheels it toward us. Blue scales. Wagging tail. Cute little wings. It's Boris, all right. But now he's almost twice his original size, and he's been souped up with fancy new wheels and some mysterious new toggles at the handlebars. It even looks like he's had a good polish.

"Whoa!" Emmett exclaims. "What happened to *him?*"

Taeyo grins. "Our engineers gave him an upgrade this morning. He was returned to your room, but you must have missed him."

Emmett pulls Boris protectively toward him and narrows his eyes at Taeyo. "Is this some kind of trick to bait us? Did your mom put you up to this?"

Taeyo frowns. "My mom?"

"Sora," I say. "Did Sora tell you to follow us?"

Taeyo looks confused. "Sora's not my mom. Not really."

Not really? What kind of answer is that?

Taeyo glances at me. "My parents were killed in the conflict, too. Sora and Austin and some of the other adults took me in, so, in a way, they're all my parents, I guess."

Emmett and I exhale sharply. Yesterday, Sora had looked at me and Taeyo weirdly when she was talking about the innocent lives Sookhee had taken. Was this why?

"I made it clear I don't want to join your clan, so if that's why you're here, you can go back to campus." I feel bad speaking so bluntly, but there's no time to beat around the bush. "Unless you can help find the last fallen star, you're not much use to us. No offense."

"Well, actually, I think I can help with that."

Emmett and I look at him suspiciously. If he knew a way to find it, why was he telling us instead of his clan?

"Elaborate," Emmett says.

Taeyo holds up his phone. "I've been working on an app. It's still in beta phase, but if I've programmed it right, it should allow us to talk to gwisin."

"Gwisin?!" Emmett and I both yelp.

Gwisin are hungry ghosts that haven't been able to pass through to the Spiritrealm because of unfinished business on Earth. Sometimes, when they had a particularly gruesome end to their life, you get hungry *and* angry ones (aka hangry ghosts), and you *really* don't want to be haunted by those.

"Yeah," says Taeyo. "It's kinda like a ghost-whisperer app. It puts out a beacon to gwisin. If they match with someone who's willing to help them, they'll finally get to pass into the Spiritrealm. Hopefully, anyhow."

"*No way.*" I am genuinely impressed by both his altruism and his coding ability. "That's kinda awesome." Then I remember he's from the cursed clan. They're supposed to be selfish and greedy. "But what's in it for you?"

He shrugs. "Nothing, I guess. Just a good feeling from knowing I helped a ghost pass on."

Hmm. A charitable Horangi. I shake my head dubiously. "And what has this got to do with our search?"

He looks at Emmett. "I thought maybe we could use the app to find your mom. Like you said yesterday, she's the only one who seems to know the truth. If she's a gwisin, she might be able to tell us who really wanted the sunstone ax, why the council framed us, and maybe even where the last artifact is being kept."

My eyes dart to Emmett. What Taeyo is suggesting is a really big deal. Emmett has wanted to meet his mom his entire life. If we look for her and don't succeed, he will be devastated. On the other hand, if we *do* find her, Emmett will learn that his mom had spent the last thirteen years haunting the Earth because of unfinished business. No kid wants to find out that their mom is a hungry ghost. On top of all that, what if what Sora said about Mrs. Harrison is true? That she was the one who stole the sunstone ax and destroyed innocent lives?

I shake my head. "Nope, it's too risky," I say. "It's a creative idea, but we won't do it."

Emmett puts his hand in front of me as if to say, *Hang on a second.* He turns to Taeyo. "What's your angle, Bow Tie? Why would you work with us? You don't even know us."

Taeyo straightens his blazer over his shirt. "I never knew my parents, but I'm told they were some of the bravest scholars the clan has ever seen. They always jumped at the chance to help people in need. I know it might sound corny, but I want to make sure their legacy lives on. I want to make them proud of who I've become."

That makes Emmett and me go silent. We both have parents we didn't get to know, either. It's understandable that he wants to do right by his.

"If it works and we find out where the last artifact is being kept," Taeyo continues, "we have a real shot at stopping the prophecy. And of course, we could save your sister, too."

I bite my lip. Taeyo's idea may have legs, but it's not worth putting Emmett through potential devastation to risk it. He's been through enough already.

"Thanks, but no thanks," I start. "We don't—"

"I'll do it," Emmett interrupts.

I reach over and squeeze his arm. "You don't have to do this. We can find another way."

He turns to me and shakes his head. "I made a decision yesterday that I'd find justice for my mom. If this is how I have to do it, then so be it." He exhales loudly and squeezes Boris to his chest.

"Are you sure?" I ask quietly. *What if you don't like what you hear?*

He nods. "We're doing this."

Taeyo adjusts his bow tie. "Great news!"

A thought pops into my mind. "Have you ever tried finding *your* parents?" I ask Taeyo.

"Yes," he says, then shakes his head sadly. "But you can't find a gwisin who doesn't want to be found. I like to think they both made it to the Spiritrealm. That way, maybe one day I'll meet them again. Even if they wouldn't technically be my parents anymore."

I nod. The gifted believe that once you die and go to the Spiritrealm, you have the chance to be reborn into a new life. Some request to be reborn near their living loved ones, and they can even come back as a family member or close friend. They don't remember anything from their past life, but at times a bond can be so strong that even without the memories the love is still there.

I wonder if my biological parents are somewhere in the Spiritrealm waiting to be reborn. Or perhaps they're still here on Earth, waiting for someone to help them finish their unfinished business.

It's like Taeyo's read my mind. "We can try finding yours, too, Riley, if you like."

I don't nod, but I don't disagree, either. I just swallow the lump in my throat. I'm not sure I could be as brave as Emmett. I couldn't handle that kind of reunion right now.

"So how do we do this?" Emmett asks. "Please don't tell me we have to go somewhere haunted and creepy."

"No creepy haunted places," Taeyo assures him. "We just have to find the best restaurant in town."

"Huh?" I scowl. Is he wanting to grab a bite right now? This is *not* the time to be thinking about food.

"They're called hungry ghosts for a reason. When you die and get stuck on Earth, you get confused. Your physical self is gone, but you stay hungry, as if you were still alive. That's why they hang out at the best restaurants. Which must suck, to be honest, since they can't actually eat anything. Anyhoo, that's how you know where the food is the best. It's way more accurate than Yelp or Foursquare."

I'm impressed by Taeyo's knowledge. He obviously did his research for the app.

"Well, that's easy," Emmett says. "Seoulful Tacos."

I nod eagerly. "It's a Korean-Mexican place run by a Tokki family. It's our fave." In fact, everyone in LA knows David Kim's family restaurant is the best in town. Just the thought of their gimchi guacamole and bulgogi tacos makes me salivate.

Taeyo points to the new-and-improved Boris. "Great. Who wants to drive?"

I shake my head. "He's too small for us all to . . ." I stop in mid-sentence. "Well, actually, I guess he *is* big enough for the three of us now, thanks to you."

Emmett quickly jumps on Boris before either Taeyo or me. "I'm driving," he says. He leans into the scooter's ear and whispers, "Sorry for leaving you behind before. Nothing personal, but hey—you're looking pretty good for an old dude." The dragon's tail wags happily.

I jump on behind Emmett, and Taeyo takes out his phone and raises it above us at a high angle.

"What are you doing, weirdo?" Emmett asks, looking sideways at him.

"I'm taking a selfie of us. I've never gone on a mission with friends before, and I don't want to forget it."

He's so sincere it makes me laugh, and I'll admit—it feels good. I lean in next to Taeyo and smile hard for the camera. "*Gimcheese!*"

Emmett glares at me. "Are you serious? You guys are losers."

Taeyo and I pull him into the shot and Emmett groans. "Okay, *fiine*," he relents. "But make sure you don't get my bad side, or else I'll hurt you. My nails are sharp. Just saying."

19.
Anyone Hungry for Seoulful Tacos?

WHEN WE WALK IN THE DOOR of Seoulful Tacos, the waft of smoky barbecued jackfruit and fresh gimchi salsa has me drooling. It smells so good in here, and I can't believe how famished I am.

Taeyo grins as he looks around the restaurant. "Whoa, there's loads of people in here. It's going to be a hotbed for gwisin!"

"If you say so," Emmett mumbles.

I've been here a million times before, but today I look around nervously as if I'm entering the place for the first time. Thankfully, I only see tables of live humans eating and ordering food. *Phew.*

We grab a booth by the window, and David Kim scurries over to give us menus. "Hey, Riley, nice to see you," he says.

His cheeks are a little ruddy, as per usual, and when he smiles, his eyes disappear into his plump face. He's wearing his Gi around his wrist, so his initiation ceremony must have been successful. I'm genuinely happy for him. He deserves it.

"Can I get some gimchi guac and corn chips to start, please?" I don't even need to look at the menu.

"And a bulgogi taco for me, thanks, with extra gochujang hot sauce," Emmett says. He looks over at Taeyo, who's going cross-eyed at the size of the menu. "Actually, make that two."

Taeyo looks up, grateful for the intervention, and Emmett takes his menu from him. "Trust me. You won't be disappointed."

David hurries off into the kitchen, and Emmett turns to Taeyo.

"So how do we do this, Bow Tie? We just open the app and put out a message?" He glances around our booth and shivers. "Are the gwisin all around us right now? I'm not, like, sitting on one, am I?"

Taeyo takes out his phone and opens an app called Ghostr. "First, you need to create a profile."

He hands the phone to Emmett, who starts typing.

"Name? Emmett Harrison. What I'm looking for? My mom, Sookhee Harrison, who was killed by the Horangi thirteen years ag—"

"Allegedly," Taeyo points out.

Emmett shrugs but adds the word to the profile. "*Allegedly* killed by the Horangi thirteen years ago. Relation to gwisin? Son. Favorite food? Bulgogi taco with extra gochujang sauce." He pauses and looks over what he's written. "That should do it."

Taeyo takes the phone from him and saves the details. "Great. Your profile should now be out in the ether for all gwisin to see. You always get a bunch of random ghosts hoping for a match. But if we start swiping, hopefully we'll get a match with your mom. If she's nearby, she'll respond."

"This might seem like a silly question," I say, "but where do the gwisin get their photos taken? And how do they load them into the app?"

"Oh, those are great questions," Taeyo responds. "You know how there's always a photo on the funeral altar?"

I nod. At gifted funerals, a large photo of the deceased is placed on an altar and surrounded by flowers, lit candles, and their favorite foods. That way loved ones can gaze at the person's face and taste food on their behalf. Mourners can even write a letter and then burn it in the candle flames, which delivers the message to the other side.

"Well, I programmed the app to upload the funeral picture into the app's back end," says Taeyo. "When a gwisin decides to create a profile, it automatically syncs with that photo."

"Impressive," I say. "You're really smart."

Emmett rolls his eyes and imitates me in a high-pitched voice. "Oh, you're *so* smart, Taeyo."

I poke Emmett in the ribs—there's no need to be rude when it's the truth. But Taeyo just smiles. "Thanks, guys. That's nice of you to say."

Emmett doesn't know how to respond to that, so instead, we huddle around Taeyo's phone and wait to see what loads. The first photo that comes up is of a sour-faced man, with his name and profile below. It says his life was taken violently, and he is seeking revenge before he passes on to the Spiritrealm.

Taeyo swipes left. "That's a hangry gwisin. I learned early on it's best to avoid those."

"Didn't he read my profile?" asks Emmett. "I said I was looking for a *mom*."

The next photo is of a super-pale woman dressed in white, with long black hair partially covering her face. Her head is angled down, but her black eyes are looking up with a steely gaze, and frankly, she totally gives me the creeps.

"'My husband cheated on me, and when I tried to confront him, he killed me,'" Emmett reads out loud. "'I don't really want to pass on to the Spiritrealm—I'm enjoying haunting him too much. I'm just here to see what else is out there, and keep my options open. In my spare time, I enjoy crawling out of TV screens and taking long walks on the beach. Message me.'" Then Emmett adds with a shudder, "And there's a kiss emoji."

The three of us cringe in unison. "Swipe left, swipe left!"

We keep going until we run out of profiles. Emmett's mom was not among them. The loading wheel keeps spinning, but no new gwisin come up.

"That's a shame," Taeyo says finally. "I thought it'd work, but I guess she's not around here."

Emmett tenses and fidgets with a napkin. "I *knew* we weren't gonna find her. What a colossal waste of time. This is a stupid app."

"Maybe she already passed through to the Spiritrealm?" I try.

Emmett turns away and shrugs.

"Sorry, Emmett," Taeyo says, looking genuinely apologetic. "I really thought we could find her." He turns to me. "Did you want to try locating your parents, Riley? We can change the profile and try again."

For a moment, I'm tempted. I really am. But, looking at Emmett's face, I decide against it. Maybe what Sora said is true, and my birth parents were good people. But this is not the time for a reunion.

I shake my head. "Is that it, then? The plan's failed already?"

Taeyo sits up taller and taps his phone. "Well, there is one other thing we can try." He reopens the profile page and types in his own info. Under *What I'm looking for* he says that he's just an ordinary boy wanting to help nice ghosts reunite with their loved ones.

He looks up at us. "Sometimes a gwisin will ask if there's anything they can do for *you*. Like grant a favor for helping them out. Gwisin aren't tethered to a physical body, so they can roam the Earth at the speed of thought. I could ask one to search for the last artifact."

"A gwisin would do that?" I ask, surprised.

He nods. "A nice one would."

As he updates the profile, it dawns on me. Taeyo might not be fixing broken bodies like my parents do, but he's helping broken souls find peace. If that's not healing, I don't know what is. Maybe Sora really was telling us the truth about the Horangi being wrongly accused. They don't seem *that* bad. . . .

"Let's do it," I say.

We huddle around the phone again and wait for the new profiles to load.

The first one that comes up is a photo of a translucent boy with a bald, egg-shaped head and big round eyes. His name is Casper, and it says he wants to connect with his crush, Kat, but his ghost uncles won't let him. He needs help in convincing them otherwise.

"He seems like a friendly ghost, but those uncles sound

kinda mean," I say, frowning. "I'd rather avoid fighting with a ghostly trio if I can help it."

The next profile shows a middle-aged woman hugging her pet turtle. She says she promised Crush a trip to Disneyland, but she died before she could take him. She's looking for someone to pick up Crush from her sister's house and accompany him on the Finding Nemo submarine ride. She wants him to learn about where he came from.

Emmett snorts, looking closer at the turtle. "That's a red-eared slider. They're freshwater turtles."

"I've always wanted to go to Disneyland, but I don't know. She sounds a little . . . different," Taeyo says.

I nod. "We don't have time for that anyway. Their lines are legendary. Let's keep swiping."

The next profile we get is the face of an old woman with sad but smiling eyes. Her name comes up as *Jennifer's halmeoni* (aka *Jennifer's grandma*), and her profile is short and straight to the point.

"'I died peacefully in my sleep, but unfortunately, I didn't get to do the one thing I needed to do,'" Taeyo reads aloud. "'Please help me deliver a message so I can pass on to the next realm with peace in my heart. Thank you.'"

"Swipe right," I say. "She sounds perfect."

Emmett nods. "She seems okay."

Taeyo complies, and we wait with bated breath.

Within a few seconds, the screen lights up with a bright notification accompanied by exploding streamers and balloons. IT'S A MATCH!

"OMG, she chose us, too," Emmett says. He's trying to hide

it, but I can tell he's excited. He glances sheepishly at Taeyo. "I guess your app isn't *that* stupid."

"Now what?" I ask.

"Now we wait for her to message us."

The food arrives, and Taeyo takes a bite of his taco. He puts it down, and the grin on his face is so wide, he's all teeth. "Oh, wow! This is *so* good." He takes a picture of it with his phone. "I definitely want to remember this."

A minute later, just when the taco has been demolished, a notification pops up on his phone. He's received a message from Jennifer's halmeoni.

Dear Taeyo,

Thank you for matching with me. From your profile it looks like you are a kindhearted young man, and I am grateful for your offer of assistance. I am seeking to deliver a message to my dear granddaughter, Jennie Byun. She is a Samjogo seeing witch who lives in this area. She has recently turned thirteen years old. I cannot leave for the Spiritrealm until I communicate with her. Will you be able to help?

I almost choke on my gimchi guac. "Of *all* people, we chose Jennie Byun's halmeoni?" I groan. "What are the chances?"

I quickly shut my mouth. As much as Jennie is a pain in my butt, her halmeoni seems sincere. And if Taeyo, a cursed Horangi, can do something nice for strangers like us, then I should be able to do the same for Jennie. Plus, if it's going to help us find the fallen star, it will all have been worth it.

Taeyo's eyes light up. "Oh, you know this Jennie person?"

"I know her, all right," I say, trying not to sound too Debbie Downer. "But I have no idea where she lives."

"Neither do I," Emmett echoes.

"I do." We look up to see David Kim standing there with a tray of Milkis bottles. His cheeks go redder than usual. "I didn't mean to eavesdrop, but my eomma told me to give these to you—on the house—and I happened to overhear your conversation. I know where Jennie lives, and I'd be happy to take you there. It's super close."

Emmett's eyebrows gather together. "Why would you help us?"

"Yeah," I say. "And aren't you working?"

David smiles shyly. "The app sounds amazing, and I know how much Jennie's halmeoni means to her. So if you'll let me, I'd really like to help. Besides, my parents don't actually need me here. I'm just an extra pair of hands."

Taeyo slaps his hands on the table. "We would *love* your help—thank you so much for offering. The more the merrier."

Emmett and I share a look. David is a decent guy, but do we really want another person to join our mission? Three's already a crowd. . . .

David beams like a neon light at Taeyo's invitation, though, so I keep my mouth shut. Hattie would probably say that more heads are better than one.

Emmett shrugs, too. And so, the next thing I know, we are leaving the deliciousness of Seoulful Tacos behind and heading to the house of my least-favorite person in the world, with a half-Gom, a Horangi, and a Tokki, to reunite my sworn enemy with her hungry ghost halmeoni.

I guess this is just my life now.

20.
Halmeoni's Soul Animal
Is a Magpie

 JENNIE'S HOUSE IS A HUGE MANSION with one of those fancy electronic gates in front, and I'm not surprised in the slightest. Witches in the Samjogo clan are often wealthy because of their ability to divine money luck from their visions. Merely by touching draft contracts or shaking hands with potential business partners they can get premonitions about the future success of a deal. In fact, one of Appa's seer friends got mega rich because he put his hands on the New York Stock Exchange building and guessed which stocks would go gangbusters that day.

"We're here." David pushes the bell on the gate and I shift nervously from foot to foot. I try to keep my face angled away from the little security camera.

The bell stops ringing. "Ugh, what are *you* doing here?" my least favorite whiny voice says through the intercom.

Taeyo takes the lead. "Hey, Jennie. You don't know me, but I am here to deliver a message from your halmeoni."

I can almost *hear* her making a face on the other end.

"Are you pulling a prank on me, Riley? Because it's *not* funny, and I will tell on you if you are."

I am horribly offended by this accusation. Why would she jump to the conclusion I would do such a thing? *She's* the one who's always mean to *me*!

"It's not a prank, Jennie," David assures her. "They're telling the truth."

There's a long pause, and for a second I worry she's written us off and walked away. But then the electronic gate starts to open with a humming buzz.

The front door opens and a fat fawn-colored pug comes running out. He tries to bark, but to be honest, it sounds more like an old man's snore. Emmett squeals with delight and picks him up immediately. Boris is still tucked under his other arm, and the dragon-on-wheels' tail wags, too. I guess he also likes dogs.

Jennie appears in the threshold with a distinctly suspicious look on her face. "What are you dawdling out there for? Come in or leave."

We take off our shoes and follow Jennie through the main foyer, which is huge, with double-storied high ceilings and a fancy chandelier. It also has one of those majestic staircases that princesses walk down in the movies, only for her guests (who are there for a fancy ball, of course) to go silent and watch in awe.

"Thanks for letting them in, door-sin," Jennie says.

"Your floors are so shiny, door-sin," David says.

"Your chandelier is amazeballs, door-sin," Emmett coos.

Taeyo and I also give the door spirit a compliment each. I'd hate to be hit in the butt by such a heavy door.

Jennie leads us into a side parlor room with lavish gilded couches. It looks like something out of a K-drama where the parents are the rich, stuck-up owners of an international company. Not that I'm stereotyping or anything...

Jennie takes a seat on one of the couches but doesn't invite us to sit down. Instead, she bites her nails nervously. "So what do you mean, a message from my halmeoni? I don't have all day."

"This might sound a little odd," Taeyo starts, "but she wants to say something to you so she can finally find peace and move into the next realm. You can reserve judgment until afterward, if that makes you feel better. Let me deliver her message to you first."

I notice he doesn't introduce himself as Horangi, and a part of me feels bad for him. It sucks feeling like you have to hide who you really are. Especially when what happened thirteen years ago wasn't his fault.

Jennie doesn't seem to notice, though. "How do I know you're not jerking me around?" She scowls at *me* even though it's Taeyo who's talking to her. She pulls her legs up onto the couch, huddling into a ball.

"I think you should give them a chance," David says, sitting next to her. "I heard them talking about it at the restaurant, and I don't think they're kidding around."

Good thing he came with us.

Jennie scowls some more but doesn't say anything, and

Taeyo takes that as agreement. We perch ourselves on the plush couch opposite her and David, and Taeyo opens Ghostr.

"First I'll tell your halmeoni that we found you." He starts typing into his phone. When he finishes, it buzzes with an alert. "Oh, she says she's already here!"

I glance around the room, but there are no foggy outlines of an old woman that I can see. Jennie looks around nervously, too, and curls herself into an even tighter ball on the couch.

Taeyo's eyes scan from left to right as he reads the message appearing on his app. "Your halmeoni says, 'Don't be angry at your parents. They work hard to provide for you. I know you wish they were home more often. It's no fun eating dinner alone, and it can get lonely in this big house always by yourself. But you mustn't forget how much they love you. You must always remember that.'" Taeyo speaks in chunks, reading as fast as the words come through.

Jennie shrinks. It's like she has turned into a child and is going to start sucking her thumb at any moment. David calmly pats her back.

"Halmeoni?" she whispers, her throat closing up. "Are you really here?"

Then, just as quickly as she softened, she hardens again. She looks at me and glowers. "I bet you're enjoying this, aren't you? Seeing me like this. Is that why you're here? To watch me squirm? Because I've got news for you. I won't break so easy."

Her outburst takes me by surprise. Sure, I can't say I've ever liked her. I mean, would I ever choose to hang out with her? *Heck no!* Has she made my life miserable every weekend at Saturday School, and would I like her to stop being such a bully? *Heck yes!* But that doesn't mean I want to see her suffer—especially over something so serious. That's not how I roll.

I hear the bearded man's words in my head. *There are always two sides to every story.*

The thing is, I've only ever seen the nasty side of Jennie, and I'd assumed she just hated me for some reason. But then I saw her being nice to David at the temple. And now this. Maybe there *is* more to her than meets the eye.

I keep my mouth shut and signal for Taeyo to keep inter-preting for the gwisin halmeoni.

"There's more: 'I'm sorry for leaving you without saying a proper good-bye. I had a good life, a long life, and it was my time to go. I felt no pain at the end. But my biggest regret is not having told you how much I love you. I wish I'd told you every morning and every night.'"

He pauses as a new paragraph loads. "'One of my favorite memories was when I taught you how to make a kite. You were only five, but you picked it up so fast and you were so proud of your creation. You cried when the one I made you—Mr. Magpie—got caught in the tree and ripped. I know you fly a kite for me every year on the date of my passing, and it makes me so happy to see it soaring in the sky.'"

Taeyo takes a breath. "'I want you to know that all the meals I cooked, all the times I picked you up from ballet les-sons, all the times we watched K-dramas in bed together, and even all the times I scolded you—those were all expressions of my love.'" He smiles. "'I wish I had said the words more often, though, which is why I am saying this to you now.'"

Tears start falling down Jennie's cheeks, and the pug jumps from Emmett's lap to hers to lick her face. "Halmeoni, you were the only person I ever felt loved by," she whispers hoarsely. "Everyone else thinks I'm this hard, confident person, but you knew better. You knew the real me. And sometimes I miss you so much I can't breathe. Some days it hurts so much, I can't get out of bed. Why did you have to leave me? It just makes me so angry. *So, so* angry."

I didn't *ever* think I'd cry for Jennie Byun—not in a million years. But soon, my leaky-bladder eyeballs make a grand appearance. One of their best shows yet. I steal glances at the others, and David and Emmett and Taeyo look teary-eyed, too.

Taeyo isn't writing Jennie's responses back into Ghostr, but Gwisin Halmeoni must be hearing them, because soon there's another response from her.

"She says to let go of your anger," Taeyo continues, so focused on the screen that his eyes look glazed. "'Anger will only make it hurt more. Know that you are loved, more than anything in the entire three realms, and I will be watching over you from the Spiritrealm and beyond. True love knows no boundaries.'"

"Please tell her I love her, too," Jennie says between sobs. "Halmeoni, even if the skies fall and the world ends, I will love you forever. Don't forget that when you get reborn, okay?"

Taeyo stands up from the couch. "She says it's time."

We all stand, because that's what it feels like the moment requires.

Then, before our eyes, a translucent figure materializes. At first, her form reminds me of an egg white before it's cooked.

Then, slowly but surely, her body becomes clearer and more defined. Solid, even. Soon, I recognize the face we saw earlier in the Ghostr app. Except she doesn't seem sad anymore. Halmeoni's eyes are warm and brown like honey. She looks like she's at peace.

"Halmeoni!" Jennie runs to hug her, and we all watch between blurry tears as they hold each other tight.

And in that moment, I learn two things:

(1) There is no excuse for Jennie to be the mean bully that she is. But I can see now that her anger never had anything to do with me. It had only to do with herself, and she chose to direct it at me for some reason. And while that is *not* cool, I kind of get it. Sometimes it's easier to blame others than blame yourself.

(2) Everything I've ever been told about the Horangi is wrong. I might never get to the bottom of what happened with the sunstone ax and the attack, but I know in my gut that Taeyo is a good person. He just helped a gwisin find peace, and by the look of things, he helped Jennie find solace, too. And all that was to help me save my sister and to stop the prophecy from coming true. If the other scholars are anything like Taeyo, then I have no reason to be ashamed of my heritage.

And with that realization, something blooms inside me.

Gwisin Halmeoni turns to Taeyo and smiles warmly. "Thank you, my son. For your help, I would like to offer you a favor in return. Is there anything I can do for you before I cross over?"

"Actually, there *is* something. . . ." Taeyo looks at me and nods.

I open my mouth to ask her to locate the last fallen star for us. But something stops me. Instead, I look over at Emmett, who is desperately pretending that he's not crying. (Spoiler alert: He's defo crying.)

"I understand you can travel the Earth at the speed of thought," I say gently. "Does that mean you can find anything—or anyone—that may be stuck here as well?"

Halmeoni considers this. "Yes, I believe I can."

Taeyo and Emmett look at me with confusion on their faces, but I nod defiantly. "In that case, we would be grateful if you could find Sookhee Harrison, a Gom, and mother of Emmett Harrison. Her son would like to talk to her. This is the favor we ask of you."

Emmett gasps and covers his mouth, but I reach out and squeeze his hand. I know he could still be disappointed, but I also know how much courage it took for him to decide to find his mom. He put himself out there, realizing he could get hurt, because seeing her again was so important to him. After everything he's done for me and I've done to him, it's the least I can do. He deserves this.

Gwisin Halmeoni nods and closes her eyes for what feels like only a passing moment. But when she opens them again, her eyes are tired, as if she has traveled a long distance. "I am so sorry, children, to be the bearer of bad news. I indeed managed to locate Sookhee Harrison. She is stuck here on Earth, unable to pass through to the next realm. But she is no longer the woman she once was. She has become a vengeful ghost, too overwhelmed by the wrongs done to her in life. And she is not willing to talk to you."

Emmett falls to his knees, and I hold him in my arms. *Oh no. I've made everything worse.* "I'm so sorry, Em," I whisper into his hair. "I'm so, so sorry."

"However..." Halmeoni looks conflicted. "When I was with her, Sookhee had one small moment of clarity. I can tell you what she said, if that will be of use to you?"

We all look to Emmett, and he nods once.

The ghost closes her eyes again, and her voice changes. It becomes younger but shrill, like someone who's desperate. Like someone who's lost her way. *"I didn't want the artifact. I didn't want to hurt anyone. I was possessed. I just wanted magic for my son, and that was used against me. I didn't kill those Horangi scholars. I was betrayed by someone I trusted. It was their fault all those people died. I was wronged!"*

Emmett covers his face and shakes his head. This is too much for him to handle. "Mom," he whispers under his breath, "I'm gonna get to the bottom of this." Then he slowly rises to his feet, looking determined. "I will find out who did this to you, I promise."

I grip Hattie's vial and hold it close to my own heart. Before, I thought it surely couldn't be Auntie Okja. But now, I can't ignore my suspicions. She *was* Sookhee's best friend. She could've been the one working with the council, the one who coveted Sookhee's position as elder, so she could get her hands on the artifact. Plus, it was Auntie Okja who told me all those horrible stories about the Horangi. And now I know she was wrong.

My head spins as I swallow the bitter pill. My auntie and the council really *did* falsely accuse the Horangi. They framed the scholars so the other clans wouldn't find out that the council had tried to steal the artifact. Then Auntie Okja stole me from my birth clan.

My whole life has been a lie.

Gwisin Halmeoni opens her eyes, and they look apologetic. "I'm sorry again for delivering such news."

Then her human body shimmers and changes, shrinking into the form of a magpie. Her black-and-purple feathers are glossy, and she utters a soft, chattering call that makes me feel warm and gooey inside.

Jennie gasps, and Taeyo explains, "When we pass into the Spiritrealm, we can choose to shed our human bodies and take on our soul-animal forms. Our bodies will change with each new life, but our soul animals will always remain the same. This is your halmeoni's true soul form."

As we all watch, Jennie's halmeoni opens her wings and flaps them, slowly at first, but then stronger and faster, until soon, the parlor room is full of wind. We cover our eyes as a warm light blooms inside the four walls, and suddenly, with a great burst of energy, Jennie's halmeoni disappears.

"She's gone," Jennie murmurs. "She's really gone." But she doesn't look sad. Nor does she look like her normal, mean self. She somehow seems softer around the edges. Fluffier. Nicer.

David takes two vials from his pocket and gives one to Jennie and one to Emmett. "These are calming tonics. I figure you guys might need one right about now." When Emmett frowns, David quickly adds, "They're totally natural and non-addictive. I help my mom make them for the Gom clinics around town."

When I corroborate David's claim, Emmett accepts the vial and swigs it in one go. "How are we gonna find the fallen star now?" he asks quietly. "We wasted the favor on me, and we don't have the time to match with another gwisin."

I put my hand on his shoulder. "We didn't waste anything. It was worth asking, wasn't it? For the chance that we could help her?"

Emmett nods imperceptibly. "Thank you," he whispers to me. "For trying. I know how much you sacrificed to give me that opportunity."

He looks at his feet, and I feel another lump forming in my throat. "You would have done the same for me."

It's not exactly forgiveness, but it feels like a start. I'll take it.

"Besides," I say, "I have a plan."

"You do?" Taeyo asks.

I breathe in deeply. "I'm going back to the campus to do the initiation. I'm gonna pledge my allegiance to the Horangi."

The whole room gasps, and even the pug seems to look surprised (although that could just be her buggy walleyes).

"This is a circle of trust, right?" I ask Jennie. "We helped you, so you'll help us? Because I'd rather you kept this information to yourself." I hold up both palms. "I promise I'm not planning a takeover or anything. I just want to save my sister."

"The Horangi aren't what they've been made out to be," says Emmett, putting his hand on Taeyo's shoulder. "This guy is one, and he brought your halmeoni."

"You can count on us," says David. "Right, Jennie?"

Jennie doesn't nod or agree, but she doesn't give me the snide comeback she normally would, either. Something in my gut tells me she'll keep my secret. I mean, stranger things have happened of late.

"What made you change your mind?" Taeyo asks me.

"Yeah," Emmett echoes. "I thought you said you'd never do that in a million years."

"I did say that." I think of Taeyo and his altruistic app. I think of Hattie and her quest for choice. I think of what it means to be Gom. "But I feel different about things now."

"How?" Emmett asks.

I take a big breath. "You'll see, Em. You'll see."

21.
Make Way for the Bionic Girl

DAVID, BEING THE TOP-NOTCH GUY he is, decides to stay with Jennie to make sure she's okay. She seems grateful, and I finally understand why the two of them are friends. It's just like in Adeline's monologue, when Mago Halmi said to the goddesses: *There is light within us all, as there is darkness within us all. These two absolutes make us whole.* Jennie may have some dark bits, but there's light inside her, too. Just as there is in the Horangi.

"So I guess I'll be seeing you around," I awkwardly say to Jennie as I put on my shoes and give the door-sin a farewell compliment.

She scowls. "Not likely."

"Really?" I say. "We're back to this already?"

She gives me a sheepish smile in return. "Sorry, old habits die hard. Yeah, I guess I'll be seeing you. And uh, thanks for today."

When we get back to the campus, there's a nervous energy in the air. People have started to gather in one of the forest clearings by the lake, milling about in groups and whispering anxiously to one another. It's like they're waiting for something to happen. Something bad.

"Do you know what's going on?" I ask Taeyo.

He looks down at his phone. His notifications have been going off like fireworks since we left Jennie's house. "It looks like we have a pest problem. Several of our offices have been destroyed already. Everyone's talking about it on our community Slack channel."

Emmett and I share a look. What kind of pest is big enough to destroy buildings?

"She's an inmyeonjo," Taeyo elaborates. "They think she was drawn to the campus because of the magic we've been doing, and then she found all the mirrors. Now she's dead set on demolishing every last one, and people are getting hurt in the process."

Emmett looks confused. "What's an inmyeonjo?"

"They're part bird, part woman," I explain, remembering Professor Ryu mentioning them once in class. "They're one of the only creatures that can fly between the Godrealm and the Mortalrealm. They're wild but not dangerous, unless they've got their eyes set on a mirror and you get in the way. Then you're in trouble."

"Ugh, not another bird!" Emmett says, curling in his fingers protectively. His hands are still red and swollen from being pecked by the book-birds. "What's her beef with mirrors, anyway?"

"It's actually a really interesting story," Taeyo says excitedly. "They say the first-ever inmyeonjo was a beautiful woman. She was so breathtaking that bachelors would line up at her door each day for a chance to win her hand. But she was young and vain, and careless with her affections. So one day, a scorned lover—who happened to be a Gumiho illusionist—cursed her to become an ugly, human-headed bird. Now, every time an inmyeonjo sees herself in a mirror, she's reminded of the beast she's become."

"Hence her obsession with destroying them," I add.

Emmett looks up at the light reflecting off the mirrored buildings. "I see why this is a problem."

Taeyo nods, his excitement fading. "She won't leave until every last shard of mirror is shattered."

"Shirtballs . . . Good luck, I guess," Emmett says. "Sucks to be you guys."

Taeyo leads us through the maze that is the campus, and we eventually find Sora in a glass-walled meeting room inside the HQ. She and Austin are having a conversation with some older scholars, and if their body language is anything to go by, it looks serious. Sora is standing with her arms crossed, and Austin is scowling.

Taeyo knocks on the transparent wall and opens the door. "Sorry to disturb your meeting, but we have visitors."

Sora signals for us to enter, and I take a quick peek at the vial hanging around my neck before I step through the door. A third of Hattie's heart has now decayed, and the sight of it gives me the impetus for what I need to do next.

Sora raises an eyebrow at me. "I thought you left this morning?"

"I did." I clear my throat. "But I've changed my mind. I've

come back to initiate into the Horangi clan. I'll be honest—I don't really want to. But I need your help to find the last artifact, and I'm willing to do whatever it takes."

She studies me for a moment, and I assume she's going to give me a lecture about how I can't just initiate for the sake of it. How I need to want it. *Mean* it.

But she doesn't. Instead, she smiles. "That's good news."

Austin whispers something to the other scholars, and when they nod in approval, he turns to me. "And it just so happens we have the perfect initiation task for you."

I hold my breath. I suddenly picture myself having to learn how to write code and design an entire app within an afternoon. I cross my fingers behind my back. *Please don't let that be my task.* My failure would be guaranteed.

"Once we insert the biochip into your wrist, you will help us take care of our pest problem," Austin announces.

My jaw drops. "You want me to kill the inmyeonjo?!"

The adults widen their eyes, surprised. "Why would you think that?" Sora asks.

Confused, I look to Austin. "Didn't you say you wanted me to *take care* of her?"

Austin laughs, and heat rises up my face. That *is* what he said. . . .

"I should have been clearer with my words. My apologies," he says. "What I should have said is that we are volunteering you for the inmyeonjo-taming exercise."

"Why tame her?" Emmett asks. "Why not just frighten her away, or something?"

"We've tried that," Austin answers. "But she keeps coming

back. It seems our mirrored buildings have struck a nerve with her, and she's taken it upon herself to destroy them all. We've managed to contain her for the time being, but we won't be able to hold her for long. Taming her is our only solution."

I swallow. "But I've never tamed anything before, let alone a cursed bird-woman. How will I know what to do?"

Sora pats my shoulder. "Others have volunteered for this task, so you'll have a chance to watch them—and the inmyeonjo—in action. If they don't succeed, it'll be your turn. And if we deem your behavior appropriate, we will invite you into our clan."

"Will I need to use magic? With the biochip?" I ask. I rub my wrist tentatively and let out a hiccup.

Sora smiles. "If you can, sure. But I understand that you won't have had a chance to practice beforehand. So just do the best you can."

If someone had asked me two days ago to put myself in front of a crazed humanoid bird creature and attempt to tame her, I would have quickly tiptoed away. But, as I clutch Hattie's heart vial to my chest, I realize I've come a long way from being the frightened, hesitant girl I used to be. I may have made some foolish decisions, which got me into this mess, but I'm not going down without a fight.

I take a big breath. "Okay. I'll do it."

"Great," Sora says. "In that case, when you're ready, Austin will take you to get your biochip inserted."

Austin motions for me to follow him, but Emmett stops me. "Just a sec before you go."

He pulls me over to a quiet corner outside the meeting

room, away from the others, and looks awkwardly down at his feet. "Are you *sure* you want to do this, Rye? You still haven't explained why you changed your mind."

My heart warms at his concern. "When Sora first told me I had to initiate, I thought I'd have to betray the family that raised me. Be a traitor or something, you know?"

He nods. "And now?"

"Now I've realized it's not a betrayal. It's a *sacrifice*. Just like our clan motto. By sacrificing my Gom identity, I can save Hattie."

"Service and Sacrifice," Emmett echoes under his breath. "I get it. Well, I just want you to know you're not alone. I'm here for you." He tips the dragon scooter up so that a little flapping wing can give me a high five. "Me and Boris both."

"I'm so grateful for you. For both of you." I sniffle.

"Geez, you don't have to get all mushy on me now. Ugh." He takes off his cremation ring and shoves it into my hand. "Don't ask why, just take this, okay? It's not for you—it's for me. It would just make me feel better if you were wearing it."

He looks away, his nose in the air. He's getting worse at hiding his feelings with each passing day. Emotions look good on him, though. I put the ring on my finger and draw him in for a hug. "Love you, boo."

"Guess you're not a bad egg, either, Riley Oh."

Austin comes over to our quiet corner. "Shall we go?" he says to me.

I nod.

"Emmett, you come with me," Sora says, ushering him away. "We'll wait for Riley outside."

With that, Austin leads Taeyo and me to a smaller tree house in the south end of campus. It's separated from the rest of the buildings in the network, as if it was designed to be hidden. The door is highly secured with what looks like ten separate metal locks. Austin rubs his wrists, and, as his gifted mark glows, he waves his hand over each of them. One by one, the locks move like clockwork until all of them have clicked open.

He pushes the door wide. "After you."

It looks like a science lab inside. People are sitting on benches at various tables, working with microscopes, mini blowtorches, and tech parts I can't identify. A small group in the back is crowded around a 3-D printer that's spitting out something too small for me to see. AKMU is playing softly in the background, and no one is talking. Everyone is intently focused on their work.

Austin leads us to a man huddled over a table in the front. He's wearing a head light and squinting through a magnifying glass attached to the rim of his glasses. As he works on a minuscule chip with tiny tweezers and pliers, his movements are so painstaking, I have to stare at him for a good ten seconds to make sure he's a human and not a robot.

He finally raises his head. "Yes?"

Austin gestures to me. "We have a new initiate."

The man doesn't even look at me. Instead, he turns back to the chip he was working with. "Sit."

Taeyo grabs a stool from a nearby workstation, and I take a seat opposite the man.

"Wrist," he commands. I guess he's not much of a talker.

I hesitate. As Hattie says, it's all about choice. I am *choosing* to do this. But I still waver. What if my Gom parents reject me after I do this? What if the gifted community shuns me even more?

"Wrist," the man says again, his tone impatient. "I don't have all day."

I take a big breath. This is for my sister. And for stopping the prophecy. For service and sacrifice.

I lay out my wrist in front of him. "Is it going to hurt—?"

Click!

Before I even finish my question, the man has held a syringe-shaped metal tool above my wrist and pressed it down onto my skin.

"Done," he says.

"Wait, that's *it*?" I ask, surprised. "I hardly felt it." I run my finger over my left wrist and feel a tiny little bump where it was inserted.

"Rub them," the man commands.

I look at him blankly and he scowls. "Chop-chop. Let's make sure you're not faulty, or else I'll need to take it out. Rub your wrists."

I wince at the insinuation I could be deemed faulty. Tentatively, I rub my wrists together. It's an action I've watched my entire life—a movement I've wished over and over again I could perform, too. And finally, I'm doing it. Even if it's in this weird science-tech lab with the Horangi clan.

The little bump scratches a little as I put my wrists together, and suddenly there is heat on my right wrist. It feels as if the sun is shining directly on that patch of skin. I gasp as the heat intensifies and the gifted mark of the two suns and two moons appears on my wrist. It glows red like a siren, reminding me of the clan I'm about to enter.

"Oh my Mago," I whisper. "I can't believe it actually works."

I know it's the wrong color, and seeing red instead of gold makes my stomach churn in a weird, homesick kind of way. But at the same time, the feeling is momentous. I've spent my whole life thinking I was devoid of magic. Now I know—no, now I can *see*—that I am gifted, too.

"Congratulations," Austin says. "You are now officially biochipped."

Taeyo grins and claps his hands. "Congratulations, Riley! Now all you have to do is channel your inner dominant element, and you'll be able to wield it." He studies me curiously. "What *is* your element, by the way? How rude—I never asked you."

For a moment, I recall my Gi ceremony. The way my elemental profile of four fires had branded me a freak of nature. Then I remember what Sora said—that the Horangi cared about what I had in abundance, and not what I lacked.

I puff up my chest. "Fire," I say to Taeyo. "My dominant is fire."

"Cool!" he says. "Uh, I mean *hot*."

I groan and then ask, "But how exactly do I channel it?"

"Well, everyone activates their chip a little differently, so you'll have to find your own way of making it work. But for me, I think of floating in the sea and feeling completely weightless. Like I'm a part of the current. Then I just relax and put my mind to what I want the water to do. Then *bam*, it yields."

As Austin ushers us out of the room, he says, "For me, it's single-mindedness. I laser my focus on the metal and imagine my hand around it, melding it, shaping it, moving it the way I want it to act. The more I concentrate, the more effective it becomes."

I must look concerned, because Austin pats me on the back. "Don't worry too much. It might not happen on your first go, but you'll figure it out. We all have."

A flicker of anticipation passes through me. A part of me is excited for the challenge. I'm eager to try out my new gift.

But as Hattie's rapidly cooling heart vial rubs against my skin, I also think of everything that's at stake—my sister's life, my parents' gifts, the prophesied end of days. . . . The burden feels like too much to bear. What if I fail? What if, no matter how hard I try, it's not enough?

As Austin leads us to the lakeside, where the challenge will be held, Taeyo takes something out of the pocket of his yellow chinos and slips it into my hand.

"This is for you," he whispers. "For good luck."

I open my palm to find a beautiful round compact made of shiny gold. Cool and heavy to the touch, it reminds me of how my onyx teardrop stone used to feel in my hand.

"What is it?" I ask.

"It's a compass I found a long time ago. I want you to have it."

I push the small button on its side and the compass flips open. It's intricately designed with tiny black detailing around the edge and a slender golden arrow hovering inside.

"Why are you giving this to me?"

He smiles openly. "I saw what you did for Emmett back at Jennie's house. How you gave up what you wanted so he could have a chance to speak to his mom. And now you're putting yourself through this initiation to save your sister and to stop the prophecy. You're a good person, Riley. You came a long way to find us, and I thought maybe, one day, if you ever get lost, this could help you find your way back to us."

He adjusts his bow tie, and something flutters inside my chest. This has to be the nicest gift I've ever received.

"It's beautiful. Thanks, Taeyo."

I close the compass and feel a rough patch against my palm. I turn over the compact and see a small faded outline of two overlapping triangles on its back. I press the symbol, and suddenly the compass makes a slicing sound as triangular blades release from the edges, forming what looks like metal rays around a golden sun.

"*Whoa!*" Taeyo breathes. "I didn't realize it was a weapon, too."

I carefully spin the compass on my palm. "Let's hope I won't need that part."

22.
Taming of the Inmyeonjo

 By the time we make it to the lakeside, the forest clearing is full of people. I'd say there are at least a hundred folks milling about, waiting for the call for volunteers.

I can't see Emmett anywhere, but he must be somewhere in the crowd. What I *can* see, however, is a terrifying bird creature probably seven feet tall, with a wingspan the cheol-lima guard would die for. Her body is covered in a shock of dirt-colored feathers, and her talons are so large they look like pitchforks. The most disconcerting thing about her, though, is her face. It, too, is covered in brown plumage, but it is distinctly human. She has high cheekbones, a well-proportioned nose, and two large eyes. Except the "whites" of her eyes are amber, and her lips stretch out unnaturally into a hardened beak. She really should have treated those bachelors better. . . .

Like Austin said earlier, the inmyeonjo is trapped inside a metal cage near the edge of the lake, but it doesn't look like it's going to hold her for too long. Because if I could use one word to describe her, it would be *furious*. She is flapping her wings aggressively against the metal bars, clawing the ground with her talons, and screeching at the top of her lungs.

"Come forward, volunteers!" Sora stands next to the metal cage and ushers people closer. "If you are brave enough to attempt the taming of the inmyeonjo, step up now."

Two kids who don't look a day over eight walk forward, holding hands. "We volunteer!" they call out.

Sora smiles but waves them back. "You're very brave, Henry and Grace, but perhaps not today."

Three older scholars from the crowd bravely raise their hands as Austin pushes me toward Sora.

"Good luck," Taeyo whispers.

I steal another glance at the metal cage. The inmyeonjo is glaring straight at me while ramming the bars, and I'm sure she's out for my blood. I gulp.

"I'll go first," one of the volunteers announces. The man—who has a well-groomed beard and a man bun—takes a lighter out of his pocket. He ignites the flame, and then rubs his wrists.

"Good luck, Jo," Sora says.

Austin magicks the metal cage so it lifts into the air by itself, leaving the inmyeonjo free on the ground. The empty trap hovers above the volunteer and the inmyeonjo like a steel spiderweb.

My heart speeds up as I watch Jo. His dominant element must be fire, same as me. Seeing him with the lighter, I realize the Horangi's magic only works if the element is nearby. That's why the training hall we were first detained in was full of water—because Taeyo needed it for his watery shackles. Unfortunately, I don't have a lighter handy.

The man concentrates on the inmyeonjo, who has started to flap her wings like she's going to charge any second. He swirls one hand over the open flame as if making a soft-serve cone, and then blows on his open palm. Fire shoots from the lighter in an impressive spiraling wave and torpedoes toward the bird-woman.

The inmyeonjo sees it coming and acts immediately. Her eyes burn with hatred and, by fanning her wings, she redirects the flame straight back at Jo, screeching angrily as she does so. The volunteer's hair catches on fire and the inmyeonjo cackles.

"You will never tame me!" she shrieks.

I cover my mouth. Wait, she *talks*?! Her voice is so screechy and warbly, it makes me wince. The sound reminds me of those woodcutting saws that people wobble and play like a stringed instrument, except it's three octaves higher.

Jo jumps into the lake to kill the flames and comes out a few moments later looking decidedly less well-groomed than before. His man bun is scorched.

Sora looks disappointed. "Next!"

The two remaining volunteers step forward together. One of the women has a pixie cut, while the other has a side shave and walks with a cane, but apart from that, they're identical. They're both wearing T-shirts with wingless fairies on them and the text TWINS BEFORE WINGS underneath.

They whisper something to each other, and then the pixie-cut woman manipulates the earth, making it move and rise around the inmyeonjo. It swallows the bird-woman until she is trapped in a mountain of soil and only her head is visible. A look of pure hatred passes over the inmyeonjo's face as she fights to get free, but the witch has her hand clasped tight, and the earth stays firm around the bird body.

That's when her twin sister strikes. She animates her cane, which I realize now is actually a wooden staff. And with a swift Spider-Man gesture of her wrist, the sharp end of the staff slices through the air, scraping past the inmyeonjo's face.

The bird-woman lets out a bloodcurdling scream as blood gushes from her cheek. The sisters high-five each other, and the crowd cheers.

"Now yield to us, inmyeonjo!" the earth-witch yells.

The bird-woman stays unmoving, still trapped in the soil mountain, and for a moment the crowd goes silent. This could be it.

The inmyeonjo closes her eyes and takes a big breath. I hold my breath, too.

"Never!" she finally cries. "I will shatter every one of those mirrors, and you can't stop me!" She *caw-caws* as she tornadoes out of the mound like a corkscrew.

She flies at the sisters, her talons outstretched. They cover their heads, but the inmyeonjo has the element of surprise on her side. She dips low and swipes at them both with one sharp movement of her talons. Side Shave trips and stumbles onto the soil mound, and the bird-woman goes for her again.

"Stand up, Yumi! Run!"

Pixie Cut helps her sister up just in time, and together, they run for their lives. Austin magicks the cage back down over the bird-woman.

Sora's face drops. "Good try, Yumi and Yuri, but not quite."

The clan leader finally turns to me. She gives me a small smile, then addresses the crowd.

"Everyone, I'd like you to meet Riley Oh. She is a Horangi, daughter of the late Mina and Yoon Seo." Murmurs of recognition and curiosity ripple through the crowd. "But unbeknownst to us, she was taken from our clan and raised by a family of Gom." The crowd gasps. "Fortunately, she has, defying all odds, returned to us of her own accord. And she wants to pledge her allegiance to our clan. She's going to volunteer herself today in this task as her initiation, so I ask that you show her a true Horangi welcome."

She raises her arms and the crowd breaks into applause. As they cheer, something cracks open inside me. There is no backing out now. I am actually doing this.

Sora quiets the crowd with her hands. "Riley, we know you've only just been biochipped today, and you may not have had a chance to unlock your power yet, but tell us, what is your dominant element?"

"Um, fire," I mumble.

"The symbol of transformation and will. How fitting for this occasion. Well, good luck. I hope you burn bright today!"

I gulp. She hopes I burn bright? With four elemental fires, she has *no* idea. . . .

The crowd applauds again, and Henry and Grace—the two kids who volunteered earlier—cheer the loudest. Jo steps forward and tosses me his lighter. "May you have beginner's luck, kid," he says. The lighter has one of those flick tops and the words NOT YOUR AVERAGE JO engraved on the front. I throw him a grateful look.

Then, as Austin raises the metal cage back into the sky, I cautiously approach the inmyeonjo.

Her eyes are piercing and unnaturally still. They blink once in the time that I've blinked ten. And I suddenly realize it was a bad idea to go last. She is now angrier than ever, having been singed, squashed, and scraped by the others. The creature lowers her head in a predatory way and opens her wings to their full width. She lets out a snarl/squawk and scratches the ground with her talons.

"Make your move, child," she says with a hiss.

I look down at my hands. The lighter is shaking, and I realize it's because I'm trembling. There are over a hundred pairs of eyes on me, and I have *no* idea what I'm doing. In the absence of a plan, I decide to take my new gift for a test drive. What have I got to lose?

I grab hold of Hattie's heart vial. Then I repeat her line under my breath. "Sometimes you gotta burn your fingers to enjoy the s'more."

I rub my wrists together, and, as the heat ignites on my right arm, I watch the gifted mark glow red. I flick the lighter until a small flame appears, and then close my eyes.

Taeyo said to imagine floating in the sea—to be one with the water. So I visualize lying on my back in the Pacific, looking up at the sky. I try to relax and stoke the flame. But when I think of the Pacific, I remember the summoning gone wrong and my sister's unconscious body floating in the ocean. I recall dragging her limp body onto the sand and feeling more frightened than I ever had before.

The inmyeonjo chuckles and my eyes snap open. The lighter flame hasn't grown—it has died out.

"Is that all you've got?" the bird-woman calls out. Her movements are rapid and jerky, taunting me.

"Don't give up!" I hear someone yell. I think it's Taeyo.

I grit my teeth and try Austin's method. I reignite the lighter flame and stare intently into its core. I don't blink, I don't breathe, I just channel my entire concentration into the small flickering fire and will it to grow. Just a little.

As an awkward hush falls over the crowd, the inmyeonjo laughs heartily. "I know it isn't fair, child," she croons, "but we can't all be heroes."

Something in me snaps. She's right. It *isn't* fair. It's not fair that both my birth parents were killed. It isn't fair that Emmett lost his mom. It isn't fair that Hattie was taken as collateral because I got greedy. And it's not fair that my parents have to choose between me and their gifts.

As anger fills my body like a poison, the lighter's flame begins to pulsate. The crowd gasps, and Man Bun Jo calls out from the crowd, "That's it, kid! Whatever you're doing, keep doing it!"

In that moment, I realize that, for me, the key is anger. I need to be furious in order to activate my element.

So I let it build. I let the frustration and pain and injustice expand like air in my lungs, and I channel it all toward the lighter flame. I take one deep breath, and then let it out, releasing it toward the inmyeonjo. A fireball flies straight at her. . . .

But it only makes it two-thirds of the way before it loses steam.

The bird-woman's eyes widen as a small lick of flame bounces forward and singes a talon. She's surprised, but she doesn't let it show for long. I used everything I have on that one move, and she knows it. She shrieks and flies over my head, swiping at me with a sharp claw. She misses, but I think she does it on purpose. She's just showing me she has the upper hand (or wing?).

I rub my wrists again, trying to activate more fire. But my anger is draining away, and even though the crowd is roaring encouragement, I can't make the flame do anything more than flicker. I am *spent*.

The inmyeonjo is on the ground now, and she fluffs up her feathers, preparing to attack again. Blood is still seeping from the cheek wound the twins gave her, but she can see she's already won the fight against me. She throws me a victorious smile and charges. I cover my face with my arms, but one sharp talon still manages to clip me.

Argh!

I clamp down on the trickle of blood from the wound. This is pointless. *I can't do this.*

The crowd lets out a gasp, and I look to Sora for help. She frowns slightly but doesn't intervene. Her words echo in my ears. *If we deem your conduct in the task worthy . . .* And *What we're looking for is your commitment and loyalty.*

As the size of the task overwhelms me, I do what I do best. I cry. Tears roll down my face as I realize I was wrong. I thought, by pledging allegiance to the Horangi, I could sacrifice myself and save my family. But I can't even do this right. Even here, even with my birth clan, I'm still the one who's not good enough. *The outsider.* I'm a failure, and they will never let me be initiated after this performance.

Instead, I decide to rely on what I know rather than what I don't. I grew up in a family of healers, and I was taught to stop pain, not inflict it. If I'm going to fail this initiation, I'm going to do it in style. Gom style.

I take one step forward and the inmyeonjo screeches. I look her in the eye with as much calmness as I can muster. "I'm not going to attack you," I say quietly. "I am going to pick some of those flowers over there"—I point to the patch of calendula and goldenrod near her talons—"and then get some stones from the water. Will you let me do that?"

The bird-woman's eyes become slits. "Why?" she asks with a snarl.

"Because you haven't stopped bleeding," I say. "And I want to heal your wound."

She squawks and rips a chunk out of the earth with her talon. "Don't you *dare* play tricks with me!"

I shake my head. "I'm not. I swear I'm telling you the truth. No tricks. I just want to get to those flowers."

Her eyes are full of suspicion, and she has started to make a weird chattering sound that can't be good news for me. But slowly I make my way toward her, one step in front of the other.

"Be careful!" I hear people murmur from the crowd, but no one stops me. I guess this is what they call watching a train wreck. You don't want to look, but you can't *not*, either.

I don't know how I do it, but somehow I get closer, inch by inch, until my hair is blown back by the inmyeonjo's beating wings. My heart is pumping so hard I can feel it pulsating in my head. Keeping my eyes glued to hers, I crouch down and cautiously pick some of the calendula and goldenrod. I may never have had a Gi, but I know that these two flowers have natural healing properties, because I've seen Eomma use them at the clinic.

With the petals in hand, I slowly stand back up. "*Shh*," I whisper, trying to keep the inmyeonjo calm as her feathers bristle anxiously at my closeness. "I'm just going to step sideways now to get to the lake. I need some stones to grind the flowers."

I start taking small side steps, shushing her the whole time. Somehow I manage to get to the waterside unscathed, and when I'm sure I'm not going to get mauled, I put the petals on a flat stone and use a smaller rock to grind them into a paste. I scoop up the salve and carefully make my way toward the bird-woman once more.

"You will never tame me!" she cries again as I near.

"I don't want to tame you," I say honestly. "I just want to help you. Will you let me do that?"

Her stare could burn holes, but she lets me approach. And, somehow, I find myself reaching up to spread the healing balm on her cheek with a trembling hand.

When my fingers first touch her feathery face, she lets out a high-pitched whine, and a shiver runs down my spine. Every instinct in my body tells me to turn and run. But I stay put. And when she realizes this is not a trick, she starts to calm down.

Eventually, she lets out a deep sigh, and her bird shoulders relax. Her feathers settle and her eyes soften until they look like molten syrup. "Thank you," she warbles, and it almost sounds melodious.

I think of the third answer to the cheollima's verification question. How the sun was mightier than the wind. I guess it's true that empathy is more powerful than brute force. In a moment of trust, I reach out and stroke her feathers. And instead of screeching or screaming or slashing, the inmyeonjo coos and edges farther into my touch.

"Let go of your anger," I say quietly, echoing the words Gwisin Halmeoni had said to Jennie. "Anger will only make it hurt more. And I know you don't like mirrors, but these are people's homes that you're destroying."

She whines and lets out a sad *caw-caw*. "But it is part of who I am. The curse of my ancestor makes me this way."

I stroke her wing feathers, now tucked snugly into her body. "Don't let a curse define who you can and can't be. Only *you* have the power to decide that."

She twitches her head to the side as if contemplating my words, and I realize how true they are. She and I aren't dissimilar, if you think about it. We're both trapped in a story someone else wrote about us. But we have the power to take the reins. If we want to.

"You're beautiful just the way you are," I say, "and you should be proud of your reflection." I picture my smiling face in the library's pond water, and I'm reminded of the journey that's brought me here so far.

"My name is Riley Oh, and it's nice to meet you," I say. "What's your name?"

A sad chattering noise escapes from the inmyeonjo's throat. "I do not have a name."

"Would you like one?"

Her eyes widen. "Yes. I would like that very much."

I ponder what a fitting name for this formidable bird-woman might be. She watches me expectantly. And suddenly, it comes to me.

"What about Areum?"

"*Ah-rihm.*" She tests out the new word in her avian mouth.

"It's a Korean name that means *beautiful*—like you."

She bows her head in gratitude. Then, to my surprise, she begins to shrink. She retains her bird body and her human-like face, but she becomes the size of a dove. She flies up and perches on my shoulder.

"Riley Oh, I yield to you."

"Wait, what?" I blurt out. "What do you mean, *yield* to me?"

The crowd lets out a loud exhale. I'd almost forgotten they were there.

"You did it!" Sora announces, clasping her hands together. "You demonstrated bravery and commitment to the task and even taught us a lesson along the way. You tamed the inmyeonjo!"

Whoa. My mind reels. Did I just *domesticate* Areum?

Sora beams proudly. "I now invite you, Riley Oh, to pledge your allegiance to the Horangi clan. Do you accept?"

I think hard about what I'm about to do. I succeeded in

my initiation, but I did it using what I'd learned from my Gom upbringing. The scholars, on the other hand, had been more than happy to use violence to try to control the inmyeonjo. Am I prepared to leave the healers? Do I want to give my loyalty to the Horangi clan for the rest of my life?

Areum looks at me with complete openness, and something broken inside me puts itself back together. It's like I'd thought earlier. I won't have to rely on someone else to write my story if I'm brave enough to take the pen into my own hands.

I turn to Sora. "Yes, I do," I confirm. With over a third of my sister's heart shriveled, and the survival of the world at stake, retreating is not an option. I will take the best of both clans and complete this job.

"Congratulations, Riley. Welcome to the clan!" Sora exclaims.

And just like that, the crowd goes wild. It's not as regal as an initiation at the gifted temple with all the elders and the entire congregation watching. I didn't even get to wear a cool bear crown or dress. But still, *I did it.*

"Welcome home, Riley!" I hear from somewhere in the crowd.

"You're a hero!" someone else shouts.

It's kind of ironic, to be honest. Because now that I've formally become a Horangi scholar, I feel more Gom than ever before. Go figure.

Suddenly, more than anything, I'm desperate to find Emmett. I haven't seen him since before I got my biochip, and I want to share this moment of triumph with him. I search the crowd and, finally, I see his familiar face. I look at him with a bittersweet mix of emotions, trying to convey how I'm feeling. But he's clutching Boris to his chest with fear in his eyes.

I frown, trying to understand why he's scared.

Then I see.

Standing next to him in the crowd are none other than my parents.

And next to them is my auntie Okja.

23.
Are Family Reunions Always This Awkward?

WE ARE BRISKLY USHERED AWAY from the crowd and into a shed by the lake that's full of kayaks and life jackets. Before Austin can even close the door, I jump into my eomma's and appa's arms and bury my head in their shoulders. Their eyes are bloodshot and they look terrible—like they haven't slept since Hattie's initiation ceremony. Their familiar scents remind me of home, and I sob inconsolably. I have missed them so much.

"I can't believe you're here. You're really here," I cry.

Appa kisses the top of my head. "Thank Mago you're okay."

"We were so worried about you..." Eomma whispers, stroking my back with trembling hands.

"I'm so sorry," I splutter between snotty tears. "I made a *huge* mistake, and now, Hattie is...She is...She—"

"*Shh*, we know, sweetheart," Appa says, stroking my hair. "Emmett filled us in on everything when we got here."

I look at Emmett gratefully.

"How did you know where we were?" I ask my parents.

"We hired a Samjogo seer to locate you," Eomma responds. "The Horangi firewall made it a challenge, but she managed to find you in the end."

"How *dare* you come here?" Sora demands, interrupting our family reunion.

"You kidnap our child and then have the gall to ask why we're here?" Eomma retorts. "You're lucky we didn't bring reinforcements."

Emmett is sending death glares at Auntie Okja after what his mom said through the gwisin halmeoni, and Taeyo and Austin are standing staunchly with Sora. Judging from the way Taeyo keeps glancing at his water bottle, I'm half expecting a water snake to burst out of there if things go south. It's not a great reunion by any means.

Sora scoffs. "*You* stole her from us thirteen years ago! She should have been raised with us, not the people who killed her parents."

"We did *not* kill her parents," Auntie Okja clarifies. She's standing near the door, keeping her distance.

"What lies have you told our daughter?" Appa jabs his finger in Sora's face. "How did you deceive her to join your cursed clan? And what is the purpose of all this?"

"No one forced me to do anything. Least of all Sora," I interrupt, trying to pull myself together. "I made a conscious choice." Appa's accusation makes me feel protective of the Horangi clan, and it surprises me. "It's all a huge misunderstanding."

Eomma's and Appa's grips on my shoulders momentarily

tighten. It's clear they have no idea that the Horangi clan was framed by the council. I steal a glance at Auntie Okja. But she is putting on an innocent face, and something inside me kindles with frustration. How can she pretend she knows none of this when she is responsible for so many deaths—including those of my own birth parents? How could she have betrayed me all these years?

Eomma spins me around and holds my face in her hands. "You *chose* to initiate into the Horangi clan? Why would you do such a thing?" Deep lines are etched into her face, and I have to avert my eyes.

"I did it for Hattie." I reach into the neck of my top and pull out the heart vial. The whole room gasps and my blood curls at the sight. The decaying must be speeding up, because over half the organ is black rot now. "And I did it for all of us. To stop the prophecy."

"But why didn't you come to us?" Appa asks, his face pained. "We're your family, and families tackle things together. As a team. You know that."

"I know . . ." I say, looking at my feet. But how do I explain all the complicated feelings I have? That I love them and yet hate the fact that they kept my roots hidden from me. That I wanted to show them and the council I was more than what they said I was, and prove I could be a Gom, too. How do I admit that maybe I was too scared to tell the truth because once they heard it they might not want me anymore . . . ?

"But it doesn't matter," I say, running my finger along the bump on my wrist. "What's done is done, and now the scholars are going to help us find the last artifact so we can save Hattie and destroy the star. Then all of this will be over."

"No thanks to you," Emmett finally blurts out at Auntie Okja, who has been unusually quiet this whole time. Sora, Austin, and Taeyo all glare at her, too. If eyes could scream, Auntie Okja would be deaf by now.

"What is Emmett talking about, Okja?" Eomma asks. Her eyebrows are knit together.

Auntie Okja frowns but stays silent, which fires up Emmett even more.

"Go on, Auntie Okja," he eggs. "Tell them. Tell them how you were the one working with the council to steal the seventh artifact for your own use, and you framed the scholars. Tell them how you wanted my mom's position as elder and how that got her *killed.*"

"I did *what?*" Auntie Okja looks stunned.

Eomma and Appa shake their heads, clearly thinking this is some kind of sick joke.

"He's right," I say, backing up Emmett. My heart is beating in triple time, but I try to speak calmly. "The prophecy says:

'When the blood moon and black sun appear to the gaze
To mark the start of the end of all days,
In the one last divine, a weapon shall rise;
Unless the gold-destroyer ends the soul who lies.'

"I've been thinking a lot about the last line, and I'm starting to wonder if it's talking about *you,* Auntie O. The way I see it, it's saying the end of all days is coming because of the last artifact, unless we stop *the soul who lies*. Are *you* the liar?"

Everyone stares at her expectantly, but she remains speechless.

"Well? What do you have to say for yourself?" Sora asks in a steely voice.

Austin bristles. "Do you know how many of our people died because of your actions?" There's so much pain in his voice it makes me shudder.

After a moment, Auntie Okja moves. Austin starts rubbing his wrist in preparation for an attack, but she just grabs a nearby wooden crate. She smooths out her skirt in one long movement before sitting on it. "When Sookhee died, I was so grief-stricken over having lost my best friend that I believed what the council told me. That the Horangi were responsible. It was easier that way—to have someone to blame."

Sora and Austin growl.

Auntie Okja gives them a guilty look, massages her temples, and continues. "But the truth is, I always thought something was off. The pieces didn't add up. It was too convenient that the scholars were there at the wrong place at the wrong time when they were the keepers of the artifact in the first place. But it wasn't until things went sour at Hattie's initiation that I started digging. And no matter where I looked, the same answer kept coming up. It all centered around one person who was adamant about keeping the scholars in the community's disfavor."

We all lean in. "Who?" I demand. "Who was it?"

"Bongjoon Pyo. The Samjogo elder. The chairperson of the LA council."

I let out a yelp, and then feel a weird sense of relief wash over me. I want so badly to believe Auntie Okja. "So it wasn't *you*?" I ask. "You weren't the one who wanted the sunstone ax? You're innocent?"

She hangs her head. "I'm far from innocent. I should have spoken up about my doubts a long, long time ago." She looks at Emmett and the three scholars. "And that's a burden I will forever carry on my shoulders. But I swear on my life, I didn't want Sookhee's position, and I never wanted the sunstone ax."

"Why do you think it's him?" Emmett asks dubiously. "What proof do you have?"

Auntie Okja's forehead crinkles in concentration. "He claimed that as chairperson of the council, only he had the authority to report illegal interactions with the Horangi clan to the Godrealm. But it was odd, considering that council elders always communicate collectively with the goddesses. Plus, he's always been dead set against my attempts to bring more diversity and inclusion into the community. I thought he was just old-fashioned, but after Hattie's ceremony, when I tried to reason with him, I saw a different side of him. A *darker* side." Her eyes crease with concern. "And then, the other day, when he told the council about his vision of Sora breaking into and entering the temple—"

"I never did such a thing!" Sora interrupts. "I tried to meet with Gumiho Elder Kim to warn her about the prophecy, but she wasn't willing to talk to me, so I left it at that."

Auntie Okja nods. "I know, I know. And that's what I figured out. Elder Pyo *claimed* to have seen you breaking in, but the next time he described the vision, the details were different. Each time he told us the story, it changed. That's how I knew he was making it all up."

"So why come clean now?" Sora asks, her face somber.

Auntie Okja looks at me and Emmett, and then Hattie's dying heart. "Because if these young people can be brave, then so can I. I believe Elder Pyo has been after the artifacts the whole time. He's the one responsible for all the deception, encouraging Sookhee Harrison to steal the ax, the deaths, and the banishment of the Horangi clan." The three scholars tense, and I see Austin clenching his fists. "Furthermore, I believe he is on the hunt for the last artifact as we speak. And we need to stop him before he finds it."

Austin puts his hand on Sora's shoulder and whispers a few words. He must not be sure about Auntie Okja's testimony, and I can't say I blame him. Not after everything they've suffered.

But Sora shakes her head. "If the end of days really is coming, and the last artifact will bring it on, then we need to find it before anyone else does."

She looks at Auntie Okja, her eyes like pinpricks. "I don't trust you, Okja, but I do believe you. So let's go find this monster of a human and stop him before he destroys the world."

24.
Let's Get Down to Business

 My parents, Auntie Okja, the three Horangi, Emmett (with Boris), and I all drive to the Woori America Bank's LA headquarters. When we park and I jump out of Eomma's SUV, the sky goes dark. I frown and look up, only to find that it's not a storm cloud that's blocked the sun, but a bird. A ginormous bird with a human woman's face.

"What are you doing here?" I ask Areum. "What if the saram see you? You don't exactly . . . well, blend in."

She shrinks to dove size and gently lowers herself onto my shoulder. "I yielded to you, Riley Oh. Wherever you go, I now go."

That alarms me. I'm flattered that this mighty bird-woman has decided I'm important enough to follow around, but I'm finding it hard to imagine having her on my shoulder for the rest of my life. It's a bit too pirate-y for my liking.

Taeyo studies Areum's shrunken form curiously, but all the adults keep a safe distance. They've seen her in fury mode, so I can understand why they're wary.

Emmett nudges me in the side. "Come on, Rye, you tamed her. You gotta take responsibility for her now. Besides, she might come in handy—you never know."

Areum turns her little head and stares expectantly at me. I guess it can't hurt for her to stay with us for the time being. "Well, you can't come into the building with us, or else the saram are gonna think they're hallucinating," I say. "But maybe you can stay outside until we come back? And keep out of sight, if you can?"

She squawks in response and flies toward the roof of the bank.

Auntie Okja ushers us to the front of the mid-rise office building, and then she turns to Sora, Austin, and Taeyo. "I'm sure you already know this, but Elder Pyo, when not acting as chairperson of the gifted council, is also chair of the Woori America Bank." Then she addresses the rest of us. "I called his assistant earlier, and he said Elder Pyo is here for a board meeting today. I say we go in there now and strike while the iron's hot."

"That's all good and well," Eomma says, "but how are we going to get past security? They won't let us through unless we have an appointment."

"Already ahead of you." Taeyo holds up a slim laptop that he brought from campus. "On the ride over, I hacked into Mr. Pyo's calendar and added an appointment with his relatives from out of town. His assistant won't know any better."

I slap him on the back. "Great work, Taeyo!"

Emmett crosses his arms and mumbles under his breath, "Guess the dude's got some skills."

I can tell my parents are anxious, but they dutifully follow

Auntie Okja to the entrance. The three scholars, on the other hand, are so ready they've already walked through the revolving doors. Emmett and I exchange a determined look and follow them inside.

When we get to the reception desk, Sora tells the security guards about our appointment with Mr. Pyo. We glaze on the cheesy smiles, and Taeyo puts on a class act, telling one guard how excited he is about visiting his "favorite uncle, Pyo." That earns him a compliment about his colorful attire and bow tie, at which he grins sincerely.

The guard calls Mr. Pyo's assistant to let him know we've arrived, and if the muffled voice on the other line is anything to go by, he seems surprised by the last-minute appointment. Taeyo must have done a convincing job, though, because before we know it, we are handed visitor passes and directed to the top floor.

Once we're upstairs, Mr. Pyo's assistant meets us at the elevator, and his eyes widen as all eight of us file out, one by one. "Oh wow! There are so many of you. . . ."

He leads us to a reception area that's furnished with fancy leather couches. Hardcover copies of the bank's annual strategic report have been artfully arranged on the glass coffee table. "His board meeting should be wrapping up soon. Can I get you some coffee, tea, or water while you wait?" He takes our drink orders and hurries off.

Emmett waits until the assistant has disappeared around the corner and then leaps to his feet. "Okay, let's make our move."

We sneak through the doors to the inner offices and pass row upon row of impersonal cubicles just big enough to fit a laptop surface and a chair. We file past the cramped kitchenette, where people are making bowls of instant ramyeon, and enter the client-meeting area with a series of small conference rooms separated by glass walls. As we make our way down the hallway, we spot Mr. Pyo running a meeting in the biggest boardroom. He is lounging in his black leather chair at the head of the table, nodding absently as young executives in tidy suits go through stacks of papers. I'm pretty sure he's starting to doze off.

"There he is!" I say, pointing.

Pyo must get that weird feeling of having eyes on him, because he suddenly sits up straight. We probably look like quite a sight just standing there in the hallway, staring at him.

At first he quirks his head to the side, as if trying to figure out who we are and why we're here. But once he sees Auntie Okja, then me, then Sora, his eyes widen. And before we can register what's happening, he has leaped out of his chair and made for an exit on the far side of the room. His employees stare at his retreating back, practically scratching their heads.

"He's getting away!" Emmett screams. "Everyone, after him!"

We chase him down the hallway as Mr. Pyo stumbles ahead and shoves anything within his reach into our path. Flower vases full of lilies, decorative statues of semi-clad ladies, and perfectly groomed bonsai plants fall to the floor as if an earthquake just struck, and we jump over them like we're in a hurdle race. If I was in any doubt before, I know for sure now. This is one guilty man.

He makes it to a window and tries to budge it open, which would have been bad luck for him if it *did*, since we're on the top floor. But it doesn't, which is also bad luck for him, because we're quickly closing the gap. He panics, searches for any escape route, and then, in a moment of inspiration, jerks open the fire-exit door and flees down the stairwell.

We chase after him and, even though the emergency siren is blaring in my ears, I can hear the man wheezing like an accordion all the way down the stairs. Still he somehow manages to get to the ground floor and out into the fresh air before we do.

By the time we all file out of the exit, Mr. Pyo is by a car parked out front.

"What do you want from me?" he shouts, sweat dripping down his face. Auntie Okja and Sora both take a step forward.

"We need to talk," Auntie Okja says.

Sora nods. "We *definitely* need to talk."

"I have nothing to say. I'm innocent. Leave me alone!"

"A bit hot under the collar for an innocent man..." Emmett comments.

Appa nods. "Definitely looks like he needs to cool off."

Austin smirks and rubs his wrists together. Instantly, the water hydrant next to the parked car unscrews itself, and water shoots into the sky. Taeyo cups his hands and animates the water to snake around and dive straight for Mr. Pyo's head in one big flow. The water pressure is so great, the man's body thumps to the ground under its impact.

"That should do the trick," Taeyo says, grinning.

Mr. Pyo gags on the water and gets drenched from head to toe before Austin shuts off the stream and allows him to get back up.

Mr. Pyo glances down at Austin and Taeyo's empty wrists. "How did you *do* that?" he asks, fear clouding his face. Then his eyes light up as if he's suddenly remembered something. He scrambles to the trunk of his car and takes out a baseball bat. "Don't come any closer, or I'll use this!" He waves it around like we're mosquitoes about to give him malaria.

I shake my head. Too bad he doesn't know what Sora's dominant element is.

Sure enough, she rubs her wrists and snaps her fingers. And just like that, the baseball bat breaks into two clean pieces.

Mr. Pyo's jaw drops. Then, finally admitting defeat, he falls to his knees and starts begging. "Please don't hurt me. I'll tell you anything. Just don't hurt me!"

Sora steps forward and glares down at him. "Tell us why you did it. Why did you frame our clan and get us banished? Why did you go to such lengths at the expense of so many lives?"

Austin spits on the pavement in disgust, and even Taeyo's face has gone red with anger. "And where is the last artifact?" I add.

"She made me do it! She said if I did, she would reward me with the artifact. But if I didn't, she would kill me."

"Who's *she*?" Auntie Okja demands.

"Sookhee Harrison. She made me do it, and then she killed all those people to get the ax. But after Sookhee was killed, it was too late to come out with the truth. I couldn't reveal the part I played. So instead, I blamed the Horangi. . . . What else was I supposed to do?"

Emmett gasps and I frown. That couldn't be right. Emmett's mom had told the gwisin halmeoni that she *didn't* kill those people. She said someone she trusted had betrayed *her*. Someone who was working with the council.

"You're lying!" I say. I want to shake the man until the truth rattles out of his mouth.

Then I remember something else Emmett's mom had said through the gwisin halmeoni. *I didn't want to hurt anyone. I was possessed.*

The cogs start spinning in my head. "Are you *sure* it was her?" I ask Mr. Pyo. "Are you sure it wasn't someone who just looked and sounded like Sookhee? Someone who happened to be using her *body?*"

Emmett grips my arm. "What are you talking about, Rye? The man is clearly delusional!"

Mr. Pyo gapes at me as if I've just asked him to eat his arm. But then his eyebrows merge until they look like one long caterpillar on his forehead. "Wait..." His face goes as white as Appa's makgeolli, and he drops his head in his hands. "Oh Mago, that makes *so* much sense," he mumbles.

"What makes sense?" Sora asks. "Spit it out."

He pulls his hands down his cheeks and sighs deeply. "I didn't understand it before, but I do now. The girl is right. She wasn't Sookhee. It wasn't her."

"Who was it, then?" Appa demands, his hands placed protectively on Eomma's shoulder and mine.

"The Cave Bear Goddess," Mr. Pyo whispers. "It was *her.*"

We're all stunned into silence.

Impossible.

Emmett and I have met the goddess. She is kind and benevolent. Yeah, she may have been a bit quirkier than I'd expected, but she'd given me the chance to save Hattie's life *and* become a Gom in my own right. She's the Gom's patron goddess. Would she really go to the length of possessing one of her Gom subjects to steal the sunstone ax? Mr. Pyo is just playing with us. Messing with our heads.

Then again . . .

Emmett's mom had said that she'd been betrayed by the one she had trusted most. Could she have been talking about her patron goddess? I mean, it's unbelievable, but everything that's happened over the last few days has been the definition of unbelievable. It's not *that* much out of the realm of possibility that the Cave Bear Goddess has been playing with us mortals this entire time.

"Blasphemy!" Eomma cries.

"How dare you!" Appa shouts. "You have *no* idea what you're talking about."

But Mr. Pyo has started to piece things together in his mind, and he's now on a roll, discovering truths as he says them out loud. "Yes, *of course!* The eight artifacts are the fallen fragments of the dark sun and moon, which means they're the physical manifestations of the six goddesses' original sin. It's only logical the goddess would want them all destroyed." He slaps his thigh and groans. "She was *never* going to give it to me. I should have known!"

Sora must be at the end of her tether, because she breaks the remaining two pieces of the baseball bat into tiny splinters with another snap of her fingers. "Stop mumbling. Speak so we can understand!"

Frightened, Mr. Pyo nods frantically. "Don't you see? The goddesses believe that if all the fallen artifacts are destroyed, their original sin, too, will be wiped away. They are assuming their punishment will be rendered null and void and they will have open, unfettered access to the three realms once more."

Emmett and I look at each other, trying to understand what we're being told. We'd learned about the fallen stars being symbols of the original sin, and how Mago Halmi had locked the six goddesses in the Godrealm as punishment for their actions. That's why the gifted clans were born—to do the will of the goddesses on Earth. Is that what Mr. Pyo is talking about?

"So, what you're saying," I start, my head spinning, "is that if the last fallen star gets into the Cave Bear Goddess's hands and she destroys it, the six goddesses will be free to walk the Mortalrealm?"

Mr. Pyo nods solemnly. "Precisely."

I breathe out, imagining what kind of chaos they might create. Would it mean six divine beings happily mixing and mingling with the saram over burgers at the local In-N-Out? Or six divine beings using mortals as their playthings and stubbing us out as they fancy? If what Mr. Pyo says is true, the latter seems more likely. Not to mention the potential devastation on the gifted way of life. The goddesses won't need the clans to do their will on Earth any longer, so would they even let us keep our gifts?

"We can't let that happen," Austin declares. "That would be mayhem. If the goddesses came down, the world as we know it would end."

Emmett nods. "We have to stop her. We need to stop the Cave Bear Goddess."

"I think I know what we have to do," I say, and everyone turns to me expectantly. "If the Cave Bear Goddess is possessing Gom bodies to do her business on Earth, she obviously needs us. So let's disconnect her. Let's sever her link to the Mortalrealm completely, so she can't ever get her hands on the last fallen star."

"You mean, like, *unplug* the Cave Bear Goddess from the Gom?" Taeyo asks.

"Exactly." I turn to my parents and Auntie Okja. They're definitely not going to like what I'm about to say. "That would mean losing our patron goddess and the Gom's ability to channel her power. Do you think the clan would be willing to do that?"

Sora holds up her Gi-less wrist. "If it's any consolation, we lost our patron goddess, and look at us now. We're still committed to our clan motto, and we're more powerful than ever. We don't *need* the goddesses to do good works. Magic is all around us."

Taeyo pipes up. "We can even help you unlock your own abilities."

My parents and Auntie Okja hesitate. I can see the doubt in their eyes. This would fundamentally change the Gom way of life. They look at one another, and eventually Auntie Okja speaks. "Our clan motto is Service and Sacrifice. This is precisely the type of decision we were born to make."

My heart beats proudly at their courage. They get it. *This* is what being a true Gom is all about.

"But how?" Emmett says, putting his hands on his hips. "How exactly do we unplug her?"

I bite the inside of my cheek. I think of the last two lines of the prophecy:

In the one last divine, a weapon shall rise;
Unless the gold-destroyer ends the soul who lies.

Based on what we know, the *soul who lies* has to be the
Cave Bear Goddess. But what if the one last divine weapon—
the last fallen star—isn't the thing that brings upon the end
of all days? What if it's the thing that will *prevent* it?

"I don't know how, but I think the last fallen star is still the
answer to all of this," I start. "It's supposed to be a weapon. So
maybe that's how we unplug her, by using the weapon against
her."

The sound of beating wings descends on us, and I look up
to see Areum land on the crown of Mr. Pyo's head. Luckily for
him, she's still dove size. He yelps and rolls into a ball, covering his head with his hands.

"You are correct, Riley Oh," Areum says. "Only a weapon
forged in the Godrealm—a piece of the divine itself—has the
power to sever the link between a goddess and her gifted clan.
The last fallen star is a divine weapon, and therefore an appropriate tool with which to carry out such a task. All you need
is a threading spell."

"What's that?" Emmett asks.

Auntie Okja responds. "It reveals the threads that connect
a witch to a patron goddess. The council has had to perform
this kind of spell on rogue witches from time to time, when
they weren't willing to tell us which clan they belonged to.
The spell can not only reveal the link, but also make the con-
nection vulnerable."

Areum gives a jerky nod. "Reveal the threads that connect

the goddess to the Gom, then cut them with the last fallen star. That is the way to sever the link between the Cave Bear Goddess and all the healers."

I let out a gleeful yelp. I guess being able to fly freely between the Mortalrealm and the Godrealm means you pick up some useful knowledge.

"And just by chance," I ask Areum, "do you happen to know *where* we could find this divine weapon?" I don't know why I didn't ask her earlier, but better late than never.

She squawks. "I do not know where it is, but I know who does."

Emmett comes over and nudges me in the side. His eyes are sparkling. "I told you she might come in handy!"

My heart soars as the sweet taste of hope returns to my tongue. *We can still do this.* Areum will lead us to the person who knows where the last fallen star is, and with it in our hands, we'll await the goddess's return. When the Cave Bear Goddess sees that I've retrieved what she asked for, she'll give back Hattie. And once my sister is safe and sound, we'll unplug the goddess from the Gom clan. The plan is kind of devious, sure, but no more so than a goddess impersonating a Gom.

"So, who is it?" Taeyo asks Areum, jumping up and down excitedly. He looks like he's holding a hot potato. "Who knows where to find the eighth artifact?"

Areum flies over to me and pecks affectionately at my hair. "Well, that's easy. The dokkaebi, of course."

25.
Dokkaebi Rules of Engagement

"The dokkaebi?"

"Yes," Areum confirms. "With its bang-mangi, a dokkaebi has the ability to summon any item in the Mortalrealm. All you need to do is make a deal with the creature, and it will retrieve for you what you desire."

We all stare at the inmyeonjo in disbelief. Sure, we've all heard the stories about the magical club a dokkaebi carries, and its incredible powers. But striking a deal with a dokkaebi would be like striking a deal with the devil. Except worse.

The dokkaebi are goblins that live in our nightmares. Literally. They feed off human despair (also literally), becoming more powerful each time they consume our deepest fears. Basically, if you fall asleep in the presence of one, it will step into your dreams and make you experience your worst horrors so it can eat them. Fun, right?

They are so frightening that when children misbehave,

parents sing them this song to remind them what lurks in the shadows:

With bloody skin so red, so bright,
And hair as black as darkest night;
Be good, you hear, unless you dare;
Don't let him see your deepest fear;
The dokkaebi may take a bite.

I shudder. What would a creature like that demand as payment for conjuring the last fallen star?

"Even if we wanted to consult a dokkaebi," I start, "which I'm not sure I do, where would we find one?" Everyone knows you don't go looking for a dokkaebi. They come looking for *you*.

"Well, actually," Mr. Pyo mumbles from the pavement, where he's still huddled in a ball, "there's a guest room at the temple. Room forty-four on level forty-four. My sources tell me a dokkaebi has been lodging there for some years now. No key is required, because he never locks the door. But that's because no one in their right mind dares to enter. If you fall asleep in there, you may never come out again."

Everyone frowns at him. It seems a little convenient that he happens to know this.

"And why should we trust you?" Taeyo asks.

Mr. Pyo rubs his shoulder where Areum's claws poked through his shirt. "Believe it or not, I don't want goddesses roaming the Mortalrealm any more than you all do."

It's not a bad answer. And considering Hattie's rotting

heart, time is of the essence. I look around, and it's clear every-one is thinking the same thing. We'll have to take a leap of faith. Even if it means facing our deepest fears.

"Well, what are we waiting for, then?" Emmett says, already halfway inside Eomma's SUV with Boris in his arms. "Get those butts moving, people!"

Leaving Mr. Pyo drenched and dejected on the pavement, we make for the temple.

Eomma drops Auntie Okja at Tokki Elder Lee's place to grab some sleep potion. The infusers call the mixture Knock-Out Juice, because it sends you into a deep slumber within seconds of swallowing. My parents sometimes use it at the clinic for saram patients who are extra suspicious about our methods. Add a few drops into their tea, and *bam*, they're not complain-ing anymore.

Auntie Okja meets us at the temple, and my parents, Emmett, the scholars, Areum, and I assemble near the eleva-tors. We haven't discussed it yet, but there's a gigantic elephant among us. Who's going to be the one to step into room 44 and drink the potion in order to meet the dokkaebi? Who is willing to confront their deepest fears in exchange for the last fallen star?

As soon as we jump into the elevator, my eomma clears her throat. "I know this situation could affect the fate of all mortalkind, but it is first and foremost a rescue mission for my daughter. So I'd like to be the one to face the dokkaebi, and I hope everyone can respect that."

"No, *I'll* do it," Appa says, his forehead creasing into a maze.

"No, *I* will," I say. "I'm the one that created this entire mess. Let me be the one to fix it."

Eomma and Appa both shake their heads adamantly.

"*No.* Not a chance."

"Don't even dream of it!"

By the time the elevator bell dings for level 44, everyone (except Areum and Boris) has volunteered for the mission at least once, and we are no closer to deciding who will be going under.

Eomma gets frustrated and snatches the vial of Knock-Out Juice from Auntie Okja. Her perm is frizzing up like she's been plugged into an outlet. "The potion is in *my* hand now, so the decision is mine. And I've decided that I'll be the one to do it. End of discussion."

She makes a zipping motion over her mouth, and everyone mutters but doesn't argue. I know why Eomma has volunteered. She wants to save Hattie herself, to make sure her daughter comes home safely. And as much as I want to right my wrongs, I don't argue anymore. I'd probably just mess up the rescue mission. After all, I'm the one who got Hattie into trouble in the first place. As much as I hate to admit it, letting Eomma do it is in Hattie's best interest.

"Fine," Auntie Okja finally says, also relenting. "But let's go over the rules of engagement."

We all huddle outside room 44 and agree on the details until the plan of attack is clear:

(1) Eomma, Appa, Areum, and I will enter the room together, while everyone else waits safely outside.

(2) Eomma will take the potion while Appa and I watch over her body.

(3) If Eomma looks like she's in trouble, we'll wake her up immediately.

(4) If at any point there are worrying noises coming from the room, the outside team will enter with expediency.

(5) No one will spend a second longer than they need to in that room.

"Please be careful," Auntie Okja says to Eomma. "All of you."

"And remember to call out if you need help," Sora adds. "We're just on the other side of this door."

Eomma, Appa, and I steel ourselves. And then, on the count of three, we all burst into room 44 together, with Areum on my shoulder.

I'm not sure what I was expecting, but whatever it was, it wasn't this. The plain room has a king-size bed in the middle and identical nightstands on either side, each with a tassel-shaded lamp. The lights are dim, and there's a weird haze in the air. Except for that, there's nothing else inside. There isn't even a bathroom, which is a nightmare of its own. And there's no dokkaebi to be seen.

We all exhale together, and even Areum looks relieved.

Eomma sits in the middle of the bed with her legs stretched out in front of her. "All right, I'm ready." She steels herself, looking just like Hattie when she makes her boss face. And suddenly, I miss my sister so much, my stomach aches.

Appa kisses her on the head. "Bring back our daughter, Eunha. We will be waiting for you right here."

We fan ourselves around the bed as Eomma says a quick prayer to Mago Halmi. Then she opens the vial and swigs its contents. Immediately, she drops onto her back and falls into a sleep so deep it's as if she has never been awake.

The next ten minutes are the longest I have ever experienced. Appa and I anxiously stand guard around Eomma's sleeping body, and I don't take my eyes off her chest to make sure she's still breathing.

Just when I think I can't possibly wait a single second longer, she bolts up in bed like a coiled spring and calls out, "No, no, no!" Her eyes are bloodshot and it looks like she's been crying.

"What happened?" Appa cries, hugging her close.

"Are you all right?" I climb onto the bed to get near her.

She puts her head in her hands and sobs. "I couldn't do it. I just couldn't."

"What did it ask of you?" Appa asks quietly.

Eomma trembles like a leaf. "He asked me to choose between my daughters. To pay for the cost of the last fallen star with one of their lives."

Appa gasps and buries his face in Eomma's hair. "Oh, my love, my poor, poor darling."

"I couldn't do it. I *wouldn't*," Eomma sobs and pulls me close to her. "How could I choose between my girls? How?!"

My heart shrivels to the size of Hattie's. Even with everything on the line, Eomma couldn't save Hattie, because she wasn't willing to lose *me*. The dokkaebi knew exactly what my eomma's deepest fear was.

I know what I have to do.

"*Psst.*" I turn my head slightly and whisper to Areum. "I need you to knock me out."

She blinks once. "Explain yourself, Riley Oh."

"Just do as I say," I urge. "Please. Just do it. And do it fast."

She pauses briefly, as if wondering if she's understood me correctly. But I guess the good thing about having a bird-woman yield to you is that your word is the final word.

The last thing I remember before my legs give out is Areum leaping off my shoulder and gaining size before slamming into the side of my head.

Ouch.

26.
The Dokkaebi Takes His Bite

 WHEN I NEXT OPEN MY EYES, I'm lying on the houndstooth carpet and Eomma and Appa have disappeared. I'm in the same room I was a second ago, but now the two lamps are emitting an eerie blue light. Areum must have succeeded in knocking me unconscious.

Getting onto my knees, I take some deep, calming breaths. My heart is beating so hard, it feels like the walls are pounding to the rhythm. Surely, the dokkaebi won't be as bad as I've been led to believe. Maybe he'll take pity on me and be nice?

I glance gingerly around the room. Aside from the details in the scary song everyone knows, I have no idea what to expect. I've never even seen a photo of a dokkaebi, so I don't know how big they are. Could it be small enough to hide under the bed...?

Holding my breath, I quickly lift the dust ruffle and take a peek. Dust balls and a spider are all I see, and I let out a laugh. Of course he's not hiding under the mattress—he's a dokkaebi, not the boogeyman! But then I look closer. There's a pair of feet on the other side of the bed.

What the—?! No one was there a second ago.

I close my eyes for a moment and then open them again. The feet are still there. And they're in gold open-toed sandals— just like the ones my sister had on for her initiation ceremony.

"Hattie?" I scramble to stand. Her back is to me, but she's wearing her golden hanbok, too. "Hattie!" I cry again as I lunge across the bed to get to her. I don't understand how she's here, but she's *here*. That's all that matters.

I put my hand on her shoulder and she swivels around.

"Hattie!" I say for the third time.

"Well, hello there, dear sister," she says, smirking.

My gut drops. There's something wrong with her.

As I take her in, her body starts shrinking. And her face melts into a new form.

"Ahh! You're not Hattie!" I clamber backward to get away from not-Hattie. And when I look up, I am facing the most grotesque creature I have ever seen.

He's the height of a chimpanzee, with greasy, stringy black hair and two sharp red horns sticking out of his head. His skin is the color of blood, and his steely eyes study me from underneath his thick brows. He's wearing a small gold hoop earring in each ear, and his swollen nose protrudes from his face like a pus-filled volcano.

He sniffs the air, and his nostrils flare like those of an angry bull. "Oh, how I treasure the aroma of frightened human girl!" He leers. "What excellent room service, indeed."

I retreat in disgust, and he chuckles menacingly. "I am

very much looking forward to having a taste...." He takes a bite of the air in front of him, revealing his teeth, which look like a shark's—sharp and deadly. The dokkaebi is definitely a creature from my worst nightmares.

"Welcome to my lair, Riley Oh."

I hiccup. How does he know my name?

Then I remember we are inside my dream right now. I invited him in by conking out in his room. And that means he has access to my mind. Everything I know, he knows, too.

A shiver runs down my spine, but I immediately go on the offensive. "I've come to offer you a deal."

He grins and a little bit of pus drips out his nose. "I assume you, too, are after the Godrealm's last fallen star."

I nod and try to stop my teeth from chattering. It's not even cold in here. "I am. So name your price, dokkaebi."

"I hope you are more fun to do business with than your mother was." He steeples his deformed red fingers and taps them from pinky to index in contemplation. "Now let me see." He pauses for effect, and his eyes flick from left to right as if he's watching the highlight reel of my deepest vulnerabilities.

His eyes finally stop moving and then pinpoint back on me. "For the services rendered to summon the Godrealm's last fallen star, I demand that which you hold dear. I demand the elemental magic that now flows through your blood."

I freeze. Did he just say he wants my *magic*?

I rub my biochipped left wrist against my right and watch the gifted mark glow red. I remember how it felt to channel my inner element and spit out that little ball of fire. It wasn't much, but it had given me a taste of my potential.

If the dokkaebi took my elemental magic, my gifted mark would disappear. And that means no matter how many times I got biochipped, my ability to wield fire would be gone for good.

But then Sora's words from before the initiation come back to me again. *What we're looking for is your commitment and loyalty.*

My success in the trial wasn't about my ability to wield fire. It was about the way I approached the task.

Something clicks into place inside me.

My new magic might be a part of me that I'd like to nurture and grow. But I would still be me without it. I thought I needed magic to be someone. But now I know that's not true. It's my actions, regardless of the magic, that really count. And right now, everything is riding on them.

"Fine," I say, holding my ground and standing tall. I'm eager for this to be over. "You can have my magic."

The dokkaebi's eyebrows make choppy waves on his face. He was obviously looking for more of a fight, and it's satisfying to know I've surprised him.

The goblin pauses, but only for a split second. His mouth opens again, spreading a horrible stench. "Don't get ahead of yourself, Miss Oh. The negotiation isn't over quite yet."

I suck in a breath. How could it not be over? There's nothing more he could possibly take from me!

"In addition to your magic, I require something else. Something you cherish above all else. The thing you cannot live without." His black eyes harden like coals, and I know that whatever comes next will be devastating. I can feel it in my bones.

"I demand the Horangi's and Gom's memories of you. You will be erased from the minds of your two clans *and* your two families. All of them. That is the final payment I require for delivering to you the Godrealm's last fallen star."

I fall to my knees. *No, no, no!* He has found the one way to destroy me from the inside out. My biggest vulnerability: the fear of being forgotten. The fear of being unloved by those I love most.

I pull out the vial from under my shirt and see that only a quarter of Hattie's heart is red now. It's me or Hattie. That's what this has come down to.

And it's funny, really. You'd think this would be the hardest decision in the entire three realms to make. It should be an impossible choice, like the one my eomma was faced with, having to choose between Hattie and me.

But it's not. After everything that's happened—after everything I've put my loved ones through—it is the easiest decision I've had to make all day. The only way I can make things right again is to take the deal. To be forgotten by both the Gom family that raised me and the Horangi clan that welcomed me into their arms. It's the price I must pay.

I close my eyes. I picture my eomma, my appa, my auntie Okja. I picture Emmett, who, being half-Gom, will also be affected, I'm sure. I picture Sora, Austin, and Taeyo. And most of all, I picture my sister. I imagine them all smiling and posing for a family photo, and I take a snapshot in my mind. They may forget me, but I want to remember them for the rest of my life.

"Good-bye," I whisper. "Thank you for everything."

Then, before I can change my mind, I turn back toward the creature. "Dokkaebi!" I announce bravely. "I'll do it."

The goblin rubs his horns and cackles at the top of his lungs. "Miss Oh, you have yourself a deal!"

He reaches his hand toward the vial around my neck, and I scream, grabbing the glass protectively. I will not let him get his nasty red fingers on Hattie's heart.

Instead, he clenches his fist in the air. And as something dark and icy seeps into my chest, I realize he wasn't after Hattie's heart.

He's after *mine.*

As he pulls back his fist, a beating black heart is extracted from my chest. The dokkaebi reels it in like a fish while licking his crimson lips.

"Ahh, human pain and suffering. My favorite meal."

Then, before my very eyes, he seizes my payment and sinks his teeth into it.

I cry out and shed tears for the life I've lost and the life I'll never have. I started with one family who loved me, gained another, and now I've lost them both.

"Absolutely divine!" The dokkaebi licks the final bits of my suffering off his lips. Black goo dribbles down his face. "And now to deliver you your fallen star." He flexes his small, red hand, and then calls out, "Bangmangi! Materialize!"

In a blink, a weird wooden club appears in his hand. It's half the length of a baseball bat, but at least twice as fat, and it's covered with pointy black and red spikes. While holding it, the creature closes his eyes and spits out words I've never heard before. His chanting gets louder as he waves his bangmangi in a weird dance-like motion, until finally there is an explosion of sound and light in the room.

"Well, well, well," the dokkaebi says to me, amusement dancing at the edges of his mouth. "This is an interesting turn of events. It seems, Miss Oh, that you are already in possession of the fallen star."

I'm already what?!

He chuckles, quietly at first, and then it crescendos into an avalanche of sound. "Such a shame, considering that you had to pay a price, but I upheld my end of the bargain. So I believe my work here is done. It has been a pleasure doing business with you." He starts walking toward the door.

"No, stop!" I yell. "What do you mean I'm already in possession of it?"

But he's already gone.

I hear a birdlike squawking faintly in the distance. I listen harder, and I can hear Eomma's and Appa's voices, too. The sounds are getting louder, closer, and now I feel someone's hand on my shoulder, shaking me. I must be waking up back in the real room.

And the thing is, I should be grateful that this nightmare is ending. But instead, all I feel is doom.

I have lost everyone I love, and for *what?*

No, this is a nightmare I would rather not wake from.

27.
Ticktock, Ticktock Goes the Heart

 "WELCOME BACK, RILEY OH," Areum greets me when I wake. I'm lying on the bed, and the lamps are no longer glowing blue. I must be back in the real room 44.

I rub my eyes and sit up. The inmyeonjo knows my name! Thank Mago, it was all just a horrible dream.

"Who are you?" Appa asks, frowning at me.

Six sets of eyes are staring at me. The rest of the crew must have come into the room while I was out.

A sharp pain stabs me in the chest. "It's me, Appa," I say, my voice shaking. "Riley. Your daughter."

Eomma furrows her eyebrows. "We only have one daughter, and her name is Hattie."

And just like that, the nightmarish deal I made with the goblin becomes a terrible reality. I gave up my newfound magic, as well as the Gom and Horangi clans' memories of me, in exchange for the last fallen star. Only the dokkaebi didn't keep his part of the bargain. Now, thanks to his tricks, I have nothing—no star and no family. Not one that remembers me, anyway.

I take out Hattie's heart vial and hold it up for them to see. My hand is trembling so much the cylinder swings from side to side. "I know this must be confusing for you, but I have been working with you to find the last fallen star to save Hattie, and to sever the Gom's link to the Cave Bear Goddess."

"How does she know our plans?" Emmett asks suspiciously.

"And why do you have our Hattie's heart?" Auntie Okja says.

Taeyo studies me. "If what you say is true, why don't we know who you are?"

"Because," I explain, "I met with the dokkaebi. And I had to give away your memories of me as payment for conjuring the last fallen star."

Their eyes widen, and Sora searches around me. "Then where is it? Where is the last artifact?"

I gulp. It's a good question. The dokkaebi played me. "Um, he said I was already in possession of it. But I don't know what that means."

"I don't trust her," Austin says, as he starts rubbing his wrists together. "We need to neutralize her before she becomes a threat."

Hiccups erupt out of my throat and I start to panic. *Think, think, think!* If I can't convince them we need to work together, our plans will be ruined. I will have given up everything for nothing.

I look at the inmyeonjo. "Areum, tell them," I urge. "Tell them who I am."

"She is who she says she is," the bird-woman confirms. "She is Riley Oh."

But suspicion still lingers in everyone's eyes. They don't know a Riley Oh anymore.

Austin starts approaching me, and I anxiously fiddle with the ring on my finger. Do I run? Hide? What are my options? Then I realize... *The ring.*

"Em," I say, walking up to him while holding out the ring. "You might not remember me, but until a moment ago, when your memories were wiped by the dokkaebi, you were my best friend. You gave me this before I got initiated into the Horangi clan."

I pass the ring to him, and he takes it, studying it from all angles. When he sees the secret compartment inside the band, his forehead creases into a frown. "I have no idea who you are, but this *is* my ring, and I *never* take it off."

"And that's Boris," I say, pointing to the dragon-on-wheels lying on the ground next to him. "Noah lent him to us the night of the summoning, and Taeyo souped him up." Boris's tail wags as if to verify my statement.

Emmett sidesteps and stands protectively in front of the scaly blue scooter. "How do you know his name?"

I turn to Eomma and Appa. "I know you can't remember me, either, but I promise, I'm your daughter, too." I point to Auntie Okja. "Auntie O brought me to you when I was a newborn. And you raised me. Hattie is my sister."

They both study my face and then share a confused look between themselves. And it feels like a hundred little cuts. My parents really have no idea who I am. I swallow my tears and shove my hands in my pockets. This is it. I'm done for. I wish I had my onyx stone.

That's when my hand lands on something round and cold and hard.

The compass!

"Taeyo," I quickly say before Austin activates the metal stars on his jacket. "You gave me this. For good luck. This is proof I am who I say I am."

He comes over to examine it. "How weird. It looks just like my gold compass, but why would I have given it to you?"

His *gold* compass.

Suddenly, the final two lines of the prophecy ring like a bell in my ears:

In the one last divine, a weapon shall rise;
Unless the gold-destroyer ends the soul who lies.

"This is it!" I scream, holding up the compass. "*This* is the last fallen star."

"What are you talking about?" Taeyo asks, stepping back in alarm.

I try to contain my blossoming excitement so I can explain clearly. How did I not see this earlier? "The dokkaebi told me I was already in possession of the fallen star. I thought he had duped me, but I see now. The gold compass is the gold-destroyer from the prophecy." I push on the overlapping symbol on the back, and the triangular blades eject out. "See? It's a weapon. In the shape of a star. It's *gotta* be the Godrealm's last fallen star!"

"Oh my Mago . . ." Eomma glances at Appa and Auntie Okja. "Could she be telling the truth?"

"But how can we trust her?" Austin narrows his eyes at me.

Emmett puts his ring back on his finger and stares thoughtfully at Boris's wagging tail. "I vote we give her a chance."

I think quickly. Taeyo had said when the Horangi lost their Gi, they started focusing on what they possessed rather than what they had lost. My two clans may have forgotten me, but like Areum and Boris, there are others whose memories will still be intact. "How about we go up to the Gi sanctuary, then?" I suggest. "If what I say is true, there'll be people from the other four clans who'll recognize me. If they know who I am, you'll know I'm telling the truth." I hold my breath. This is my ace card. It *has* to work.

"I believe her," Taeyo finally says. "It's too much of a coincidence that she had both Emmett's ring and my compass. The probabilities work in her favor."

Eomma gasps and points to Hattie's heart. I look down and blanch. There is only one tiny sliver of red left on the shrunken organ. "We've run out of time," I whisper, gripping the vial tight in my hand. "We need to act *now*."

And that is the final push they need. Everyone stares at Hattie's dying heart in silent agreement. I guess desperate times call for desperate measures.

"Let's go to the sanctuary," Auntie Okja says.

Sora nods. "You lead the way."

With adrenaline pumping through my body, we take the elevator up to level 88.

The sanctuary is empty today. Just my luck. I was hoping for a Gi ceremony or initiation, or at least a clan gathering so I could find someone from Saturday service who'd recognize me. Instead, the goddess statues stare blankly at us from each of the six hexagonal walls.

Austin hasn't stopped evil-eyeing me since we left room 44, and now he raises his crossed wrists in a threatening motion. "This better not be some kind of trap."

I shake my head furiously. "No trap, not at all." I hold up the fallen-star compass. "But as long as you trust me, we finally have everything we need. We just need the goddess to—"

There is a shift in the atmosphere, a sudden thickness to the air, and my words stop dead in my throat. I know this feeling. It's the same one I had at Santa Monica Pier when Hattie tried to summon Mago Halmi. A fierce gust blows over the chamber, and I cover my face. That's when I hear her voice.

"Well, hello again, my favorite new recruit!"

I freeze, and even Areum tightens her talons on my shoulder.

She has returned.

"Cave Bear Goddess?" Auntie Okja says, stunned. She bows her head automatically in reverence.

"How is she here without being summoned?" Eomma whispers to Appa, gripping his arm.

"If the goddess has an outstanding deal with a mortal,

she is able to return to collect on that arrangement," Areum explains.

Even though I saw her once before, the sight of the goddess still surprises me. She doesn't have her Winnie the Pooh apron or saucy ladle with her today, but she's still a frumpy middle-aged woman with frizzy hair and dated clothes.

She smiles at me with that soft, kindly face, and I will myself to smile back. Did this Korean Mrs. Weasley really manipulate us all so she and her sisters could freely roam the Earth again? What a shrewd disguise!

If the goddess has seen the other people in the sanctuary, she doesn't show it. Instead, she pinches my cheek affectionately. "So tell me, dearie, are you enjoying the new job? Do you think you're in the running for employee of the month?" She chuckles, and her soft belly jiggles under her knitted vest.

I keep the smile plastered on my face. I have to be careful about my next steps. Despite her convincing act, she is not the benevolent goddess we all thought she was. She's responsible for the Horangi clan's expulsion, and the deaths of Emmett's mom, my birth parents, and Taeyo's parents. She could bring on the end of the gifted clans and mortalkind as we know it. This is not a simple trade anymore.

"I don't know about employee of the month," I say modestly, "but I have found the Godrealm's last fallen star, just as you asked."

She doesn't hide her delight. Her skin glows a bright hue of solar yellow. "Well, well, my dear, you *are* a treasure indeed. Maybe even in the running for employee of the century! Go on—show me what you've found."

I hesitate, holding the star compass behind my back. I could reveal it to her first and then demand Hattie back, but my recent experience with the dokkaebi has made me wary—and weary. I look around at my Gom family, my Horangi family, and my best friend, all of whom have been through enough already.

No, this is not the time to show goodwill. I need to be smart about this.

"Come on, Goddess!" I say, hitting her jovially on the arm. "You said so yourself—I'm best-employee material. How about you bring my sister back first? Then I'll give you the star." I slip the compass into my back pocket and hold out Hattie's heart vial.

The goddess laughs heartily. "Oh my, looks like you've picked up some bargaining skills on the job!" Her eyes start twinkling. "And what if I don't? If I refuse to bring her back first, are you prepared to give up the compensation I promised you? I thought you wanted to be reborn in my image—as a Gom and a healer?"

She's testing me, but I'm not going to give in. Because if I've learned anything over the last few days, it's that healing magic isn't what makes me a true Gom. No, it's my willingness to sacrifice myself for my loved ones. It's my desire to serve those I care about.

Instead, I play her game. "Oh, Goddess, you're so funny!" I laugh so convincingly, I should get nominated for an Oscar. "You're the benevolent patron goddess of service and sacrifice. You would never go back on a promise! Besides, as I believe you once told me, compensation for a divine job completed is stipulated by Godrealm law." I wink at her. "You wouldn't break the law, would you?"

I'm not sure where I'm getting the courage to sass a divine being this way, but, if I'm being honest, I kind of like this new me. It has taken me a little while, but it feels good to speak out and trust in my abilities. It feels right. Hattie would be proud.

The goddess grins and slaps me on the back. "Well put, my dear! I'd better start wriggling, then. I don't want those holy lawyers knocking on my door—they're a divine pain in the backside!" She rolls up her sleeves and rubs her hands together. "Let's bring your sister back, shall we?"

As the last muscle of red organ tissue in the vial shrivels into black rot, the goddess plucks something out of the air. It shines like a nugget of gold between her fingers, and she places it carefully on the ground near the Gi cauldron.

The next time I blink, I see a body wearing a long golden hanbok lying on the floor.

My heart soars like an inmyeonjo.

It's my sister.

It's Hattie.

28.
Nuh-uh, She Didn't!

 "Hattie!" I cry.

"Hattie-ya!" my parents shout.

Eomma, Appa, and I run to the body that has materialized out of nowhere onto the floor of the Gi sanctuary.

I fall to my knees, burying my face in my sister's chest. My parents shed tears of joy and relief, and the feeling is overwhelming, seeing her in the flesh again. It's only been a few days, but it feels like years since I've seen my boss sister. She got so skinny in the Godrealm. Her arms are barely thicker than sticks, and her face is sunken and painted a sickly shade of gray. So much for "safekeeping," like the goddess had promised. Hattie looks barely alive.

Her eyes flick open like two headlights.

"You're awake!" I cry out. "I've missed you so much, Hat. I can't believe you're back. You're really back!"

Except something feels off.

The light in my sister's eyes is gone. There's no *Hattie* in those eyes. But if Eomma has noticed, she's not showing it. She hugs Hattie's limp body to her own, crying into my sister's bony shoulder.

"Eomma..." I warn.

My hand grasps the cold vial still around my neck, and my eyes flit from Hattie's body up to the goddess. "Something's not right!"

The goddess raises an eyebrow. "Hmm, that's interesting."

"What do you mean, *interesting?*"

Hattie twists unnaturally in Eomma's arms, as if her body is being controlled by a puppeteer. Her eyes lock like a hawk's on Emmett, and her arms stretch toward him.

"My son," she croaks, her voice sounding dusty and hoarse. "My son, my son, my son."

All color drains from Emmett's face, and he stares at my sister with frightened eyes. "Mom...?" He starts walking toward Hattie, his mouth hanging wide with disbelief.

"No..." Auntie Okja murmurs. "It can't be."

"Where is my sister?!" I demand of the goddess, dropping my cheerful act. "You promised her safe return!"

"Gone," she answers simply. "The young witch's heart perished, and it seems an opportunistic gwisin has possessed her body. What a shame." Something changes in the goddess's face. It's like her features are shedding their kindliness.

I clutch at my chest. "*No*, that's not possible." I think of what Jennie's halmeoni gwisin said—that Emmett's mom had become a vengeful gwisin stuck on Earth, too overcome by the wrongs done to her in life. She was no longer the woman she used to be, and she wasn't willing to talk to Emmett. Then what is she doing here now?

Emmett kneels down in front of Hattie. His whole body is trembling. "Mom, is that really you?"

Hattie's eyes blink once, and then, in a blur, everything changes. She is no longer limp on the ground, cradled in my eomma's arms. She now stands, her body in an unnatural position, like that of a marionette, her arms outstretched. She walks rigidly toward the goddess.

"You!" she shrieks, pointing at the goddess's face. "You did this. You used me. You made me steal the artifact, and then you made me kill all those innocent people. I was wronged!"

The goddess shrugs her off. "*Tsk-tsk*, you insolent gwisin. You have the audacity to return from the dead to accuse me of such a petty crime? Don't you know who I am?" She turns to me and shakes her head. "Can you believe the gall of this ghost? Or should I say, the *ghoul* of this ghost?" She chuckles and winks at me.

I realize with a jolt that the goddess still thinks I'm on her side.

Emmett hasn't taken his eyes off Sookhee/Hattie, and now he nears her again, fidgeting with his silver ring. "Mom, what *happened* to you? You didn't want to talk to me before. How come you're here now?"

Sookhee turns around stiffly and focuses on Emmett's face. Her sunken eyes are still midnight black, but now they shed fat tears. "Oh, my sweet, sweet boy. I was lost in my anger for so many years. But when I found out you were searching for me, I fought the fog with all my might. And when it cleared, I remembered everything. I remembered what it was all for. You helped me find my way back to you."

I nervously glance over at the goddess, but she isn't even listening. She has wandered over to the Gi cauldron and is running her finger along the lip of its mouth. She's whistling the tune to "Twinkle, Twinkle Little Star" while casually looking around as if she's sightseeing. I blink twice. Is it my imagination, or is the goddess getting taller . . . ?

Sookhee takes a jerky step toward Emmett. As she talks, her movements become smoother and more natural, as if she's growing more solid and real with each word. "My deepest desire was for you to be loved and embraced by my community. The goddess promised to give you magic if I let her borrow my body. But it was never her intention to help me. She just wanted the artifact for herself. She possessed me and made me do terrible, *terrible* things." Sookhee weeps, and it looks like a dam has broken inside her. And it's no wonder. Thirteen years' worth of pent-up emotion has been released, and she is finally getting the chance to clear her name.

It all makes sense now. The bearded man told me there were always two sides to every story, and he was right. I did see Sookhee take the sunstone ax from the Horangi in the vision in the Haetae's bell. But it wasn't her. It was the Cave Bear Goddess. She'd been behind everything the whole time.

"I'm sorry I wasn't there for you, my baby," Sookhee sobs. "But please know that everything I did, I did for you. I love you more than you could ever know. And I am *so* proud of how you've turned out, my son."

Something cracks in Emmett and he pulls Sookhee into a tight hug. "You came back from the dead to find me," he whispers. "I love you, too, Mom. Saranghaeyo." He openly weeps into her shoulder, and my own leaky-bladder eyeballs do what they do best.

Now I realize that tears are nothing to be ashamed of. I'd always considered them a flaw—something that made me weak. But now I see that they are a part of who I am—a part of who we all are. They come because we care. It's a way of saying *I love you.*

As Emmett, too, embraces his emotions in a way he's never done before, Hattie's body glows bright from every pore. Then, as she crumples and falls softly to the floor, the light pulls away, like skin being shed by a snake. The glow re-forms into the shape of a leopard standing next to Hattie's body, and it shimmers like a holograph.

"Mom?" Emmett stares at the cat with wide eyes.

The leopard pushes her snout into Emmett's hand. "Now I can finally leave in peace," she whispers. "Never forget, my son—you were made in love, and you will live a life full of love. Don't be scared of letting it in. You are worthy of it all. Good-bye."

And just as Jennie's halmeoni gwisin did, Sookhee's soul animal disappears in a burst of warm light. Emmett wipes his eyes. And for the first time since I met him, he looks completely at peace. His perpetual pout has been erased, and it's as if the weight of the world has been lifted off his shoulders. "Good-bye, Mom," he whispers.

Eomma, Appa, and I run to Hattie once more, to cradle

her lifeless body in our arms. And, with an aching heart, I face the truth. Hattie—the real Hattie—is gone.

"Hattie," I breathe into her hair. "I'm sorry. I'm so sorry I failed you." The words seem meaningless as I gaze at her still face. A deep pain erupts in my chest, and I clutch at it. My rib cage feels empty. There's a Hattie-shaped hole inside, and I'm never going to be able to fill it.

The goddess returns from her sightseeing trip to the Gi sanctuary and puts her hands on her (slimmer?) hips. "All right, subjects, that's enough with the sob stories. I believe I've been *more* than generous with my patience, not to mention allowing that poor excuse for a soul to spout off such nonsense." She turns to me with sparkling eyes. "Time to talk shop. Be a good dearie and hand over the Godrealm's last fallen star, won't you?"

Bubbles of frustration rise to the surface of my skin. How can she be so nonchalant when she's brought pain to so many lives? How can she claim to be the patron goddess of service and sacrifice when all she does is create more suffering? She's nothing but a con artist!

"This is all your fault!" I scream at the top of my lungs. "You didn't even bring my sister back. Why should I give you the last fallen star?"

Her eyebrows arch as she digests my outburst. Then she purses her lips. "I wouldn't push my luck, *dearie*. You may have been a model employee so far, but my tolerance is not a bottomless cup."

As I look down at my poor parents, my grief explodes into a ball of fury. The goddess was supposed to be benevolent and good—an example of what mortals should aspire to become. But instead, she is the definition of selfish. She acted with complete disregard for mortal life just so she could erase her crime.

I dig my feet into the ground and stare into the goddess's eyes. "Will you ever stop?!" I cry, my hands clenching into fists. "Will access to the three realms be enough? When will you stop treating us mortals like we're disposable? Can't you see our lives are *worth* something?"

The goddess sighs deeply. "Oh, how you disappoint me, mortal child. I thought we had something special between us, but here you are, throwing it all away." She closes her eyes for a moment, and her body starts to glow. It looks like LED bulbs have been switched on under her skin.

"There's one thing you have to understand." She advances toward me, her frame elongating, her once soft face hardening. With each step her dowdy clothes are gradually being replaced by a flowing gold gown. "You cannot compare your lives to ours. My sisters and I are Mago Halmi's divine children. If mortals must perish to suit our needs, then so be it. It is the law of nature."

That's all the fuel I need to stoke my fire. If she doesn't respect mortal lives, then she has no right to roam our realm.

"Auntie O!" I scream, releasing the metal rays of the compass behind my back. "Do it now!"

Auntie Okja might not know who I am anymore, but she still knows the plan. At my command, she rubs her wrists together and starts chanting the threading spell. Before our eyes, tiny silver ropes start appearing between my auntie and the goddess. They look like spiderwebs touched by morning dew, glistening under the lights of the sanctuary.

"What is the meaning of this?" the goddess asks, looking between herself and Auntie Okja.

"You are the patron goddess of service and sacrifice," I start. "Yet the only one you serve is yourself. You don't *deserve* the Gom. You don't *deserve* this realm. You want the Godrealm's last fallen star? Well, here it is. Let us show you what we mortals are truly capable of!"

And with that, I run toward the threads with the star compass in hand. I run with all my might, and with Hattie in my heart. I channel all my anger and grief into my arms, and I slash at the threads with both hands. I attack them with everything in my being, desperate to sever the link between the goddess and the Gom clan.

The goddess watches me with surprise, momentarily stunned into silence. Then she looks at the compass and cackles. "Stupid mortal child, that is not the Godrealm's last fallen star. How dare you test the patience of divinity?"

"But it . . . it . . . it *has* to be!" I stop slashing and look at the threads between my auntie and the goddess. I expect to see them cut and drooping like wilting flowers. But they're still connected, firm and taut, as intact as they were when they first appeared.

"I don't understand," Auntie Okja breathes.

"It should have worked," I murmur.

I turn the compass over in my hand. The dokkaebi had said I was in possession of the fallen star, and the compass is the only thing I have on me. And the prophecy confirmed the weapon is made of gold. The compass *has* to be the last fallen star.

If it isn't, then where in the world is the *real* artifact?

The goddess locks her eyes on me, and her glowing skin starts radiating an angry orange. "You don't complete your job, and then you try to attack me. What utter insubordination! You want to know how we're different, you and I?" She sneers and all traces of the kind, frumpy woman disappear. "I follow through with my threats. You *will* feel my wrath, child. This I promise you."

Emmett runs in between me and the goddess. "You're full of it!" he screams. "You're powerless here without a willing host to use. You're nothing but an empty shell. That's why you had to possess my mom's body!"

The goddess smiles and reaches out for the threads. "Indeed. Which is why I'm lucky to have one connected already." She reels it in like a fishing line, and her catch is none other than my auntie.

"Help!" Auntie Okja calls out, realizing what is about to happen.

I run and grab her from behind, trying to hold her back. Eomma and Appa then wrap their arms around my waist, soon followed by Emmett, Taeyo, Sora, and Austin. We all pull on Auntie Okja with our collective weight, trying to prevent her from moving an inch closer.

But we're no match for a divine being. The Cave Bear Goddess wins this tug-of-war, and as Auntie Okja screams for her life, the deity reaches out and puts her hand on my auntie's head.

There is a sound like crashing cymbals. Auntie Okja's body convulses and floats in the air. Her face distorts and her limbs flail about. Then the goddess disappears, and Auntie Okja's body falls to a heap on the floor.

"No!" I scream. "Not my auntie, too!"

The goddess, now in Auntie Okja's body, picks herself up off the floor. She straightens, clicking her vertebrae into place, then puts her hands on her hips and smiles. "All right, mortals, let me show you how it's done. Who wants to go first?"

29.
Get Your Battle Gear on, Fambam!

"No, stop! Please!" I shout, as the goddess approaches my parents in her newly possessed body. My *auntie's* body.

She ignores me. Instead, she walks toward my appa and flicks her finger as if catapulting a bug. Appa is propelled into the air and lands with a thud against one of the Gom pews.

"James!" Eomma cries, running to his side. She rubs her wrists and heals him as panicked tears roll down her face.

The goddess continues moving toward my parents, ready to strike again, and my heart drops into my stomach. *No!* This is not how the plan was supposed to go. We already lost Hattie and Auntie Oh. I can't lose my parents, too.

That's when the first metal star blade flies across my vision en route to the goddess.

"Austin, be careful!" I call out, feeling conflicted. I know it's the goddess in there, but she's using my auntie's body.

"I won't hurt her," he calls out, hurtling two more stars toward her. "But we need to keep her from hurting anyone else."

The goddess momentarily halts and looks surprised. She must not have known the Horangi taught themselves a new kind of magic. But she doesn't stay surprised for long.

"Impressive," she merely says. "But I'm afraid your party tricks will not be enough to stop me." She laughs and makes another flicking motion with her hand. Austin gasps as he's lifted off his feet and thrown across the sanctuary, landing hard against the Mountain Tiger Goddess's statue.

"Austin!" Taeyo cries. He looks around, searching for any water he can animate. But all he has is the little bit in his water bottle. He makes it shoot up from the bottle and form a barrier in front of Austin's body, while Eomma runs toward them, leaving Appa recovering in a pew.

As Eomma attempts to heal Austin's injuries, Sora rubs her wrists together and makes a lifting motion with her two open hands. One of the wooden pews in the front row of the Horangi section rises into the air. "Don't you dare lay another finger on him!" she calls to the deity as the entire bench flies through the air and lands in her path.

The goddess takes a step back in annoyance, but then she simply climbs over the pew. This time she starts coming for *me*.

I gulp. I look down at my wrists and see the glaring absence of a Gi. I feel for the bump of the biochip, but thanks to the dokkaebi, that's gone, too. I want to be able to do something to protect my families, but I'm powerless. *Useless.*

"I am going to enjoy this," the goddess coos in my auntie's voice. "I'm going to enjoy this very much." She lifts her hand as she nears, preparing to attack.

I hold my breath. The fact of the matter is that I tried my best, but the goddess is right. We mortals are no match for divinity. Especially when she's using a physical body. A body we don't want to attack.

"Feel my wrath, mortal child." She locks her eyes on me and claps her hands together. I close my lids, ready to surrender to whatever comes next.

Ca-caw! The sound of beating wings fills my ears as a full-size inmyeonjo blocks the goddess's attack.

A power surge hits the bird-woman, and she shrieks and falls to the floor, her right wing bent at an unnatural angle.

"Areum!" I fall to my knees and hold her head. She shivers in pain. "*Shh*, it's gonna be okay," I soothe.

"Incorrect," the goddess declares, raising her hand once more. "Let this be a lesson to all of you. *Never* start a job you can't finish."

She makes a scooping gesture, and I hunch over Areum's body protectively. I won't let her get hurt again.

The marble floor in front me begins to curve upward like a stone wave, and I tense, waiting for it to swallow me whole.

At that moment, a gust of wind sweeps me off my feet. For a second, I feel weightless. When I regain my footing, I'm somehow on the opposite side of the room with Areum at my side. And standing next to me are Noah Noh, Cosette Chung, David Kim, and Jennie Byun.

I rub my eyes. Am I hallucinating?

Noah regards me with concern. "I told you guys to be careful. And look where you are now." His gaze flicks to Hattie's body on the floor, and his chest hitches with a sob. Noah must have lifted Areum and me up and moved us out of the goddess's path. And now that he's seen what's happened to Hattie, I can only imagine how he must be feeling.

"How did you guys know to come here?" I ask, still not sure if I'm imagining them.

Jennie shrugs. "I'm a seer, remember? I'm actually pretty good, if I do say so myself."

Cosette nods. "Jennie had a vision that you were in trouble—that all the gifted clans were in need of help. We came as quickly as we could."

I look between them and suddenly realize they remember me. They know who I am. A surge of gratitude washes over me, and I pull them into a group hug. "Thank you so much for coming, guys," I say. "You have no idea how happy I am to see you."

"Watch out!" David calls out as the goddess throws several candle stands at us. Each one is almost as tall as we are, and one of the bronze arms slices my leg as it clatters to the floor. I hiss in pain and clamp down on my thigh.

Noah picks up two of the stands with ease, as if they're made of cardboard. He leans back to throw them toward the goddess, and I shout, "Please don't hurt my auntie's body. She's still in there somewhere!"

The candle stands fall uselessly a few inches from the goddess's feet.

"We're over here, bully!" Emmett taunts the goddess as he jumps onto Boris and starts to zoom around.

Her lips tighten into a line and she makes her way toward us. Cosette glamours herself to look just like Auntie Okja, and for a second, the goddess stares at her mirror image with her mouth ajar, momentarily thrown. David takes a few vials from his pocket and tosses one to Jennie. As the goddess comes within arm's reach, David and Jennie uncork the vials and throw the contents at her. Liquid splashes into her open mouth and she wobbles on her feet, trying to keep her balance.

"It's a disorientation potion," David explains. "It won't hurt her, but it will disable her for a while."

Noah takes the opportunity to push four wooden pews into a square around the weakened goddess, and she falls to her knees. Sora uses her magic to lattice some pews on top, forming a wooden cage.

"How dare you try to imprison me?!" she shrieks.

Having been healed by my parents, Areum flies above the cage, squawking and clawing at the goddess's hands as they emerge through the gaps.

I let out a breath of relief. We've contained our enemy for now. Now we just need to figure out how to get the goddess out of my auntie's body.

I look around to see that each of the six clans is represented here. The Gom, the Horangi, the Samjogo, the Tokki, the Gumiho, and the Miru. All the gifted clans are working together for the first time in over a decade, united in a common cause. And I'm at the center of it.

I've spent my whole life thinking of myself as an outsider. I always kept my head down because I was different and never fit in. But as I look around now, something stirs inside me.

Despite not having achieved my wish of becoming a healer, I have never felt more Gom in my life. At the same time, even without my Horangi elemental magic, I feel more like a scholar than I ever could have imagined. And though I no longer belong to either clan, I feel more gifted than I ever thought I'd be.

It's just like Hattie said. It's all about choice. I don't have to feel conflicted about being Gom or Horangi, gifted or saram, adopted or born into a family. Because my choice isn't either-or. I can choose to be all of those things. It's my actions that define who I am, not who I was born to, or what blood flows through my veins, or even what magic I can wield. And the fact of the matter is that I chose all these people, and these people chose me.

Out of nowhere, the third line of the prophecy echoes in my ear.

In the one last divine, a weapon shall rise.

As the words wash over me, something ignites in the pit of my stomach. It's a new kind of heat, but it's not unwelcome. A pocket of warmth grows from my gut and spreads into my limbs and my chest, right up to the top of my head. It zings through me like pure energy—like something awakening after a long slumber.

Do you see now? a voice whispers in my head. I'm pretty sure I've heard it before, but I can't quite put a finger on who it is. *This is who you've been all along.*

I shake my head. *But I was born Horangi, and I was raised Gom,* I say to the voice in my head. *It's not possible that I—*

The mysterious voice answers the question in my mind

before I can finish the thought. *Mago Halmi did not build the world in singularity. She made us all in eum and yang—in contradiction and equilibrium. Each of us is capable of more than you can imagine.*

I think I see the flicker of something large and shiny in the opposite corner of the sanctuary. Then something weird happens. The Gi cauldron starts to tremble. It shakes and groans like it's coming alive, and thick black fire erupts from its top. The hungry dark flames burn fiercely, like a bonfire made of night, and everyone stops to stare at it.

"What's happening?" Cosette says.

"Is that supposed to be burning?" Emmett asks.

A seed of understanding begins to sprout. The star compass wasn't the Godrealm's last fallen star. I've had it wrong *all* along.

"Oh no," Sora says, her eyes widening. "The goddess is too powerful. She's escaping."

I turn to see that the deity has gotten a second wind. The potion must have worn off. "You will pay for this, you insolent mortals!" She throws up her arms in anger, and one of the latticing pews gets flung across the chamber.

"It's no use," Emmett cries. "Nothing can stop her."

The goddess breaks another bench above her head and stands up. She locks her eyes on me, and her gaze is so icy, I swear my insides freeze on the spot.

"Enough!" she yells. "Enough play. It is time to finish this." She puts her hands together and releases them toward me in a forceful gesture.

Eomma sees it coming and dives in front of me to block the attack. But it's too late. The next thing I know, I am hurtling through the air. My back hits something hard, and I fall to the marble floor with a thud. Ugh. My chest feels like it's full of rocks, and I can't catch my breath. I clutch at my throat, trying to let the air in.

Just breathe.

Breathe.

Breathe!

As the deity turns her attention to the others, I slowly get to my knees. I turn and realize I was thrown into the statue of the Cave Bear Goddess. No wonder it was a rough landing. I use it as a prop to pull myself up to my feet, then quickly close my eyes. I'm woozy from the impact, and I hold on tight to the icon. As the dizziness subsides, I stare at the likeness of the goddess.

That's when it strikes me.

The Cave Bear Goddess statue is made of gold.

I run through the prophecy in my head once more:

When the blood moon and black sun appear to the gaze
To mark the start of the end of all days,
In the one last divine, a weapon shall rise;
Unless the gold-destroyer ends the soul who lies.

As the statue's gilded eyes probe into my own, the last piece of the puzzle falls into place.

"Goddess, I might still be in the running for employee of

the century, after all," I say, my voice deeper and surer than it has ever been before. I walk up to her, rubble trembling under my feet, and I feel only strength, not fear. "I have found what you're looking for."

The goddess pauses her destruction to look at me.

Well? her eyes demand.

I look over at the cauldron and the pure power flowing from its black flames. The same power that flows from *me*.

And for the first time in my life, instead of being ashamed of my four inner fires, I embrace them. I let the embers drift down over me, become part of me. And as the licks of power engulf me, I allow myself to accept it, and accept *myself*.

Intertwined with these feelings is my love for both sets of parents, compassion for my sister, thankfulness for the companionship of my best friend, and gratitude for the unity of the Gom. I fuse it with my appreciation for the scholars' bravery, the loyalty of the inmyeonjo, the support of my auntie, and the courage of my gifted friends.

I have never felt more at home than here, right now, among all my people. So, using that feeling, I form a colorful patchwork of the diverse mortals who make me who I am. And I burn fiercely with pride.

"Choose your next actions carefully," the goddess warns as I take my final steps toward her.

The dokkaebi may have been evil, but he was right. I was indeed in possession of the Godrealm's last fallen star. I've had it with me—*in* me—all along.

Because *I* am the weapon.

I am the gold-destroyer.

And I will end the soul who lies.

"It is I that you seek," I declare proudly, and I have never been surer of anything in my life. "*I am the Godrealm's last fallen star.*"

Shock reverberates through the sanctuary at my declaration, and the goddess's skin shines a brilliant magenta.

"Oh, how the Mother works in mysterious ways." There is satisfaction and hunger in her eyes, both hands poised to destroy me. I am now her only target.

But I know what's coming.

And I am prepared.

Yes, the voice whispers in my ear. *It's time for you to shine, my little fallen star.*

I smile. I gather all the dark and light, love and hurt, good and bad from my life into one monumental ball of fire. Above all, I think of Hattie, the best sister anyone could have *ever* wished for.

And as the goddess comes for me, I counter her with a unique cocktail of divinity and human experience. I release the inner heat from every pore of my body, and, in a blinding blaze, simultaneously let go of and embrace my potential, channeling it all toward the gold statue of the Cave Bear Goddess. The black flames explode out of the Gi cauldron and fly toward the statue, their sheer force shattering the sculpted gold into a thousand little pieces.

"*Nooo!*" the goddess cries, as she is ripped out of my auntie's body. She stands in her frumpy mortal guise once more, fear gripping her eyes. And as she looks at the shards of her statue littering the floor of the sanctuary, she, too, begins to shatter.

The deity shrieks. And in that moment, the world seems to hold its breath and gasp at the same time. Time stands still and is simultaneously full of motion. It is thunderous and silent, chaotic and calm. The very fabric of the atmosphere rips open as the goddess explodes into a dazzling shower of light. And when our eyes finally recover, it all becomes ever so clear.

I am the last divine star that fell from the Godrealm's sky.

I am the one who was destined to stop the end of all days.

I have lost, but I have gained.

Because I am strong. And I am brave.

My name is Riley Oh, and I was born to shine.

30.
The End Is Also the Beginning

To be honest, everything feels sort of anti-climactic after that. I find myself standing awkwardly among everyone, twiddling my thumbs and trying to find the right words to say.

Just to recap, I've found out I'm a piece of the divine—the Godrealm's last fallen star (which is kind of awesome), and I've managed to vanquish the Cave Bear Goddess (which is also kind of awesome, since I pretty much saved the world).

But as the excitement dies down, I realize my two families still have no memory of who I really am. And, more important, Hattie is still gone. Her body remains lifeless on the floor, surrounded by my crying parents. Nothing I can do or say will change that. And despite my having stopped the end of all days, it hurts deeply to know that I failed her.

I drop my head into my hands as my leaky-bladder eyes make their appearance. I miss Hattie *so* much.

"Thank you for all that you have done for us," Appa says to me between tears, a weird sense of formality clipping his tone. "For stopping the goddess, and for trying to save our daughter . . . I mean, your sister . . . uh . . ." He trails off and gives me this awkward half hug, half pat on the back. Auntie Okja, who is now recovering, also gives me a small grateful smile.

"Yes, the Horangi thank you, too," Sora agrees, calm but solemn. "You showed great courage today, and we will always remember that."

Jennie, Cosette, David, and Noah try to comfort me, banding around me in a circle of friendship I never thought I'd have.

"Don't worry, star girl," Jennie says. "We still remember you, and there'll be a way to restore their memories of you, I'm sure of it."

Cosette and David nod. "We'll help you. You won't have to do it alone."

Noah nudges his fogged-up glasses up the bridge of his nose. "Hattie would have wanted us to help you," he says quietly. "I know it."

Emmett and Taeyo consider me from afar, probably curious but also cautious, considering I just destroyed a goddess. It's not every day you see that happen.

Areum calls for me from outside the sanctuary. And since I don't really know what else to say or do right now anyway, I pretend I need to visit the restroom and take my leave.

I find the inmyeonjo by the elevator. But she's not alone.

Next to her is a statuesque creature with a great mane, a single blunt horn, and red eyes that shine like rubies. His bioluminescent scales glisten as he nods toward me, the bell around his neck jingling a sweet melody.

"Haetae?" I ask in surprise. "What are you doing here?"

"You have done well, fallen star."

I blink, and suddenly I see the bearded man standing before me. He's just as I remember him—well dressed and well built with an impressively bushy beard. But now, his eyes shine ruby red.

I blink again, and he's the Haetae again.

Blink.

Bearded man.

Blink.

Haetae.

"Wait, *you're* the bearded man?" I ask, starting to understand. "You were pretending to be a guard at the laundromat? You're actually the *Haetae?*"

He tips his head. "At your service."

"It was you, wasn't it? You were the one talking to me today. In my mind."

A warm smile spreads across his face. "Indeed it was."

"But why?" I rub the back of my neck. "Why did you help me?"

"I am Mago Halmi's guardian. I made a grave mistake when I bit the dark sun and the dark moon at the goddesses' request. I have been roaming the Mortalrealm since the pieces fell here, to ensure that the remaining stars do not get into the goddesses' hands. Something at which I admit I have not been very successful."

I frown. "But why didn't you just tell me you were the Haetae when we were at the library? You knew what I was looking for. Why not tell me the truth about who I really was?

You could have saved me so much time. I could have saved my sist..." I trail off, choked by my tears.

His ruby eyes soften. "Mago Halmi wanted you to discover the truth for yourself. This was your journey to take. I was just here to guide you in the right direction."

He solidifies in Haetae form, and my eyes lower to the shiny bell around his neck. A scene materializes in its reflection like it did at the library, and I recognize it like I remember an old dream—hazy and fragile, drifting just beyond my grasp.

I'm falling from the sky—a screaming ball of pure, divine heat. A piece of the Godrealm's dark sun. I burn through the Earth's atmosphere and, as the Haetae's voice guides me, I fall into the Mortalrealm.

The Haetae flickers back into his human form, and I blink a few times, the scene receding back into the cloudiness of my memory.

"So I'm a piece of the dark sun that fell to Earth, and you hid me in my Horangi mother?"

"That's correct," he confirms. "You now know the full truth. And like I said, you performed your prescribed duty beautifully. But listen well, because you must remain vigilant. You may have destroyed the Cave Bear Goddess today, as the prophecy predicted, but there are five more goddesses in the Godrealm who crave access to the three realms. Now that one of their sisters has fallen, there is no knowing if, or how, they may retaliate."

"But, Haetae, my families don't remember me anymore. What do I do now? I have nowhere to go. I'm all alone."

"Do not despair, fallen star. There are ways lost memories

can be recovered. Nothing is ever truly lost, after all. And as for being alone, I think you already know how wrong you are."

He removes a marble from his pocket and holds it up to me. I immediately take a step back, remembering the blue-and-purple gas that knocked Emmett and me unconscious.

The Haetae smiles sheepishly. "There is no need to be afraid. Biting the dark sun and dark moon burdened me with many troubles. But it did provide me one gift, and that is the ability to manipulate time. Now that you have successfully completed your journey, I would like to grant you one divine favor. By turning back time, I can restore one thing of your choosing to its original form. But choose wisely, fallen star, for you may use this once and for one thing only."

I open the sanctuary door slightly and peek inside. My parents are grieving over Hattie's still body. But I also see Austin showing Jennie how his biochip works. Cosette and Emmett are giving each other cheesy salutes, and Noah and David are asking Taeyo to do another water trick. Auntie Okja is speaking with Sora, and at one point, they share a warm handshake. This must be the first time in a long time the Horangi are standing as equals among fellow gifteds, and in the temple at that.

I imagine being there with my families, being remembered by them, and being welcomed home. My heart physically aches to be a part of that picture.

I know more than anything what I want to reverse.

"Haetae," I start, removing the vial from around my neck that now contains nothing but a charred remainder of my sister's heart, "I want you to restore this."

The Haetae takes the vial but lets it hang like a comma between us. Areum coos from her perch on my shoulder.

"Are you sure that is what you desire?" the Haetae asks. "You could ask me to restore what the dokkaebi took from you."

I shake my head. "I'm sure. Like you said, there are other ways to recover lost memories."

"As you wish, fallen star."

The Haetae makes his way into the Gi sanctuary, and Areum and I follow.

Everyone starts whispering as he gets near. I'm sure they're wondering who this strange man is. But no one bothers to ask. I guess after everything they've seen today, there isn't much that will surprise them anymore.

The Haetae takes the vial over to Hattie's lifeless body, and Eomma and Appa look uncertain. But I nod to them, and they silently move aside, allowing him to get close to her.

He puts the vial on top of her chest, above her heart, and steps back. Holding his marble in his open palm, he starts chanting ancient words under his breath, and blue-and-purple smoke wafts from the sphere, swirling like a small tornado in his hand. He blows on the storm as if wishing on a dandelion, and the clouds fly obediently toward Hattie, enveloping her entire body in the colors of the divine.

Suddenly I feel a bit nauseated, as if I'm on a rocky boat ride. The ground seems to be slipping under my feet, as if we're literally moving back in time.

Then, just as quickly as the feeling came, it's gone.

And the Haetae with it.

I rush over to Hattie, who remains still and unmoving. The vial on her chest is now empty—no red, no black, no nothing. I shake her shoulders.

"Hattie, wake up, wake up! Come back to us."

Emmett and Auntie Okja join me at Hattie's side, with Eomma and Appa opposite me. Taeyo, Sora, Austin, and the rest of my friends surround us in a circle. And together we repeat Hattie's name over and over again like a prayer.

Then, like a miracle, her eyes flicker open. And this time they're not pitch-black. They are warm brown—the color of healing-spell training sessions, the color of Saturday night tteok-bokki and K-drama marathons, the color of late night gossip-a-thons under the covers. . . . They are the eyes of my sister.

"Oh my Mago," she croaks, coughing and spluttering as she comes to. "Where am I?"

We all cheer—the witches and the fallen piece of the divine, together as one.

"Hattie!" Noah cries, kneeling down and hugging her tight. "You came back! I'm so glad you came back!"

He suddenly realizes everyone is watching him, and he quickly gets up and walks backward, step-by-step, until he's completely out of the circle. "I mean, I'm pleased you've returned safely, just like everyone else is. . . ."

Hattie smiles weakly, but I see some much-needed color flash on her cheeks. They are *so* getting together, Mr. and Mrs. Oh-Noh. I'd bet the Haetae's bell on it.

"Thank you so much for bringing her back to us," Eomma cries, looking at me the way people look at firefighters after a blaze. Grateful but respectfully distanced.

Appa says nothing but reaches over Hattie's chest and takes my hands, resting his head on them. And that gesture says more than words ever could.

"Hat," I whisper, tracing my finger along her pale, gaunt face.

She looks at me blankly, and a burning heat builds behind my eyes.

She has no idea who I am.

One lone fat tear falls from my face onto her heart vial. It splashes off the glass and drips down onto her chest.

"I know you don't remember me," I whisper, "but I just want you to know that I love you more than anything. And you are the best sister a girl could ever dream of."

She blinks once, as if to clear her vision. A pause. Then her blank look disappears and is replaced by one of puzzlement. "Uh, Rye, why in the three realms wouldn't I remember you?" She breaks into a wide, toothy grin. "But thanks for the nice words. You're the best sister I could ever have dreamed of, too."

My heart stops, and I clutch my chest with both hands. "Wait, you remember me?! Do you really remember me?!" I pull her into a bear hug and I hold her so tight, she coughs a few times.

"*Whoa*, easy does it!" she croaks, smiling. "I'm not going anywhere."

I don't know how, but against all odds, my sister remembers me. I wonder if the Haetae had something to do with it. Or if it's because she wasn't technically in the Mortalrealm when the dokkaebi and I made the deal. But Areum offers her own theory from my shoulder.

"It is a well-known fact," she says into my ear, "that true love conquers all."

Hattie squeezes my arm, and I feel the weight of the last few days melt off me. With Hattie by my side, there's nothing we can't do.

"So, it's Riley, right?" Taeyo asks, adjusting his purple bow tie. "Maybe at some point you could give us a blow-by-blow of everything that happened today? It was, well, out of this realm."

Emmett nods, hugging Boris close and tickling behind his ears. "Yeah, what he said! Also, has anyone ever told you you're a badass?"

I chuckle as a new warmth fills my chest. There is definitely hope. And, as always, it tastes ever so sweet on my tongue.

I don't know if I'll ever get my elemental magic back, or whether everyone will remember me again. I don't know what it means to be a fragment of the Godrealm's dark sun, and I definitely don't know what the rest of the goddesses might do now that I've destroyed one of their sisters.

But the truth is, right here, right now, none of that matters. Looking around at the diverse group of people surrounding me—the people who fought for me and stood with me—I understand just how right the Haetae was.

Because if there's one thing I know for sure, it's that I'm not alone. I am surrounded by people I love and who love me.

I belong.

Despite everything that's happened, my heart has never felt so full.

"BTW, I had a premonition dream this morning," Jennie starts.

"Wow! Go on," Taeyo encourages earnestly. "Tell us. Knowledge is best shared."

"OMG, isn't that totally the type of cheesy thing Professor Ryu would say?" Jennie says, smirking at Taeyo.

Noah and David nod in agreement.

"Totally."

"Absolutely."

Cosette stands up for Taeyo. "Hey, let the dude be cheesy if that's his jam."

Jennie shrugs, but I see a small smile on the edges of her lips. "Whatever. Anyway, as I was saying, I had a premonition dream, and even you were in it, new kid."

Taeyo beams, obviously chuffed he's now part of this gang.

"We were on a mission to find the lost memories of Riley."

Areum rustles her feathers and squawks. And I can guess what she's thinking: This is proof.

This can't be where the story ends. No way, not today, definitely not when there is hope on the horizon. I *will* restore my families' lost memories, and it looks like I won't have to do it alone.

"So," Hattie says, pulling on my hand and searching my eyes. "Did I miss much?"

I lie down and rest my head in my sister's lap. "Oh, you have *no* idea."

She pouts. "Guess I missed out on all the fun then, huh?"

I chuckle. "Oh, don't you worry about that. This is only the beginning."

Epilogue

When the fragments of the dark sun and the dark moon fell from the Godrealm's sky, the Haetae noticed they fell in pairs. One piece of the sun and one piece of the moon, falling together as one.

As the six goddesses became consumed with their desire to destroy the fallen pieces, Mago Halmi grew worried. "We must ensure my children do not destroy them all," she said.

So she commanded the Haetae to find one of the fallen stars and separate it into its two parts. "Leave the dark-sun piece in the Mortalrealm," she said. "But take the piece of the dark moon and hide it well, my loyal guardian. For when the day comes that the dark sun and moon are united, a new era will be born. They will call it the Age of the Final Eclipse. This is my prophecy."

And so the Haetae did as Mago Halmi commanded.

He separated one of the fallen stars and left the piece of the dark sun in the Mortalrealm. Then he took the piece of the dark moon and hid it in the safest place he could find—the Spiritrealm.

Glossary

aegi-ya (EH-ghee-yah) What my eomma calls me when she's about to deliver bad news. *Aegi* is Korean for *baby,* and the *ya* on the end is what you add when you're calling out to someone.

appa (AH-bbah) Korean for *dad.*

Areum (AH-rihm) A Korean name meaning *beautiful.*

bae (beh) a delicious Korean pear that's big and round (sometimes as big as my face). It's super crunchy and refreshing, and supposedly one of the Cave Bear Goddess's favorite things to eat.

bangmangi (BAHNG-mahng-ee) a magical club covered with pointy black and red spikes that dokkaebis use to summon any item in the Mortalrealm.

Battle Galactic a video game that's similar to *Fortnite Battle Royale,* but set in space. My BFF, Emmett, is *obsessed* with it.

bulgogi (BOOL-goh-ghee) a super-yummy marinated beef dish. David Kim's family restaurant, Seoulful Tacos, makes the *best* bulgogi tacos in town.

Cave Bear Goddess the patron goddess of the Gom clan.

cheollima (CHOL-lee-mah) winged horses that are the preferred mode of transport for the goddesses in the Godrealm.

Cheollimas are known for being too big, too swift, and too majestic to be mounted by any mortal being. Interesting fact: Ages ago, a cheollima who lost his wings and fell from the Godrealm became the first horse on Earth.

dojang (DOH-jahng) a formal training hall for Korean martial arts, like Taegwondo.

dokkaebi (DOH-ggeh-bee) really scary goblins that enter your dreams and make you live out your worst fears so they can eat them (literally). They have magical clubs called bangmangi that can summon any item in the Mortalrealm. Pro tip: Avoid them at all costs.

eomma (OM-mah) Korean for *mom*.

eum and yang (ihm) and (yahng) the Korean way of saying *yin and yang,* which is the idea that seemingly opposite or contrary forces may actually be complementary and interconnected.

Gi (ghee) a cylindrical glass charm filled with one of the five sacred elements, worn as a bracelet by all initiated witches. When rubbed against the wrist, it activates a witch's magic by channeling the divine power of that witch's patron goddess.

gifted witches who are members of the six gifted clans and descendants of the six patron goddesses. Basically, those with magic in their blood.

gifted mark the symbol of the two suns and two moons that appears on a witch's inner wrist when they do magic. It's often used to prove one's gifted identity—for example, to get into the temple for Saturday service, because it glows in the witch's clan color.

gimbap (GHEEM-bahp) Korean sushi. Gimchi and cheese are the best combo for fillings, in case you're wondering.

gimchi (GHEEM-chee) a spicy fermented cabbage side dish that makes whatever you're eating infinitely tastier. The gimchi guacamole at Seoulful Tacos is my jam!

gimchi jjigae (GHEEM-chee JEE-geh) a hearty stew made with gimchi, which happens to be Eomma's favorite meal.

glamour the type of magic that witches of the Gumiho clan (illusionists) practice. It allows people, places, and things to be hidden, transformed, or disguised. Pretty awesome.

gochujang (GOH-choo-jahng) A spicy-sweet chili sauce used in a lot of Korean cooking. Emmett loves it and puts obscene amounts on his tacos.

Godrealm the realm where Mago Halmi, the goddesses, and other divine creatures live.

Gom (gohm) Witches of the Gom clan, like my parents, my auntie Okja, and my sister, Hattie, are healers and descendants of the Cave Bear Goddess. Our clan color is gold, and our motto is Service and Sacrifice. Healers often run clinics hidden in plain sight, like holistic medicine centers, well-being retreats, or like my parents' Traditional Korean Medicine Clinic.

Gumiho (GOO-mee-hoh) Witches of the Gumiho clan are illusionists and descendants of the Nine-Tailed Fox Goddess. Their clan color is silver, and their motto is Beauty and Influence. This may sound like a generalization, but their good looks often lead them to become K-pop and K-drama stars. True story.

gwisin (GWEE-sheen) hungry ghosts that haven't been able to pass through to the Spiritrealm because of unfinished business on Earth.

Haetae (HEH-teh) a uni-horned lion-like beast, and Mago Halmi's guardian pet. He's known for his incredible loyalty, and his ability to manipulate time.

halmeoni (HAHL-mo-nee) Korean for *grandma*.

hanbok (HAHN-bohk) the traditional Korean dress or suit that witches wear in their clan colors for special occasions.

Horangi (HOH-rahng-ee) Witches of the Horangi clan are scholars and descendants of the Mountain Tiger Goddess. Their clan color is red, and their motto is Knowledge and Truth. They used to be the keepers of the sacred texts at the gifted library, but were cursed and excommunicated from the gifted community almost thirteen years ago.

hotteok (HOH-ddok) cinnamon-y sweet pancakes with a gooey brown-sugar center that Appa makes. Hands down, my favorite meal.

house-sin (house-sheen) spirits that protect the gifted's homes. The door-sin, the kitchen-sin, and the toilet-sin are the main ones, but you can have others, too. You have to give them compliments every time you use them, or they might make your life miserable.

inmyeonjo (EEN-myon-joh) a wild creature with the body of a bird and the head of a woman. They can fly between the Godrealm and the Mortalrealm at will, and are obsessed with destroying mirrors because they hate their own reflections.

Joseon Chalice (JOH-son) a 600-year-old sacred artifact that belonged to King Sejong the Great, who ruled as the fourth king of the Joseon dynasty. He also happened to be gifted, but not many people know that.

K-drama the short way of saying *Korean TV shows*. Hattie, Emmett, and I have K-drama marathons every second Saturday.

K-fry a nickname for Korean fried chicken. If you haven't tried it, you are totally missing out. Just saying.

Knock-Out Juice a sleep potion, infused by the Tokki witches, that my parents sometimes use at the clinic for saram patients (so they don't realize they're being healed with magic). A few drops in a cup of tea knocks you straight into a deep slumber. Useful stuff.

K-pop the short way of saying Korean pop music. Random fact: All but one of the BTS members are Gumiho. You heard it here first.

Mago Halmi (MAH-goh HAHL-mee) the mother of the three realms, mother of the six goddesses, mother of mortal-kind, and mother of all creation. Basically, the head honcho who made the world.

Memoryhaze a potion, infused by the Tokki witches, that can wipe a saram's mind of the magical things they've seen. It's important for protecting the privacy and sanctity of the clans.

Miru (MEE-roo) Witches of the Miru clan are protectors and are descendants of the Water Dragon Goddess. Their clan color is blue, and their motto is Provide and Protect. Thanks to their superhuman speed and/or strength, they often guard our secret portals and entrances. They usually give off a jock-like vibe.

Moon Rabbit Goddess the patron goddess of the Tokki clan.

Mortalrealm the realm where we mortals live, aka Earth.

Mountain Tiger Goddess the patron goddess of the Horangi clan. She disowned the clan when the witches were excommunicated, though.

Nine-Tailed Fox Goddess the patron goddess of the Gumiho clan.

noraebang (NOH-reh-bahng) a Korean karaoke room. *Norae* is Korean for *song*, and *bang* means *room*.

nunchi (NOON-chee) the word you use to describe someone's ability to pick up what's going on or someone's feelings without being told. Essentially, one's ability to read a room. Surprisingly, despite his being allergic to emotions, Emmett has amazing nunchi.

Samjogo (SAHM-johk-oh) Witches of the Samjogo clan are seers and are descendants of the Three-Legged Crow Goddess. Their clan color is purple, and their motto is Leadership and Wisdom (although my appa says it should be Power and Ego, because they're so full of hot air). Seers can get visions of truth simply by touching an item, and have premonitions in their dreams.

saram (SAH-rahm) the word we use for people who aren't gifted with magic.

saranghaeyo (SAH-rahng-heh-yoh) Korean for *I love you.*

Saturday School school for witches, held only one day a week.

Spiritrealm the place we go after we die.

Taegwondo (TEH-gwon-doh) a Korean martial art. Noah Noh's dad is a Taegwondo grandmaster and runs a famous dojang in Koreatown.

Three-Legged Crow Goddess the patron goddess of the Samjogo clan.

Tokki (TOHK-ghee) Witches of the Tokki clan are infusers and descendants of the Moon Rabbit Goddess. Their clan color is green, and their motto is Kindness and Heart. They infuse all the potions and tonics the clans use. They also run the best restaurants in town, because of their ability to infuse food with magic.

tteokbokki (DDOK-bohk-ghee) a spicy rice-cake dish that Hattie, Emmett, and I eat every other Saturday while watching our K-drama marathons. It's even better if you melt cheese on top.

Water Dragon Goddess the patron goddess of the Miru clan.

Korean passages with English translation:

Jega gajingeon, dangsinege jumnida.
That which I have, I give to you.

Dangsini gajingeon, jega gajyeogamnida.
That which you have, I take from you.

Nae nunape inneungeot,	The thing that is in front of me,
Geurimsoge inneungeot.	Inside the picture that I see.
Nuneul keuge tteugo boseyo,	Use your eyes, look carefully,
Muni jamsi yeollyeoyo.	A door opens momentarily.

Acknowledgments

One of my fondest memories growing up was visiting the local library every week with my appa. I would come out the doors with books stacked up to my chin, grin on, my fingers itching to explore the pages as soon as I got home. We couldn't afford to buy books then—my immigrant parents were already working three jobs each just to put food on the table—but our weekly trips to the library made me feel like the wealthiest girl in the world. All those worlds, all those lives, all that *magic*, right there at my fingertips . . .

Three decades later, not much has changed as far as my thirst for books go. Words are still everything. Except at some point, I realized something was missing. In all the books I read and treasured as a child, I never saw myself. The message was clear: People like me didn't belong in books—and nobody wanted to read our stories.

The thought festered, making me increasingly frustrated. *But why not?* I asked myself. *We have so much to share with the world!* So, I woke up one day and decided I was going to be part of the change. I would write the books younger-me would have wanted to read. And now here you are, reading my book. Whoa! Yay! Is this a dream? (Please don't wake me if it is. . . .)

Books aren't written by merely one person, though, despite what the name on the cover might suggest. They are intricate patchworks made by many talented, passionate, and generous people. I am proud to say that *The Last Fallen Star* is no exception.

First and foremost, I have to give a huge shout-out to my agent and secret long-lost doppelgänger, Carrie Pestritto. Thank you for being my biggest advocate. You believed in my words even before I did, and for that I will eternally be grateful.

My deepest gratitude to my editors, Hannah Allaman, Stephanie Lurie, and Rick Riordan. Hannah, the day you shared your vision for my book, I swear the clouds parted and a rainbow appeared in the sky. Steph, having you to guide me to the finish line was like having my own Haetae by my side. You are both #braingoals and I am in awe of you. Rick, I'm still pinching myself that I get to be part of your RRP family. As Emmett would say, *holy shirtballs*—what an incredible honor! Thank you to all three of you for taking a chance on me.

To my publisher, Emily Meehan; Guy Cunningham and his copyediting staff; creative director Joann Hill; cover artist Vivienne To; Marybeth Tregarthen and her production group; Seale Ballenger, and the marketing, publicity, and sales teams; and all those who worked tirelessly in the background: Thank you so much for helping me bring Riley and the gifted clans to the world. Maybe we should summon Mago Halmi and ask her to create a seventh Disney clan?

A special thank-you to Beth Phelan and #DVpit for giving marginalized writers like me a platform to be seen; and to Alexa Donne, my mentor Rebecca Barrow, and AMM for being the first real edge-piece to my writing journey. Becky, I still have nightmares about that roundabout in Swindon. . . .

To all the AMM R3 alumni, thank you for being my first writing community. A shout-out particularly to the #WritersFightClub and my amazing CPs who wouldn't let me give up: Julie, Sarah, Tara, Chelsea, Jordan, Laura, Susan, Emily, Kathy, Leanne, Heidi, Erika, Carolyn, and Louisa, I heart you all. We've got this!

To all the talented humans in the #yaysquad for your friendship and wonderfully wacky profile pics, especially Adelle, Ana, Anna, J.Elle, Moniza, Naz, Robin, Sonora, and Taj. Thinking of you guys makes me hungry. Is that weird? Also, Jess, my publishing twin, you are all around #goals. Can you please teach me how to life?

All the beautiful souls I met at the Madcamp BIPOC Retreat, I miss you! Natalie, Tess, Justina, thank you for organizing what was a dream-affirming experience for me. Zoraida, *Labyrinth Lost* was my muse for the virgin draft of this book—I am indebted to you forever. To my cabinmates, Yas, Elise, Susan, Christina, Yamile, Tracy, and Kyndal, my belly still hurts thinking about our late-night laughs. Can we do it again? And Tracy, OMG, you called it!

To all my Kiwi writing whānau, especially Claire Donnelly for being the first person who *got* it and reminded me I wasn't alone; my Meetup group for our Saturday morning sessions at Catalina Cafe; Tim Owen and the North Shore writers; and Amy Martin and Teresa Herleth for their support and encouragement.

I can't forget about my Welly Wonkadoodles: Mel, Vivienne,

Emma, and my Pitchwars co-mentor, Karah. It's mind-boggling how four such exceptional creators and humans got to be in one tiny city together. Lucky me! I can't wait to eat with you all again. And sorry not sorry about the group name—I take full responsibility.

To my SCBWI critique group: Jen, Kerstin, Lynley, and Catherine, for all the tireless hours you put into helping me improve my craft. To David Hill for the manuscript assessment and encouraging words. To my writer friends in the MGicalMisfits, DiverseInk, The21ders, and the Class of 2K21. To Swati, June, and Naz for your precious feedback in the latter stages. And to everyone else that has been part of my wordy community, I am so grateful for you.

I would be remiss to not mention the first-ever teen and tweens who were forced to read my words when I was still in training wheels. Sian Allen, Nikka Caraig, Hannah Jones, you are angels for being so constructive and supportive.

To the soulful Giulia Mazzola, and my half-orange BFF, Jamie Vulinovich, for reading some of my earliest attempts at writing and not telling me I sucked. I hope all people in the world know the joy of having friends like you. So many hugs and kisses xx.

And of course, my dearest Kimchingoos: Sarah, Jess, Grace, and Susan. I actually don't know where I'd be without our snug little family pod. We have so many in-jokes I can't remember half of them, but for the record, I raise my glass to our buddy Mack Gully. Hope you enjoyed the inmyeonjo-taming scene . . . :)

Speaking of family, my love to the ever-growing Cribbens

clan—especially Mum and Dad Cribbens—for always showing such interest in my writing, even if my response was always a variation of "I'm getting there..." or "Not quite yet..."

To my sisters, Ally and Joya, for being the inspiration behind Riley and Hattie's unbreakable sisterhood. Growing up with you two was the best childhood I could have asked for. Thank you for being my best friends, and for being co-sufferers of the leaky-bladder eyeball syndrome. No, I'm not crying, *you* are....

Eomma and Appa, there are no words that can even begin to describe the gratitude I feel for the sacrifices you made for me. You are my biggest heroes, and I count my lucky (fallen?) stars that I get to be your daughter. I strive to do you proud in all that I do, each and every day. Saranghaeyo. Oh, and look! It's our name on the cover!

And, of course, to my Spudman: my baby daddy, my hippocampus, my person. Thank you for reading every single draft, for being my biggest cheerleader, for the (many) late-night brainstorming sessions, and for your eternal well of patience. You are my home and my paradise, and I genuinely don't know how I got so lucky. If I had a chest full of time-reversing Haetae marbles, I would re-choose my life with you. Every. Single. Time.

Last but not least, my biggest shout-out to you, dear reader. To all the adoptees, the diaspora kids, the misfits. To anyone who's ever felt invisible, or felt like they don't belong. Real magic lives inside all of us—in the choices we make every single day. This book is for you.

Coming in Summer 2022

The Last Fallen Moon

A Gifted Clans Novel
Book Two